GENESIS CODE
BOOK 1, GENESIS SERIES

ABOUT THE AUTHOR

Eliza Green tried her hand at fashion designing, massage, painting, and even ghost hunting, before finding her love of writing. She often wonders if her desire to change the ending of a particular glittery vampire story steered her in that direction (it did). After earning her degree in marketing, Eliza went on to work in everything but marketing, but swears she uses it in everyday life, or so she tells her bank manager.

Born and raised in Dublin, Ireland, she lives there with her sci-fi loving, evil genius best friend. When not working on her next amazing science fiction adventure, you can find her reading, indulging in new food at an amazing restaurant or simply singing along to something with a half decent beat.

For a list of all available books, check out:

www.elizagreenbooks.com/books

BOOK 1 IN THE GENESIS SERIES

GENESIS CODE

ELIZA GREEN

Second edition 2020

First edition originally published December 2012

Copyright © 2012-2020 Eliza Green

The moral right of the author has been asserted in accordance with the Copyright, Designs and Patents Act 1988.

All rights reserved. No part of this publication may be reproduced, stored in a retrieval system, or transmitted, in any form or by any means, without the prior written permission of the author, nor be otherwise circulated in any form of binding or cover other than that in which it is published and without a similar condition being imposed on the subsequent purchaser.

All characters in this publication are fictitious and any resemblance to real persons, living or dead, is purely coincidental.

ISBN: 9798650538509

Cover: Deranged Doctor Design
Editor and Proofreader: Nerd Girl Edits

To Christopher Nolan.

Yes, you may turn this book into your next success and I will accept your truckloads of cash. Now, please stop calling.

"A hard-hitting blend of 1984 and Blade Runner... Green's storytelling goes far beyond your average sci-fi yarn—she writes brilliantly "human" characters and crafts intricate conspiracies that kept us guessing."

iBooks Editorial Review

PROLOGUE

Dazzling lights brightened the dark sky. Hundreds of gazes looked up as a new string of lights flashed behind the thick grey cloud. A screeching sound followed.

Curious Indigenes watched silently as the sky turned from a murky grey to acidic yellow. Around them, their young played a game of run and catch. A flare brightened the yellow in the sky to an almost white. Those with the strongest empathic abilities breathed hard, picking up on the moods that had switched from curious to panic.

A distant rumbling grew closer; it was loud enough to send several groups running back to the underground tunnels. The scientifically minded among them stayed put. A thousand pinpricks of light brightened the sky again. Sounds of heavy breathing and scuffling feet from the playing young broke through the silence.

A sharp whistle followed sounding like an echo in the distance, as though it had travelled along a current of air. Pieces of hot metal crashed to the ground. Indigenes jumped out of the way, barely dodging the air assault. The young jerked to a stop, eyes wide.

A thick gas floated down, not quite making it to the

ground. It darkened the space above them, as if lying in wait.

Those too drawn in by the spectacle watched the sky for more evidence. New lights appeared, bigger than the pinpricks before and moving as fast as the projectiles that had crashed moments ago.

The young tugged on the sleeves of the adults. Nobody moved.

Then the rain hit, searing a hot trail of pain along their skin and burning their eyes. Screams and gasps punctured the heavy silence. Chemicals transformed the air into static, something that aggravated their skin.

Don't touch the soil.

Weeping adults and their young defied one scientist's warning and dropped to their knees, smearing soggy earth over their exposed skin. The contaminated ground only made their condition worse.

New screams pierced the thick air. Hot, salty tears leaked from inflamed eyes. The young wailed and crawled around blindly on their hands and knees. Perfect spheres slammed into the earth, splitting apart and unleashing the chemicals inside—chemicals that were rapidly altering the air into something less breathable.

Unbroken bombs transformed into mini projectiles, destroying any structure they came into contact with. With heavy legs and weakened bodies, the Indigenes staggered back to their sanctuary. The young clinging desperately to their backs slowed down their escape.

New lights appeared in the skies, brighter and bigger than the ones before. Something turned the sky a beautiful orange.

That beautiful something burned away the last remaining air.

Tight chests heaved. Bodies collapsed feet from

their sanctuary. Broken.

1

Year 2163, Exilon 5

Thirty years later

A fucking alien hunter.

Twenty years of working for the World Government had led to this moment. If his wife hadn't gone missing, Bill Taggart wouldn't have agreed to this gig.

But here he was, hunting down an alien race on a planet thirty light years from Earth. Bill was a damn good investigator. He could coax the worst criminals out of hiding. But this race?

It had been a year since anyone had last seen one of the creatures the children called 'Shadow People'. For the last two years, he'd tried to get information on his wife's whereabouts only to have every door slammed in his face.

By Charles Deighton, especially. The CEO of the World Government on Earth. The one who paid his wages. He was a strange individual with a flair for the dramatic and love of a good scene. He also believed Isla Taggart was dead.

Bill pushed the food around on his plate. Cantaloupe

was busier than he would have liked for a Thursday. The crowded restaurant bothered him more than usual.

New London had only one Cantaloupe restaurant. Real—not replicated—ingredients made its old-fashioned fare popular with the elite. He stabbed at his steak that cost more than he earned in a month, but the World Government was paying, so what did he care? Charles Deighton ate meals like this once, maybe twice, a day on Earth. The biggest powerhouse on Earth controlled everything back home and here, on Exilon 5. Twelve leaders could make or break society and Bill was their lead investigator.

He brought his next hit of caffeine to his lips. Some might say four cups in an hour was too many, but without it Bill couldn't function. The caffeine jolted him into life and set his hands to shake, worse than they had after his third. He put the cup down and made two fists to control the shaking, brought on in part by his nerves.

This restaurant had recently been visited by one of the 'Shadow People', a race also known as Indigenes. A weird static in the air—one caused by the race—made the hairs on his arms and neck stand up. They'd been in here recently, after a year of nothing.

His pulse quickened with a new hope that he might find his wife. Two years ago, Isla Taggart had disappeared on this planet while monitoring the movements of the Indigenes. That was twenty-eight years after the first stage of terraforming to prepare this planet for human occupation.

His position gave him the power to arrest anyone deemed to be a threat. That included the Indigenes. But he feared the secretive race could not be caught easily—if at all. Worse, he was certain this scumbag species knew exactly where Isla was. For that reason, he needed to learn as much about them. With time, maybe they would lead him to her.

But patience was not his strong point.

He took another hit of coffee. The caffeine set his heart to pump faster. His hands shook like a city junkie's, but junkies weren't the worst thing to fear on Exilon 5. Yes, the new cities required better policing, but something else made it dangerous to live on Exilon 5.

The residents were being fed half-truths about their new home.

His wife, the love of his life, was gone. Taken from him by a group of feral creatures who had been living on this planet, long before humans knew this place existed.

A pain gripped him as he pictured Isla: her rosy cheeks, waist-long brown hair and dimpled smile. She had a positive attitude. She also took no shit from anyone. Isla was the polar opposite of his cynical self. She was the reason he got out of bed, because life without her wasn't worth a damn. Yet his mind nagged at him that this might all be for nothing. It had been two years and still no contact from her.

'I promise you, Isla, I'll never give up.'

Bill's communication device shrilled. The noise made him flinch. Customers flicked their eyes to him in disgust. He eyeballed them as he stuck the earpiece in his ear. 'Yeah?'

'Bill? Daphne calling. Have I caught you at a bad time?'

He straightened up. The CEO of the Earth Security Centre. Deighton's second in command.

'No, just doing some recon.' He pushed his plate away.

'Bill, I'm worried.'

Fuck. 'About what?'

'About how you're handling your first solo investigation.'

'I'm fine.'

He heard what sounded like a fingernail tapping on wood—one of Daphne Gilchrist's habits. While he didn't trust the woman, she was easier to deal with than Deighton.

'I don't mean to intrude so late in the day, but I need to make sure you're on form. We're concerned about you.'

Bullshit. He might be considered young at forty five, but he had experience. There was nobody better to handle this case.

'Deighton cleared me for duty.'

A short pause followed. 'Actually, Mr Deighton asked me to check in with you. This is an important mission and we want to make sure you're up to the task.'

'Of course I am.' He felt his anger slip. 'Seems a bit late for Mr Deighton to have second thoughts.'

'It's just... your wife, and what happened. You still haven't dealt properly with her death.' Gilchrist laid on the charm so thick, Bill wanted to vomit. 'Mr Deighton knows you're capable, as do I. We like to keep a close eye on our best people.'

The CEO of the World Government sending Daphne Gilchrist to do his dirty work? That didn't surprise him. Deighton had assigned Isla Taggart to work on this planet. That made him partly responsible for her disappearance.

'If he's so concerned why doesn't he call me himself?'

'You know that's not possible. Charles Deighton is a busy man.'

Bill bit his tongue. He needed out of this conversation before he said something he might regret.

'I don't want anything to go wrong tomorrow,' Gilchrist added.

'I'm ready, and so is my team.'

'What are your plans?'

'To observe the Indigene and see what it does.'

'That means no interference from you or your team.'

'I understand that.'

A brief silence followed. Then Gilchrist said, 'Are you absolutely sure you're up to this?'

'I'm fine,' he said a little too fast. 'My job is to monitor their activity and that's what I will do. My personal feelings will not affect my work.' As soon as he'd said the words, he knew it was a lie.

'Look, Bill, I won't sugar coat it. This could be a turning point in the investigation or an all-out disaster. Whatever happens, I need to know I can count on you to keep it together.'

Bill's pulse thrummed in his throat. 'Yes, you can.'

'Good. And remember why we picked you. It was because of your success with Hunt. Mr Deighton's expectations are high.'

'Understood.'

Gilchrist clicked off, leaving Bill to ponder his most high profile case on Earth.

Larry Hunt. Just hearing his name made his shoulder throb with the memory of when one of his henchmen had knifed him. Even while incarcerated, the man refused to go away. To say the World Government regretted its involvement with the man who controlled seventy percent of the food replication business was an understatement. The government had a lot to lose, but also plenty to gain from its majority stake in Hunt Technologies. But what it would not tolerate was shady dealings and undervalued share prices threatening that investment.

He yanked the earpiece out of his ear and tossed it on the table. The other patrons hadn't paid his conversation any mind. Not that he cared. His pretence of being in control was to appease Deighton, so he wouldn't take him off the case. Despite Bill's promises to Gilchrist, he planned on doing his own investigation on the species.

A tear fell. Bill thumbed it away, and shook off his lingering anger. With plenty still to do, he tuned in to his surroundings.

Cantaloupe restaurant, with its trademark red-and-white chequered cloth-covered tables, was full for the dinner-time rush. He watched as over-friendly servers took new orders and wealthy patrons settled their bills at the counter with a scan of their identity chips. It chilled him to think one or more of the Indigenes had been here, in this very restaurant. Nocturnal creatures by nature, their sudden appearance during daytime hours marked a change in behaviour for them. They were becoming bolder and riskier in their choices.

He knew that to get answers was to get inside the head of the species he hunted. That began with shelving his anger, and putting himself in their shoes to understand their motives. Easier said than done.

Why choose this place? Are they hunting for their next victim?

He rubbed the lingering static from his arm. They had been here in, what, the last hour or two? World Government intel had reported an Indigene had attempted contact with a boy the previous week. Signs were strong that the same Indigene would try again soon. The thought of these freaks walking around New London sickened him.

Bill ate what he could stomach and checked the

time. It was early evening and he still had a bunch of confidential files on the Indigenes to comb through before tomorrow.

He stood up. 'Time to study these fuckers.'

Habits. Behaviours. Motivations. Every piece of information the government held on the creatures mattered. Every small detail on the species who, until a year ago, nobody had known existed. That same species had survived the brutal terraforming efforts thirty years ago.

At the counter, he scanned his identity chip and charged the meal to his World Government account.

He walked out of the restaurant, worried about one thing. The information the government had on the creatures was hyperbole at best. What did he or anybody really know about the Indigenes?

2

Stephen paced the length of District Three's laboratory. His mouth had gone dry and he couldn't shake the chill in his bones. He was hours away from doing something the Indigenes had never tried before. No better time to have second thoughts.

Exposing his skin to the blistering Exilon 5 sun was both a risky and stupid move. The cold-blooded Indigenes could not tolerate the sun, unlike the Surface Creatures.

Previous attempts to contact the race living above ground had always been at night. But this daytime mission defied their usual strategy, because that's where Stephen's next target would be. His success or failure the next day would determine his species' future on this world.

Everything had to go well. He must get the information fast, before a Surface Creature noticed him in their world.

A familiar voice tickled his mind. He stopped pacing.

Failure is not an option, Stephen.

Anton, his childhood friend, stood at the entrance to his lab, arms folded.

Don't you think I know that? Stephen replied to his telepathic conversation.

Shadow People. That's what they call us. Anton entered the room.

The Indigenes—probably shadowy figures to some—preferred to hunt at night. In weaker moments, Stephen had considered joining one of the groups that hunted more than animals.

What are you doing here, Anton?

Anton switched to his voice. 'I thought you'd like a hand getting ready for tomorrow. It's what they do, right? Talk out loud? They don't have telepathic abilities like we do.'

His friend, born after the terraforming, had not witnessed the early changes to their society—changes that had later killed Stephen's parents. The district tunnels running beneath Exilon 5's surface had preserved what was left of their species, allowing them to start over.

Anton was not consumed by thoughts of revenge, like Stephen was.

Stephen made two fists. 'I have nothing in common with those brutes.' Anton responded with his usual eye roll. 'My hatred of their kind is valid.'

If you say so. I just think you've let it consume you for too long.

Stephen strode over to his workbench, where he'd left the artificial skin. He pressed a piece of the silicone, designed by Anton, to his face. Changing his appearance bothered him, but to blend in with their kind required him to change. The target must not become suspicious.

His fingers grazed the delicate silicone; it yielded to his touch. Despite it weighing almost nothing, it felt heavy, like an additional layer on his skin.

'It's good, yes?' Anton slid in next to him and

handled another piece of skin on the workbench. 'I adapted their silicone at the molecular level to make the skin lightweight and wafer-thin. And, it also cools the skin. How great is that?'

It *was* great. With the ability to manipulate the Surface Creatures' technology, Anton could do amazing things—or dangerous things.

I also added pigmentation to match the Surface Creatures' opaque appearance. It's not perfect, but it's the best I could do without a sample of their skin to compare the density. You should blend in well enough.

Stephen liked how he looked, but to meet with the target he had to look less like himself. The Surface Creatures had controlled life on Exilon 5 for too long. What happened the next day could put power back into the Indigenes' hands.

'Are you nervous about going alone?' said Anton.

'Terrified.'

Any prior trips to the surface had always been with other Indigenes. Safety in numbers: that's what Pierre, the Central Council elder, had always said. But more than one Indigene showing up the next morning could spook the target.

'Having my tech will make it feel like I'm right there with you.' Anton squeezed Stephen's shoulder, a gesture meant to reassure him. It had the opposite effect.

He'd been close to their kind before; close enough to feel the heat from their warm-blooded bodies. His body emitted a static electricity that appeared to irritate them. It was a weak defence, but one nonetheless. The Surface Creatures' skin could handle fluctuations in temperature, something Stephen's body could not. He hoped the silicone skin would protect him from any sudden rise in temperature, both inside and out.

'It will,' Anton replied to his private thought. Stephen could usually mask his thoughts from others, but his current distractions made it hard to think straight.

'Hey, do you remember when they first arrived on the planet?' said Anton.

Stephen nodded. 'We were just a pair of curious Evolvers back then.'

From a distance, they had watched as automated cranes removed pallets of materials from several spacecraft. A piercing screech had accompanied their downward drilling equipment. Fires, from burning materials, had released noxious gases. The elders had worried about them finding the locations of the tunnels, but their constructions had not made it that far below ground. More Surface Creatures had followed after that day, a number that soon overtook that of the Indigenes. Ten thousand years of peace had been stripped away in a few years.

Stephen shook the negative thoughts from his mind and grabbed an air filtration device from the table.

Anton clapped his hands in excitement. *Oh good, I was wondering when you'd test this out.*

Stephen left the laboratory. A giddy Anton followed close behind. In a nearby tunnel, Stephen touched the rock face made of insignia. The rock, with its ability to trap cocoons of surface air in its wall, vibrated in response. He set up a device powered by the amplifying strength of gamma rock in front of the wall. The device drew a single cocoon of air from the wall and stretched it, until it was large enough for Stephen to stand inside.

He drew in a deep breath from District Three's strictly controlled atmosphere and opened his hand. The air filtration device came in three pieces, clear in colour. Two smaller pieces slotted into his nasal cavities and the third larger piece fitted at the back of his throat. He pushed through the cocoon until he stood inside.

A wide-eyed Anton watched as Stephen tested out his equipment.

The first breath of contaminated air burned Stephen's lungs. The intensity lessened as the single-charge micro filter restricted the flow of oxygen to his lungs. When the burn vanished, he exited the cocoon and carefully removed it.

'I get just an hour with this thing?'

Anton nodded. 'How did it feel?'

'Painful at first, but fine once the filter kicks in.'

His friend looked relieved. 'Stick to the time. Yes, you could swap a depleted device for a new one, but the longer you're exposed to their air, the more dangerous it is. My team and I are working on a better, rechargeable version using the body's kinetic energy, but it could be months before that's ready for production.'

'This will work fine, Anton.'

Fine? Anton switched to telepathy again. *It's the best thing I've invented, besides the skin.*

'I'm sorry, Anton. It's perfect.'

'It's better than that. It will help to keep you safe.'

Stephen had other skills that would do that. 'I'm already the fastest runner in this district.'

'No arguments there.' He clapped him on the back. 'But how about you stick to the time limit so you don't need to test that out?'

3

The evening sun warmed Bill's naturally aged skin. He relished the feeling, so different to the dark and gloomy Earth he'd left behind. On his walk through a dialled-back replica of London, he passed by its residents enjoying the sweet, clean air. Nobody wore breathing masks or oxygen canisters here. Not like on Earth, where the poisonous air demanded the masks be used. This planet made it easy to forget the bloated and poisonous planet thirty light years away. But Earth would be a part of him forever. It was where Bill had met Isla.

He arrived at his ITF-issued apartment in the New Westminster area of New London. The hierarchy went: World Government, Earth Security Centre, and International Task Force. But the ITF, the people Bill worked for, were far from soft touches. They had Deighton's full backing to make sure protocol was followed.

A chair dropped from a window above his head to the pavement, just missing him. Bill jumped out of the way and cursed.

He looked up to see a man following up with a

couple of garbage bags down after it.

'This isn't a fucking collection point,' he shouted.

The man flipped him off and slammed his window shut.

Yeah, things were going great on this utopian planet.

Bill grunted as he tossed the chair and both bags into the alley, on top of more discarded waste. The cleaning autobots weren't scheduled for a few days. Scheduled rubbish collections, like on Earth, was one of the World Government's ill-thought-out plans to smooth the transition from old to new planet. But without anyone assigned to police the efforts, waste collection had become a problem.

Bill pinched the end of his nose and hurried inside.

Exilon 5 was supposed to be a fresh start for the human race. Six cities to start, each one a nod to their twin cities on Earth, and a fraction of their size. Not nearly enough to accommodate twenty billion people. Terraforming efforts had made the planet livable in five short years, but only a fraction of the population had been transferred to Exilon 5 in the last twenty-five years.

If the World Government was serious about transferring all inhabitants of Earth, then Exilon 5 needed more cities, more housing, more of everything.

And better rules.

With a heavy step, Bill climbed the stairs to the third floor where his apartment overlooked Belgrave Square Gardens, a close replica of the same gardens once seen in London on Earth. Green open spaces, taken over to build apartments on Earth, had been included in the city's limited design plans.

He opened his front door, but didn't enter.

His job as investigator made him more enemies than

friends. Bill had gotten used to living out of a suitcase and sleeping for two, maybe three, hours per night. The paranoia had become a steady companion in his fight against crime and desire to put things right.

Hunting and catching bad people didn't always live up to the sexy reputation it had garnered on Earth. Yeah, it felt good to put the bad guys away, but it was a lonely existence. Being good at his job had earned him a ticket to Exilon 5 and an opportunity to search for Isla. That's all that mattered to him.

He examined the apartment that looked the same as it had when he'd first moved in, over a year ago. One sofa, one Light Box, and one kitchen table with four chairs next to the window made up his home. If he could even call it that. The kitchen, bedroom and bathroom were separate rooms. These apartments weren't huge, but they beat the studio shoeboxes on Earth for size.

Bill crept into his apartment. The virtual Light Box didn't greet him; he'd disabled its security function a while ago. A thick layer of dust covered every surface. That tip from an informant made it easier to see when things had been moved. Old circular imprints from legs of chairs remained hidden. He sloped to the bedroom to check on the only thing of value: his suitcase. Hidden in his bedroom wardrobe, it contained personal items belonging to him and Isla.

The ITF owned this apartment and was on their radar. So was his life. He kept what he could private.

Gilchrist's call still angered him. Bill had worked hard to separate himself from the politics and to focus on what mattered: learning more about the Indigenes and the location of their lairs. Caves. Wherever the savage creatures liked to congregate.

But her lack of faith in his ability had brought Isla

into play—a topic Gilchrist knew was off limits. Her warning not to make a move on the Indigenes made him want to do the exact opposite.

Watch and wait. Gather information, and strike at the right time.

Yeah, it made sense. But this was no ordinary mission for him.

Bill retrieved the files on the Indigenes from a wall safe hidden behind a bookshelf in his bedroom. To open the safe, he scanned his identity chip and security chip, in his left and right thumb. To operate the digital pad and access the private folder containing the files, he repeated the same steps.

He returned to the living room with the DPad, equal in size to his hand. The Light Box flashed once and he grunted. Bill had disabled the virtual information system with programmable artificial intelligence the second he moved in. But the flash of light told him someone had found a way to reconnect it.

One of Gilchrist's people, no doubt. He'd already located some of the ITF's bugging devices: two in the base of the table lamps, one inside a disused cupboard in the kitchen and one underneath his bed. And those were just the ones he could find. The head of the Earth Security Centre and Charles Deighton's second in command trusted nobody. She was another snake with a reputation for getting what she wanted. Bill had been vague about his reasons for wanting on this mission. Gilchrist's pep talk earlier told him he was not hiding those reasons well enough.

But he was their best investigator.

Their best, ill tempered, wayward Scottish investigator who hated authority more than he did liars. And snakes.

Bill set the DPad down on the glass coffee table and walked over to the Light Box. He studied his reflection in its shimmering facade that was just a virtual representation of an actual screen. The skin around his tired eyes aged him more than the flecks of grey in his dark brown hair. Nothing a little genetic modification couldn't fix. Improved medical procedures had made it possible to live longer. But he despised dishonesty, and those who modified their appearance were lying to themselves. Deighton and Gilchrist were both fans of the treatment.

He'd worked hard to convince Gilchrist to put him on this mission. Given that Isla had disappeared on this planet, he thought his chances were slim but something, or someone, had changed her mind. The ITF handled the grunt work for the ESC—investigations, arrests, policing—and nothing ever happened without Gilchrist's say-so.

Isla had once told him that no matter what advances were made in age alteration, he should always be able to recognise himself in the mirror. He hadn't given too much thought to it over the years, but the advice seemed more pertinent now that she was gone. Thinking of her tore a new hole in his festering wound. He turned away from the screen, refusing to allow whoever watched him to see his grief.

His hands shook again. Only one of two things could settle his jitters.

In the kitchen, he ignored the food replicator and made a pot of coffee the old fashioned way. He filled his "I heart Boston" mug to the brim, something Isla had bought for him in an antique shop a few years back. The aroma filled the room and he licked his dry lips. Actigen—pills that allowed him to skip sleep—and coffee were his go-to diet on missions. Sleep only made him dream of Isla. The last thing he wanted was to imagine what the

Indigenes had done to her. He'd survived without sleep for the last two years. And that's how he'd continue until he found her.

Bill carried his mug with the cracked rim and faded heart back to the living room and his waiting files. The Indigene's meeting was rumoured to happen the following morning and, if World Government intel was correct, it would occur in the hour after dawn. These cold-blooded Indigenes with a low tolerance for high temperatures had found a way to surface safely.

Bill wanted to know how.

He placed his DPad on one knee and balanced the mug on the other. With a flick of his index finger, he pulled the information from the screen. It became a 3D image before him. He resumed his review of the government's files on the alien race.

The problem with the indigenous race was a difficult one to solve. Humans had no choice: move to Exilon 5 or die on a resource-exhausted Earth. At the point when everything looked like it might settle down, the Indigenes popped up out of nowhere. Even Gilchrist had been shocked.

But not Bill. He knew they'd come. Intel had reported bands of Indigenes were targeting humans during their nocturnal trips. He estimated it wouldn't be long before they would surface again.

The wait was almost over. Soon, one of the creatures would make a mistake and walk right into Bill's backyard. And when they did, he would be waiting.

4

Stephen leaned against the tunnel wall outside his lab. What advantages did he have over the Surface Creatures that would guarantee his safety the following day? Speed? Strength?

The Indigenes fared better on intellect, but the Surface Creatures understood cunning and deception in a way that put him at a disadvantage. He pushed off from the wall and paced the length of the tunnel. What else could he use—his vision?

An Indigene's vision worked best in low levels of light. It allowed them to make sense of the dark and was the reason they preferred hunting at night.

Relax, said Anton leaning against the entrance to the lab. *It'll be fine.*

You wouldn't say that if it were you going.

Anton grinned. *Yes, I would. I have faith in my inventions.*

Stephen hid his jealousy; his friend's easygoing nature was hard to take sometimes. Seeing his parents die had made Stephen anxious about everything. But the upcoming trip was too important to mess up over his insecurities. Insecurities that made him want to tear the silicone skin from his face and cancel his plans. His last trip to the surface to study the Surface Creatures hadn't gone so well. His group of three had used a cheap disguise and no silicone skin to hide their real identities.

On the back of Central Council orders to find out more about them, his group had started their search just inside the city border for New London. Outside a closed food replication terminal building, they'd found group of seven boys. Even from a distance, he'd caught the pungent smell of alcohol in the air.

Their approach reduced the boys' loud chatter to whispers. A skittish Stephen hung back while the other two Indigenes moved closer.

What could he say to them? How about, *your parents are murderers and you will grow up to be one, too?*

Not exactly the best way to get them to talk.

To his relief, one of the other Indigenes started the interrogation. The mood started out light, but turned heavy when the questions to the boys became more personal. Stephen's finely tuned hearing allowed him to pick up the boys' utterances.

'Who the fuck are these losers?'

'I know. I'm losing me buzz.'

'I'm bored.'

'C'mon, let's show these clowns what dirt tastes like.'

'Yeah!'

'I wanna go home.'

'Stay where you are, Jason. Everybody's stayin' put.'

'D'ya think they're some kind o' military?'

'Dunno. They're not wearing uniforms.'

'Don't wanna to get into no trouble.'

'Don't be an idiot, Jason. Do as I say.'

'Seven against three. Easy.'

The boys came at them, arms flailing and legs kicking, fuelled by a mixture of alcohol and stupidity. Stephen retreated into the dark night. The other Indigenes followed. But instead of leaving, they stopped a short distance away and listened.

'Where'd they go?' said one boy.

'What the fuck?'

'It's like them Shadow People I keep hearing 'bout.'

'Don't be an idiot. That's just legend. A story to scare the little kiddies so they don't fall 'sleep.'

'No, I heard them people's real. They hunt late at night and they eat kids and adults if they sleep. Sometimes they catch them out here.'

'That don't even make sense, Jason. We're out here ev'ry night, and I haven't seen no Shadow People.'

'Well what'dya call them people just here then?'

'Fucking losers.'

It was the first time Stephen had heard the term "Shadow People" and Central Council had no idea whom among their race was hunting Surface Creatures. Any future contact with the race on the surface needed to be planned out.

Why is Pierre letting you go and not me? Anton's voice broke through his thoughts.

Because it was my idea to target one of them during daylight hours.

He must have been crazy to suggest such a thing. But all he could think about was avenging his parents' death. To do that, he needed to learn more about the race's weaknesses. While Pierre had agreed with his logic, Elise, Pierre's wife and the second elder of District Three, had not.

He had a target in mind: a loner boy who he'd been observing for a while. He'd promised Pierre he would use the boy's natural curiosity to gain his trust.

You're not exactly the friendliest Indigene around, said Anton.

Only two Indigenes could say that to him: Anton, and his other friend, Arianna.

And the elders.

I can pretend for a day.

Stephen took out a box and rummaged through the items that had been 'acquired' from the Surface Creatures over the past few months. He fished out a thumb-sized digital recorder that Anton had stolen from a female's bag.

'Took me a few tries to get that.' Anton switched to his voice. 'She kept moving her bag around. I had to move faster than she did.'

Stephen located to a new room off from the tunnel where he'd tested the air filtration device. A metal table sat in the centre of the square shaped room, flanked by two chairs. A soft hue illuminated the white walls; the light was facilitated by tiny solar-powered discs embedded into the wasteland above. He placed the tiny recorder on the floor, near one of the table legs, and waved his hand over the device to start the first recording.

A high-resolution 3D image of the restaurant burst out of the device, filling the otherwise plain room with a soft light. The wall's surface bounced the images back into the room. Stephen watched as Cantaloupe restaurant came into focus. It felt strange to sit in a place where people served other people food. Stephen ate nothing he didn't kill himself, but the decline of the primoris—a native animal on Exilon 5—had forced their race to seek alternatives to a raw-meat diet rich in iron. Animal hunting satisfied their primal urge while a synthesised protein substitute kept them alive. The animals the Surface Creatures had brought with them tasted strange; the composition of their blood was different to the primoris. While the taste of warm blood and fresh meat from the new animals suppressed their desires, it did not satiate their hunger.

Stephen sat at the table and aligned his body to mirror one half of a Surface-Creature couple. He immersed himself into their timeline as they ate. Anton sat opposite him with the 3D image of the second person overlaid on his upper body and face. Sitting down was an unnatural position for Indigenes who preferred to stand. He gripped the steel edges of the chair and studied the recording, observing the way they used their hands to gesture. He concentrated on their conversation. When he watched the Surface Creatures in this way, he could be clinical in his observations; no hate, or panic or fear to upset his preparations. His lips moved in perfect synchronicity with theirs.

'I remember this scene. I sat right over there.' Anton pointed to a spot off camera. 'I was lucky nobody bothered me.'

Stephen's gaze settled on a lone male in his forties with dark brown hair sitting by the window.

'He watched me for a while,' said Anton. 'But I'd hidden the camera well enough. Then he gave up and just went back to looking out the window.'

'What would you have done if he'd approached you?'

Anton smiled. 'I have no idea.'

The recording looped, and Stephen glanced around the restaurant he'd seen too many times now. A much older male sat to his right.

'How long do you think they live for?' asked Anton.

The oldest living Indigene on record was one hundred and ninety-eight. He knew the Surface Creatures' bodies were the same—one heart, one liver, two kidneys and one brain—but fundamental differences still existed between the two species. The Indigenes' bodies and minds didn't suffer deterioration due to the regeneration of all cells. An injury that could take weeks to heal in a Surface Creature would only take minutes in an Indigene's body. Having studied their physical composition from books, Stephen discovered that the cells in their brains and spinal column possessed no regenerative ability. The Surface Creatures relied on the production of synthetic cells to combat brain injuries, old age and paralysis. Disease was uncommon among the Indigenes, because an infected cell never had time to manipulate a healthy one when the body was already expelling it.

The lone male by the window with the salt and pepper hair drew his attention again. A sudden hate for him forced Stephen's concentration back to Anton and the image of the companion superimposed over him.

Anton was mimicking the movement of his doppelganger's hands. 'See how they do that? It's like he's playing out a musical score.'

Anton continued to copy the movements while Stephen watched and learned.

The recording looped for the third time and, right on cue, a female came to the table and filled their glasses with water. He'd read somewhere that Surface Creatures' bodies contained sixty per cent water, although they didn't always drink it in its purest form. The same female handed a beer to the male by the window. While the Indigenes could drink water, it didn't "quench" their thirst as it seemed to do for the Surface Creatures. Initially when the

Surface Creatures first relocated to the barren planet, they had brought their own water with them. What little supply they did find on Exilon 5, however, they replicated using chemicals.

How had the Surface Creatures with their lesser intelligence come to destroy so many Indigenes? It was almost as if they knew of the Indigene's existence.

He kept that thought from Anton who watched him carefully now.

I think you should take a break, Stephen.
I'm fine. I need to rehearse this.
I think you've got it.

Stephen ignored his friend and allowed the scene to loop for a fourth time. He rehearsed their movements and studied their familiar ease with one another, ignoring eerie similarities between their species. There were plenty of differences, too; like the speed at which both species moved. The Indigenes regularly conversed in thought alone; words weren't always necessary to convey a message. Since Stephen rarely spoke out loud he would have to slow down his speech for this mission. He loosened up his stiff posture and turned off the recording.

'I need a set of your lenses.'

Anton stood up and stretched out his back. 'I really hate chairs. I'll get a set for you now.'

The lenses would protect his retinas from the harmful daytime sun.

With Anton gone to get the lenses, Stephen cast his own chair to one side and pushed the table against one wall. In the box, he picked out a half-length mirror and propped it up against the wall. The silicone skin he'd tried on earlier still clung to his skin. He looked past his strange image and practised his eye movements, then his speech, and last his hand gestures. He kept rehearsing until the movements felt a little less obvious and more natural.

Anton stood at the door with a box in his hand. *It's just for an hour. No problem.*

Just an hour. So why was Stephen nervous about the trip the next day? Was it because the Surface Creatures had killed his parents? Every fibre of his body screamed at him to stay.

But he had to go. Central Council needed answers.

The time for waiting, the time for hiding, was over.

5

Laura O'Halloran dashed across the road to the nearest food replication terminal for lunch, one of many located close to the Earth Security Centre, in Sydney. She stepped inside the entrance area, along with fifty others. The doors closed behind them and fans whirred overhead as the harmful Earth air was decontaminated. A second set of doors opened giving her access to the environmentally-controlled terminal.

She popped off her gel mask from her face and placed it in her pocket. Next, she tugged at the Velcro strips that covered the zipped part of her grey ESC uniform. Her fine blonde hair fused with the strip and she worked it loose. That tight feeling around her neck lessened the moment she released the top section.

A breath of relief rushed out of her, but a new scent spoiled her joy. She spluttered as the smell of body odour and sickly sweet lavender hit her—the latter designed to mask the noxious smell. Sucking in a new breath, she joined the queue of people waiting to use one of the replication machines. A hunched-over woman in her nineties stood to the front of her; crooked postures were a common side effect from overuse of the genetic manipulation clinics. A large sweaty man pressed up against her back, causing her to squirm in the cramped space. But the more she moved, the more the air toxins clung to her pale and clammy skin. People eyed her suspiciously, as they often did when she displayed her ESC uniform.

The queue inside the confined corridor moved forward quickly. At least efficiency and speed rated high in a world with twenty billion people. The old woman selected a beef stew and a glass of water. Laura ordered a chicken sandwich and a Coke, a choice which caught the woman's attention.

'Don't order that, dear. There's something wrong with the chicken replica. Looks and tastes like solidified porridge. Quite disgusting.' Her nose wrinkled.

'What's good?' Laura asked to be polite. Truth was she was too hungry to care.

The woman leaned in. 'Anything except the chicken. Larry, who runs this place, says they're trying to get replacements for some of the particle cards but the companies won't replace them. The graphic cards need fixing too, he says. They're years old now and don't work properly. Have you seen how unappetising some choices look? Should take those foods off the menu, if you ask me.'

'Thanks.' Laura changed her order to lamb slices with potato cakes and mint jelly. The woman smiled as Laura collected her food from the base of the machine.

The line progressed towards the pay station.

She had felt eyes on her the moment she walked into the replication terminal, but now one hot set burned a hole in the back of her skull. She turned around to see a man in his early forties, with slicked-back hair and a beanpoleshaped body, staring at her. His loose jeans were secured with an old belt. She'd seen many junkies like him before, but she didn't know if he was a druggie or a tech over loader. Both types had one thing in common: wild eyes.

'Can I help you?'

The man said, 'You lot over there think you're so fucking great.'

She braced herself for another verbal attack, usually brought on by the uniform she wore. 'Is there something you want?'

'My mother is in debt because of you,' the man almost hissed at her. 'Owes your crowd a ton of money. Can't sleep 'cause she's expecting your lot to break down her door and arrest her.' He pointed at her. 'What are *you* going to do about it?'

'You need to take it up with the World Government. I work at the ESC.'

Laura worked on Level Four of the ESC, where she'd spent too many hours filing away boring information about tax matters. In other sections, workers checked, processed and filed traffic violations and countless transactions that the inhabitants of Earth had charged to their accounts. ESC had nothing to do with setting taxes or chasing down tax-evaders. That was the World Government's job. But that detail didn't matter to most people.

'Same fucking thing if you ask me.'

The junkie left his place in the queue and got in her face. Laura shrank back from the smell of his putrid breath. She noticed the track marks on his right arm as he used it to block her path.

Jabbing a finger in her face he said, 'You lot are all the same, sucking the goodness out of innocent people like me and my family. You make me sick.'

Hot spit landed on her face. She tried to wipe it away, but the junkie had pinned her against the counter.

The large man, who'd been queuing behind her, stepped forward suddenly and pulled the junkie back by his collar. 'Looks like you're queue-jumping and we don't tolerate that in here. So either you go back in line or I throw you out the door. Your choice. If you're lucky, I might not break all your bones when I slam you into the pavement.'

The junkie squirmed out of his restraint and rejoined the queue, his eyes seething with hatred.

Laura released a breath.

'Thanks,' she said. The man grunted and returned to his place in line.

At the pay station, she scanned her identity chip. Her legs shook as she entered the common eating room, still shocked by her confrontation.

The square room was standing room only. She found a not so quiet—but much coveted—spot by the window. There she nibbled at her tasteless lunch, hoping to avoid any more drama.

The large man entered the room and stood between her and the entrance to the corridor. When the junkie finally entered, his eyes searched the room, but he lost interest when he saw the hulking figure in his way. For once, Laura couldn't be happier for the packed room conditions.

She picked the fat off her lamb slices and gazed out at the dark, smog-filled day. It had been ten years since she'd seen the sun, when she was twenty-six years old. Since then, the change in atmospheric conditions had led to a steady increase in cloud and drop in temperature. A constant chill now replaced the lack of sunlight. In the thirty years since Laura's parents had emigrated from

Dublin to Sydney, the temperatures barely surpassed ten degrees in high summer. Her golden hair no longer shone. Her previously sun-kissed complexion was now pale and pasty.

She tore off a piece of lamb and popped into her mouth, wondering if she would ever see or feel the sun again. Exilon 5 had sunlight in abundance and she dreamed of living there one day. But early selection for the World Government's transfer programme was not a guarantee. It seemed the policy changed every six months, and working at the Earth Security Centre didn't give her any special rights. What was once a volunteer arrangement had now changed to a lottery selection. But with only a small percentage of the population having transferred, she wasn't sure how to play the numbers.

The city still carried evidence of the catalyst that had changed Earth's atmospheric conditions. Their generation blamed the habits of older generations, but little had been done to stem the changes. Tattered posters on walls announcing the *Go Green* revolution served as a daily reminder of their failure to stop the problem. *Go Green*: the World Government's answer to counteracting global change. But as industries became self-sustainable, green energy had not become the cash cow they had hoped for.

It was at the turn of the twenty-second century when space exploration really took off. How to fund that exploration? Tax the *Go Green* initiative, of course. Any businesses and industries that survived were subsumed by World Government to become its new subsidiaries.

Laura picked at her lamb. Her appetite waned further when she caught the junkie staring at her. If only people could see the good work the ESC was doing. Headed up by Daphne Gilchrist, the woman not only protected the Earth from unknown dangers but from people themselves.

Laura's only chance to move to Exilon 5 would happen through promotion; she'd heard that the higher levels had a better chance of catching Gilchrist's attention for the transfer programme. The purple-uniformed workers from Level Five commanded instant respect. That's what she wanted.

Respect. From Gilchrist.

Tired of the hostile attention because of her uniform, she dropped her leftovers into one of the waste incinerators and headed for the exit.

Laura affixed her gel mask to her face. The frigid air hit her like she'd plunged into icy water. She wrapped her coat around her tighter and crossed the street, remembering when trees and plants used to grow in the city. But nothing grew in an atmosphere with high levels of CO_2 and nitrogen. She'd almost forgotten what flowers looked like. Wild animals had been the next to go, although the city had preserved some domesticated creatures. Humans were the only species adaptable enough to live in the toxic air.

She approached the ESC building, surrounded by an invisible medium-level force field that her security chip allowed her to access. The public area to the front—the newest and brightest section of the Centre—was the only part without an active force field. She bounded up the crescent-shaped steps and into the private entrance through the former Anzac War Memorial building. Recognisable by its pink granite exterior, it had remained largely unchanged since it was designed by C. Bruce Dellit and completed in 1934. The World Government had added the public section to the memorial building about fifty years ago, as part of its attempts to regenerate a declining city.

Inside, white granite covered the floor and part of the walls. Various sculptures and figure reliefs hugged the upper part, protected by a symphony of stars across the dome-shaped ceiling. The gold stars, one hundred and twenty, reminded the city of the many wars of the past, and the volunteers who'd fought during a more primitive time. A Rayner Hoff sculpture named "Sacrifice" had once stood in the centre of the room. The sculpture, with its golden sun and fiery outstretched arms, had been relocated to the public foyer of the Security Centre. In its place was the turbo lift, linking to the nine underground levels.

Laura pressed her right thumb on the flat plate beside the turbo lift doors. The system read her security chip that gave her access to the first four levels below ground. She entered the lift and within seconds the doors opened on Level Four.

A bright foyer with a glass ceiling and floor beckoned. Above her workers walked, but below, to Level Five, she saw nothing through the opaque floor.

Officially known as High Level Data Storage Facility, Five was where the World Government sent its high-security documents. Five had been christened *The Abyss* because of the joke that sensitive information was often lost, never to be seen again.

Her lunchtime experience wasn't anything new. Laura had been losing something she valued for a while now. As she walked across Level Four's foyer, she wondered if she'd ever see her bravery again.

6

Daphne Gilchrist pored over that week's data sent from the ESC overseers for levels one to six. She sat back with a sigh. Facts and figures bored her. She'd rather be commanding her troops into action than checking how many people failed to pay their taxes last month.

When had the Earth Security Centre changed from the front-line organisation protecting Earth from attack to a compiler of information on tax evaders? Okay, Charles Deighton *had* assigned the responsibility of the ITF to the ESC. But the business of investigations and policing was being handled by ITF overseers in each city. What did that leave?

Twenty years as CEO of the ESC had to count for something. She'd even tried to pass this task off to others, but her bio signature was the only one Deighton wanted to see at the end of the report. Daphne pictured a different working role for herself, one that steered the course of humanity.

Exilon 5 mattered. Making sure the Indigenes weren't a threat was paramount. But the direction things were heading under Deighton's command unsettled her.

The World Government board members had allowed him to run with plans to make Exilon 5 safe. In turn, Deighton had assigned Daphne to oversee Bill Taggart and his team.

Yet, here she was checking numbers, while Deighton was about to interfere in an operation he had told her to manage. Deighton told her he would follow up with Bill even after Daphne had assured him she could handle the investigator's difficult manners. Her strict family upbringing in Osaka, Japan, meant she understood men. She valued the Japanese no-nonsense approach to work and traditional views of home life, even if she hadn't gained the respect of being a woman in power there.

Deighton was becoming a problem. His interest in Taggart and his investigation was bordering on obsessive. Why couldn't he trust her to handle things?

Because he has bigger plans than the whereabouts of a few lousy Indigenes.

She knew it. She'd sensed a marked change in the CEO's behaviour, ever since Taggart's wife went missing on Exilon 5. Something had happened to the ex-soldier, the same woman Daphne had been warned to never mention.

Her review of data had taken Daphne to a spare boardroom with a one-way view out across Level Four. She pulled up a new memo, sent within the last hour and marked for her attention. It was a list of names, people who had reached the highest grade in their jobs and were costing money.

A note was attached from Deighton: *Find a way to save me money. I need it for my transfer programme.*

She perused the list of people who were slightly younger than her and who had been earmarked for review. One name stood out from the list: Jenny Waterson. A skilled pilot with no prior infractions. Her crime? Having experience and costing too much.

But what Deighton wanted Deighton got.

A blonde-haired woman rushed into the lobby and pulled her focus away from the list of names. From personnel files, Gilchrist recognised her as Laura O'Halloran.

Daphne turned her DPad around and looked up details on the worker. *Father committed suicide. Mother is a recluse. O'Halloran lives alone and is the first to volunteer for extra shifts.*

She admired people who worked hard. She looked up. Although seeing the girl hopping around like a jittery cat, Daphne would reserve her judgement.

O'Halloran jerked to a stop, her eyes wide as a second woman walked her way. A Level Five worker.

Daphne stood with a smirk and smoothed down her grey pants suit. Nothing ever happened on Level Seven and Eight, the location of her office and that of her overseers.

'Hello.' The glass muffled O'Halloran's greeting to the woman.

The Level Five worker glanced at her, nodded, and walked on, leaving a dazed O'Halloran in her wake.

Daphne checked her reflection in the glass wall. The feminine folds of the grey suit she wore hid her stocky frame. Her cobalt-blue eyes, framed by red hair that curled under at the nape of her neck, contained little emotion. Her eyes were her secret weapon; she could hide a lot from others in them. One side of her genetically altered face lifted into a half smile. Now in her late eighties, she looked no older than sixty-five.

Grabbing her DPad first, she left the boardroom through a door not visible to the workers and walked towards O'Halloran.

The blonde haired woman looked over, eyes wide. 'Shit...'

Daphne didn't pause in her stride. 'Laura O'Halloran?' she boomed from across the foyer.

'Y...Yes?'

'Why were you addressing a Level Five worker?'

'I... I was saying hello.'

She stopped abruptly in front of her, catching the woman in her glare. Most days she wouldn't bother, but she'd been after any distraction from reviewing the weekly updates.

'You are not cleared to talk to the higher levels.'

O'Halloran's pony tail bobbed with her nod. Her eyes slid to Daphne's stomach. 'My mistake. I apologise.'

'This is your only warning,' said Gilchrist. 'Get back to work.'

She turned and walked back to the boardroom, affording a smile as soon as her back was turned to the woman. What she'd said was true enough. Level Five workers were off limits.

Daphne slipped into the boardroom once more and checked the updates of the overseers for each level. She stopped on the data for Level Five, the one Suzanne Brett oversaw.

The Abyss. It was a crude nickname given to the level by the workers. While information didn't disappear from there as rumoured, it was kept on a separate server only accessible to those with clearance.

The information in Brett's report was light, but she expected that to change soon with Bill Taggart's current investigation.

7

Laura released a breath as she watched Gilchrist disappear through a wall, like it wasn't there. She searched for the hidden door that she assumed contained an observation room used only by the CEO.

With shaky legs she carried on to the door at the end of Corridor Ten. There, she pressed her chip to the security plate at the end of the hall. Her full name, photo and title flashed up on the screen, along with the time she'd been absent.

Gilchrist had rattled her. She entered the office space and scurried up the middle aisle, hoping to reach her chair before she collapsed. On either side, dozens of white workstations sat in neat rows, totalling one hundred. Each row was divided into sections of six. She dropped into her seat that was in the third section.

Janine, a co-worker with a bitter edge, looked her over. 'What's wrong with you?'

'Just had a run-in with Gilchrist.'

Her eyes widened. 'Over what?'

The other workers stopped what they were doing and listened. Laura gripped the arm rests. She'd worked hard to keep her nose clean. And in one second Gilchrist caught her out.

'I was caught talking to a Level Fiver.'

'Crap. And she pulled you up on that?' said Chris, another co-worker, less bitter than Janine.

She nodded. 'Came out of nowhere.'

He pursed his lips in a pitying way. 'Yeah, she tends to do that. This place is full of secret doors.'

'And some guy was abusive to me in the terminal.'

'You can't seem to catch a break today, can ya?' Janine's icy tone chilled her.

'Do you even have a sympathetic bone in your body?' Chris said.

Janine's face reddened. 'I'm just saying I'm glad it wasn't me. Laura can take it. She's Teflon. Nothing sticks to her. I'm a lot softer.' Chris blew out a disbelieving breath. 'What? I am!'

'And I'm a virgin,' said Chris.

Laura ignored Janine, the drama queen. She activated her workstation and the screen whirred into life. Thousands of documents awaited her, all from the inhabitants of Earth. Before the end of the day, there would be another one hundred thousand added to the list. Encrypted information sent electronically to the Security Centre contained thousands of layers of code that had been stripped out before reaching Level Four. Her job, along with everyone else on Level Four, was to sort the information before re-encrypting it and sending it for long-term storage in the supercomputer on Level Nine. Their orders were to redirect any material that was still encrypted to Level Five.

While the supercomputer could do her job, Chris had said the ESC considered document-sorting to be a lesson in character-building; it weeded out the workers who weren't cut out for life there. A list of people on the outside waited for her job, waited for her to slip. Loyalty meant little in a world with more people than jobs. Laura had kept her job so far by not making waves. Except for her major slip up a few moments ago.

Her thoughts went to the junkie in the food terminal. She wished she'd asked his name so she could look him up, see how much he owed and to whom. People who screamed publicly about family debts were usually careless with money, over-indulging in gambling, drug or tech addiction, unnecessary organ purchases or genetic manipulation treatments not covered by the World Government longevity programme. But genuine debt cases existed, too, but she couldn't help but wonder if his mother's debts had been caused by her son's habit.

'Are you still mad at me?' Janine asked Laura.

She closed her eyes and took a cleansing deep breath. Janine could be a handful. 'No, I'm not mad at you.'

'Look, it's not my fault you got into trouble at the terminal. What did you say to them, anyway, to go off on you?'

'I don't have to *say* anything to them. The sight of me is enough to set them off.'

Janine lifted her chin. 'I always wear my overcoat. I sweat like hell when I'm inside, but at least they can't see my uniform. You should have done that.'

Laura gritted her teeth to stop her from telling Janine to mind her own business. That would upset the semi-calm working environment she enjoyed.

'I'll keep that in mind.'

'Have you heard they're running a lottery in Darlinghurst?' said Chris.

Laura's stomach dropped. 'Not Haymarket?' She

lived in an apartment block in that district.

'Not yet,' said Chris. 'Don't know what made them pick Darlinghurst. Point Piper and Rose Bay, too.' The transfer programme was living up to its lottery rules. 'My mate says they're going to focus on Perth after this.'

'What? That's it? Just three areas?' Laura stood up and pinned Chris with a stare. 'Did they say when they were coming back to Sydney?'

He held his hands up. 'Hey, don't shoot the messenger, all right? You know how these things go—how often they change their mind? Every six months now. They'll focus on Australia again in no time.'

Laura slumped into her chair, wishing she could believe that. With a heavy heart, she resumed her review of the documents on screen. Earth was no place—and no way—to live. In a society where government discouraged free thinking and technology ruled, it became harder to find the good in life.

Her initial enthusiasm to work at the second most prestigious organisation on Earth, behind the World Government, had carried her for a while. Three years on and she'd seen many people come and go from the lower ranks. Promotional opportunities at the higher levels were rare and she was sick of being another of Gilchrist's forgotten. During her darkest days, she contemplated quitting. But staying at the ESC gave her and her mother the best shot at transferring to Exilon 5.

New documents pooled on her screen. One of them listed names for non-payment of taxes. The first was a Mrs Annette Billings of Toronto, Canada. Seventy-six years old; she had failed to pay her outstanding tax following receipt of a new heart. It was her first violation. She'd given the excuse she waited on eye replacements and had not seen the reminders. A note sat beside her name: *Has received goods. First Warning Issued.* She had paid her arrears within the extra time allotted.

Seven hundred other entries on the list all had similar stories. The seventeenth name was highlighted in red: Mr Robert Fennell, originally from Wales but now residing in Tokyo. Fifty-eight years old. *Failure to pay apartment taxes. Issued with second warning. No further failures will be tolerated.* According to the file, he'd promptly paid the outstanding balances, including arrears.

Laura sat back in her chair with a groan. She could do this job with her eyes closed. Gilchrist may have caught her just now, but she didn't care about Level Four workers. Laura needed to find a better way to catch the CEO's attention, because moving to Exilon 5 wasn't about some silly dream.

She needed it like she needed air. She needed it to relieve the clawing, incessant tick in her mind; a painful, desperate longing that living on Earth only made worse.

Laura was sick and Exilon 5 was the cure.

8

Bill's communication device shuddered on the coffee table, jolting him out of his thoughts. He grabbed it and shoved it in his ear. What did Gilchrist want now?

His patience wore thinner as he activated the device. A thin microphone unfolded to the start of his mouth.

'Yeah?'

'Mr Taggart?'

Bill almost dropped his mug of coffee when he heard the voice. 'Yeah?'

'Charles Deighton. Lovely to talk to you, old boy. It's been a while.'

Not long enough.

'What, er, can I do for you, Mr Deighton?'

'I just spoke to Ms Gilchrist about this mission and I wanted to add my support to you and your team.'

First time for everything, he supposed.

'Thank you.' Bill had only spoken to the CEO of the World Government twice before; once was to challenge his orders to send Isla to Exilon 5.

'I must admit I'm a little envious of you, stuck on a sunny planet, filled with fresh air and hope.' His breathing rasped. 'To tell you the truth, I'm sick of wearing my damn gel mask every time I leave a controlled environmental zone.'

'It's... different.'

'Bill... I hope I can call you Bill.' Deighton didn't wait for an answer. 'I must stress the importance of the events about to unfold tomorrow.'

'I'm well aware, sir.'

'But you've had trouble since your wife—Isla wasn't it—disappeared? There's still time for you to step down from the task.'

Bill gritted his teeth at the mention of her name. 'No thank you, sir. I'll be fine.'

Deighton cleared his aged throat. 'That's what I told Ms Gilchrist. She was worried about you, but I said, "Daphne, Bill is one of our best investigators. If anyone can do this, he can." Are you clear on what's not to happen tomorrow?'

He nodded, even though Deighton couldn't see him. 'At the briefing. Observe only. Don't apprehend.'

'Good. This is an important moment for all of us. It's the first time one of the Indigenes has been brave enough to surface during daytime. We don't want to scare him or her off. Just let it happen.'

Everything Deighton said had already been covered in Bill's briefing with Gilchrist over two months ago, when increased activity had been first logged within city limits. He struggled to see the reason for this call.

Deighton continued, 'Bill, you've always been a loyal servant, and you proved that loyalty when you helped us take down Larry Hunt.'

'Thank you sir.'

'Your wife would have been proud to see how far you've come.'

Okay, he was done talking.

'I really should get back—'

Deighton chuckled. 'Of course! Apologies, I'm keeping you from your work. Back to it, soldier.'

Deighton clicked off. The microphone folded back into the top of the earpiece. Bill yanked the unit out and tossed on the table.

'Fuck!' Anger bloomed in his chest. He paced the room to try and ease it. The last thing he needed was a pep talk from the man who'd put Isla on the very mission she'd disappeared from.

His breaths turned short and sharp. He punched the spot next to the Light Box, causing its 3D image to ripple. A sudden flash turned his anger into fear. Who was watching him: Deighton or Gilchrist?

Struggling to breathe, he snatched up his DPad and relocated to his bedroom, where he perched on the edge of the bed. 'Calm down, Bill.'

He couldn't help it. Deighton brought out the worst in him.

Larry Hunt. A prize scalp in the one-hundred and nineteen-year-old's eyes.

He activated his DPad and pulled up Larry Hunt's photo. Staring back at him was the criminal he'd helped to put behind bars. Hunt was an ordinary-looking man; most criminals usually were. Bill had expected retaliation from Hunt for his involvement in bringing him to justice, but more than that, he'd expected to feel relieved. The empty feeling after the catch had surprised him.

The chase had felt too easy, almost like he'd been set up to succeed. When Hunt Technologies had released their latest food replication model, the Replica 2500, the ESC had ordered Bill to intervene. Hundreds of businesses that had bought the model were touting it as a fake.

Daphne Gilchrist had ordered him to a meeting. On his arrival, she'd handed him a list of numbers.

'What do you see?'

Bill scanned the information, recognising the format of prices against amounts. 'Shares.'

'Exactly. Mr Hunt has been pulling a stroke, overvaluing his stocks to gain a better share of the replication market. Naturally, the World Government board members are upset at this revelation. If the Replica 2500 is a fake, the company's value will drop into negative equity. That's a loss nobody wants.'

Bill looked up at her. 'You want me to profile him?'

Gilchrist leaned across the table, her expression cold. 'I want you to take the son of a bitch down.'

Bill had spent months trying to get inside the head of the man who had dominated the food replication world for three decades. He eventually found his way in, through a disgruntled employee with bills to pay.

Bill recalled his only encounter with two of Hunt's henchmen shortly after his indictment. He'd attempted to shake his pursuers as they chased him through London's dark streets. After cornering him, one man grabbed his arms so roughly he'd almost dislocated Bill's shoulder. The other produced an antique knife. He'd plunged the blade into the soft area of his left shoulder.

A goddamn antique knife. There were easier ways to kill him.

The attack had come with a verbal warning attached. 'Hunt wants you to remember this.'

Bill touched the area where the knife had penetrated his skin. Although it was repaired with no sign of a scar, he still remembered the blinding hot pain from the blade tearing through his skin.

His hands shook as he flicked Hunt's photo away

and returned to his files on the Indigenes. The caffeine tremors made it hard to hold the DPad, but the Actigen worked to balance out his addiction and give him focus.

He needed answers soon. Only then would he kick both bad habits.

Bill combed through the dozens of files the World Government held on the Indigenes. With so many to choose from, one drew his attention every time. It was a year ago, when the government had captured a young Indigene. The alien had not lived long due to its inability to breathe the same air as humans. The file also mentioned details about an atmosphere-controlled containment unit in a medical facility, on the outskirts of New London. Maybe Bill would take a closer look at that facility once his mission ended.

'Watch the subject, don't approach it.' Gilchrist's warning to him at the briefing. 'And make sure those idiots we assigned you don't do anything stupid.'

Bill had requested a Special Forces team. What he got was Armoured Division, minus the heavy artillery. 'Divide and Conquer' was their motto.

What he really wanted was a chance to question the alien about Isla's whereabouts. After, the World Government, the ESC—or whoever wanted it—could do what they liked.

Memories of his wife were more vivid than usual. She'd been the optimistic antidote to his pessimism.

One of those memories had been of her beautiful dark-brown hair that hung down to her waist. As he recalled, it had required a lot of maintenance.

'Why don't you ever cut your hair?' he'd asked her once.

'Because it makes me feel feminine. It's also where my strength lies, like Samson.' She gathered up a bunch of hair. 'It took me so long to grow. If cut it, I'd feel like I'd lost a part of me.'

The memory unsettled him more than usual as he returned to the living room. Maybe it was because he was using the mug she'd given him. Or maybe it was because he inched closer to the truth about her disappearance. He trawled through past memories, searching for new clues that might explain her disappearance. Deighton had been helpful enough initially, but it didn't take long for him to lose interest.

'She's gone, Bill. You must accept that. We have all suffered a great loss. Isla was one of our best soldiers. We share in your pain.'

He walked over to the window and rested his face and hands on the cold glass. Belgrave Square Gardens sat across from his apartment. He watched an automated vehicle pull up to the entrance through a fog his breath had created. Half a dozen children and one woman—presumably their teacher—alighted from the vehicle. The children screamed as they bolted for the swings in the park. The teacher yelled after them to come back but they were running free and wild.

The window fogged up more as his breathing became laboured. Isla had been open about her desire to have children, but Bill hadn't been as keen as her. He didn't think Earth was the right environment to raised them, but had promised to think about it again when they transferred to Exilon 5. Now Isla was gone and all he could think about was having a child; a little version of her to make him laugh the way she always could. But Exilon 5 was no safer than Earth as long as the Indigenes existed. The creatures had stolen the one person from him he cared about most.

Isla was in his head. 'Forgive them, Bill.'

'Forgiveness is earned,' he said coldly. If it came down to it, would he grant it to the Indigenes?

He returned to the sofa and buried his nose in the transcripts from the previous week's surveillance operation. His heart hardened when he read the detail about one male Indigene's attempts to contact a boy in Belgrave Square. But the mother had returned early and taken the boy with her. Now the Indigene had a new boy in its sights: Ben Watson. A scrawny kid with black hair, no father and a mother more interested in virtual reality than life, according to one of his men's reports.

The last attempt at contact had occurred in the hour just after dawn. Criminals usually fell into predictable patterns. There was no reason to think this Indigene wouldn't do the same.

And when he did, Bill would be ready.

9

The sun, low in the sky and not that warm, irritated Stephen's skin. He shifted uncomfortably on the bus-stop bench that was in plain sight of anyone who passed. He had worn a long brown coat and a matching fedora hat to hide his appearance. The rim of the hat made his head sweat.

Anton's artificial skin and his costume reminded him that he did not belong here. His racing heart served as another reminder. This was a bad idea. But despite his inner warning, he stayed put.

Anton's advice last night came to him: 'Sit still and don't fidget. The Surface Creatures will be more likely to overlook you if you do.'

Easier said than done.

How had Anton sat still long enough to record that scene in the restaurant? His friend had always been more pragmatic than him. Stephen, a scientist no less, should have this level-headed business perfected. But faced with his worst fears, he could not stop clenching and unclenching his hands.

He'd spotted the skinny black-haired boy a week

ago. Now, he was sitting next to that same boy with a backpack on his lap. His target glanced at him from where he sat at the other end of the bench. He looked nervous, but Stephen also sensed his curiosity. The boy opened his backpack suddenly and pulled out what looked like a parcel of food. He followed up with a container of orange-coloured liquid.

A new fear rippled through the boy that Stephen felt like a shiver down his own back. That's how he sensed moods: as physical sensations. Fear delivered the strongest one of all. The boy clutched the bag tighter. Oddly, his worry calmed Stephen a little.

When his target glanced at the bag then at him, Stephen understood. The sun lifted higher into the blue sky and raised the air temperature slightly. He could not stay longer than an hour. More importantly, he had no interest in the boy's bag.

'Hello.' The word tumbled out as though he had no control over it. 'What's your name?'

His target sat up straight. Suspicion narrowed his eyes. 'What's yours?'

'My name's Stephen. Forgive me for staring but I've never been this close to your kind. I've only read about you or seen photos. Can you tell me what you are?'

The boy's brow creased. He looked around as if he were expecting someone. 'I'm English. And this is New London. Your skin is dark. Are you from one of the other cities? I didn't know they spoke English like us.'

'Neither place. I live here, just like you. I just don't live in this city.'

A silence followed. Stephen sucked in a deep breath but the butterflies wouldn't settle.

'Forgive me. I should rephrase my original question. What do you call yourself?'

'I suppose you mean my name?' The boy's brow creased with worry. 'Do you know my mum?'

'Who is your mother?'

'Diane Watson.'

'The name is not familiar.'

The boy released a quiet breath and shifted closer. 'My name's Ben. Pleased to meet you.' He thrust out his hand towards him. Stephen hesitated then shook it.

Ben's eyes widened, his mild shock translating into a brief tickle for Stephen. Or maybe that was his own shock he felt. He'd never shaken a Surface Creature's hand before and Ben's skin was warmer than he'd expected. He rubbed the back of his hand where the boy's fingers had rested.

'What's wrong?' asked Ben.

'Your hand is warmer than I'd expected, that's all.'

Ben smiled. 'I was going to say yours is quite cold. Why?'

Stephen sensed only curiosity from him now. 'This is a normal temperature for me. Why is yours so warm?'

'Everybody's hands are warm. You're the one that's different!'

That was true. 'I wonder what else is different about us?'

He shifted in his seat; a new wave of shivering fear from his target hit him.

'Don't go! Please,' Ben said. 'Uh, why is your skin colour so strange? I mean, your neck is really pale, but your face is brown.'

He poked Stephen's neck with his finger. Stephen jerked away from him.

'My skin cannot tolerate the sun. But the covering I wear produces inconsistent and patchy results. Why is yours is so much darker in colour?'

Ben frowned. 'My teacher says it's because I have mel... melon in my skin. It helps turn my skin to brown.' He held up his arm to examine his olive complexion. 'You should know that since you're old, like her.'

An engine-red automated bus pulled up to the kerb, interrupting their conversation. Several people alighted from the back while a queue disappeared into the front. Intermittent beeps drifted from the open door as passengers pressed their thumbs against a touchpad. Neither Ben nor Stephen moved from their spots.

Despite the child seeming harmless, Stephen's skin crawled at his proximity to one of them. But to show weakness in front of the boy could lose Ben's trust. Central Council needed answers, and that would mean pushing the boy's curiosity to get what Stephen needed. Pierre and Elise were no closer to understanding the Surface Creatures than before. He hoped his risky move would finally allow them to understand the enemy.

Uneasy gazes from the passengers on the bus settled on him, then flicked away. He wrapped his coat tighter around him and pulled the lip of his fedora down. The eliminator in his pocket absorbed the static his body naturally emitted.

Maybe he should have brought Anton with him to ask the questions. But Stephen came because he could outrun them all in District Three. His speed was legendary. So too was his lack of patience.

The boy frowned at the ground, as though he were trying to grasp the detail of their discussion. Stephen could have picked any random child. Why he settled on this one both fascinated and disturbed him.

The automated bus moved off and Stephen relaxed as the danger went with it.

He looked around at the new city, built upon the

land once occupied by the Indigenes. So much had been altered in the last thirty years; the Indigenes' living environs and the raised platforms where the Central Council had once stood to address the population were gone. He could no longer pinpoint where he used to play as an Evolver, or where the dome-shaped buildings had once stood. It was as though the Indigenes had been wiped from existence. But what the Surface Creatures had yet to discover was the infinite power beneath their feet.

Stephen checked the time left on his air filtration device. Thirty minutes had passed. He chastised himself for wasting precious minutes lamenting about a past life that no longer existed, that they would never get back.

Ben's next question caught him off guard. 'Why don't you have any hair?'

'I don't need it where I am from.'

His target leaned forward, squinting at Stephen. 'Your eyes look funny. Can you see like we can?'

Stephen opted for the truth. He had to take a few calculated risks. 'I can see better in the dark. But up here, my eyes cannot tolerate bright light. I wear lenses to protect my eyes from the sun.'

Ben nodded and frowned. Mostly confusion, and a little curiosity, dominated his expression.

'Are you cold?' the boy asked next.

The unusual question made Stephen frown. 'Why do you ask?'

'Because you've been shivering for the last two minutes. I was just wondering if you were cold.'

'Actually, the opposite. I am too warm.'

'How come?'

The child went to touch Stephen's hand. His first instinct was to pull away, but he allowed him to make contact.

'My body doesn't react well to this environment. I don't know how to regulate my core temperature here. I live within an entirely different atmosphere.'

'Why, where do you live? New Taiyuan? I hear that's hot. It's not that hot here, you know. It's only going to get to twenty degrees today.'

Had he lived in a hotter climate, his thinner blood would have made it harder for his body to insulate in a colder place. But that's not how his body worked: his core temperature was heating up while his extremities remained cold.

'That wouldn't explain your pale skin though.'

'No, it would not,' said Stephen with a smile. 'And no, I do not live in New Taiyuan. I told you, I live here.'

Ben leaned back into the contours of the bench and swung his legs. Stephen crossed his legs from right to left and rested his hands on his knee; a pre-rehearsed move. Should he keep going or organise another meeting? When he checked the time again, his priorities changed.

He stood. 'I have to leave. I need to be somewhere else.'

'No. I don't want you to go. I want you to stay here.'

'I'm afraid I will be late for another engagement if I stay.'

'I said, stay.' Ben's bottom lip quivered.

The boy's reaction was a good sign; he would be amenable to meet a second time. Whether Stephen could bring himself to show up again was another matter.

Stephen kept one eye on a group of Surface Creatures who had gathered at the bus stop. 'Could we meet again, but somewhere else?' It was far too exposed here.

Ben gave him a gap-toothed grin. 'Where?'

'A place not too far from here. Belgrave Square Gardens. Do you know it?'

He nodded. 'I go there on my own sometimes. I like to play on the swings.'

'Next Saturday at the same time—'

Ben added, '—by the bench near the large oak tree.'

Yes, it should be sheltered enough there. He tipped his hat to the boy in another practised move, and left.

His pace started out easy as he recalled the things Ben had told him. But when he remembered where he was —in their world—a shiver rattled his bones.

Injecting new pace into his slow step, he shook away his ease. No matter how well that had gone he could not let his guard down.

10

That damn Indigene must have picked up on Bill's surveillance team. The male left too fast for him not to have detected something. And now both Caldwell and Page were on the move, despite his orders to stay put.

He growled into the microphone. 'Caldwell, Page. I said to stay where you are. Do you hear me?'

No answer came. Not surprising.

Isla had trained with buffoons like these before. Their bullish behaviour had been the main topic of discussion whenever she checked in from Exilon 5. Certain ITF field operatives had a reputation for following rules, but only when it suited them. His wife could look after herself, but he couldn't help thinking one of those assholes had pushed her into danger while on mission.

Bill paced the living room, wearing a hole in the ITF-issued carpet. His stomach lurched as his best hope of finding Isla ran from the bus stop area. His orders to keep a distance from the target couldn't have been clearer. If he didn't rein Caldwell and Page in, the Indigene could disappear for good, leaving his plan to find Isla in tatters.

Bill fiddled with his earpiece. 'Caldwell, Page. State

your position now.'

An occasional crackle greeted him.

His body twitched from the stimulants in his system. Nervous energy and palpitations replaced his recent lethargy. He sat down and fussed with his ear piece as he waited for a response.

For a moment he considered joining the pursuit, but everything was happening too fast.

Bill pulled the thin microphone closer to his mouth. 'Caldwell? I know you're out there and I know you can hear me. Where the fuck are you?'

A heavy silence hung in the air. His heart pounded against his ribs, forcing him to pull in a sharp breath. Both hands quivered from a mixture of agitation and stimulants. He was sick of this shit, following Gilchrist's insane instructions not to intervene. Why weren't they capturing the alien?

'Jesus, come on...'

A voice broke through the air and startled him.

'Caldwell here. Sorry for the silence earlier. It was necessary. Over.'

'What the hell is happening down there? Where are you?'

'Page and I are keeping our distance. It appears the alien is headed for the Maglev station, in New Victoria district. Over.'

He slammed his fist down on his leg. 'You'd better not lose him. Where is he now?'

Caldwell grunted. Annoyed or out of breath? Bill didn't care.

'The alien is closing on the main entrance. He already had a strong head start. The crowds are thick here. They might slow him down. Over.'

Bill warned Caldwell, 'Make sure he doesn't see

you. We need the meeting to happen next week.' When he got no reply, Bill added, 'Understood?'

'Sure, sure. Gotta go.'

Caldwell clicked off, driving Bill to his feet and to pace the living room again.

A second voice broke through. 'Officer Page here. The alien is moving too fast. Over.' Her breathless words indicated she was on the move.

'Don't you dare lose him, Page. We need to know how he's moving around.' It wasn't much but knowing the alien's route in and out of the city might come in handy.

'It's at the entrance to the train station. I've got to go—'

Bill punched the wall. Radio silence followed without an update. His fear escalated.

Had these aliens perceived Isla to be a threat? Is that why she disappeared?

A new voice shrilled through Bill's earpiece.

'Caldwell here. We're in New Victoria station. Over.'

'Tell me you caught it.'

'It's gone.'

His hands shook worse than before. Gilchrist's instructions to observe only agitated him. He wasn't going to find Isla by sitting in his apartment. This was bullshit.

Bill looked out the window just as a red bus pulled up. Ben Watson got out. Bill broke protocol and made plans to leave his apartment.

He shoved a stuffed toy containing audio and visual equipment into his bag, from an ITF box of supplies. With his bag slung across his body, Bill exited the apartment and took the stairs two at a time to the ground floor. He burst through the main door to his apartment block and stepped off the kerb without looking. An automated car barked at him. Bill jumped back, then made a quick run for it when it passed.

The spacious park was quiet at this early hour, but he knew exactly where the boy would be. He walked to the area with the swings. There he found the boy swinging higher with each push.

Bill slowed his walk, not wishing to alarm the boy. But despite his efforts, Ben jerked to a stop and jumped off the swings.

'Who are you?'

Bill smiled at him. The boy looked like he might run.

He held his hands up. 'Easy now, I just want to talk.'

Ben's eyes grew large. He looked around. 'Did my mother send you?'

'No. I swear. I just want to ask you a couple of questions.'

'About what?'

Bill lowered his hands and stepped closer. 'About your friend from earlier.'

Mention of the alien appeared to soften Ben's mood. But only a bit. 'He didn't do anything.'

'He's not in trouble, I swear.'

A sudden breeze rushed through the trees above their heads and lifted leaves from their branches. The leaves danced and swirled around Ben's head. Ben dug his feet into the sand—a sign Bill's soft touch wasn't working.

He opted for a new angle. 'Why don't I just speak to your mother? We can ask her about your new friend.'

Ben stumbled and fell to his knees. 'No! I'll tell you what you want to know. I promise.'

The boy got to his feet and blurted out the stranger's name, recalling his own observations about Stephen's odd appearance. The Indigene's use of a human name made Bill's skin prickle. Other than the polite manner in which the alien had spoken to Ben, he learned nothing new.

'And you're sure he's going to show next week?' said Bill when Ben went off on a conversation tangent.

'He said he would.'

Bill reached into his bag and pulled out the teddy bear. Ben's eyes widened.

'A thank you for your help.'

He snatched the toy from Bill.

'Now listen to me, I want you to show off your new toy for your friend next week. Can you do that?'

Ben grinned. 'I will. Thanks mister.'

The boy ran off. At least the mission hadn't been a total disaster.

Bill turned his attention to his main problem—Caldwell and Page.

☼

His anger simmered low and dangerous as he gathered his surveillance team in the heart of no man's land. The area of red and gold-tinted stony landscape stretched between New London and New Tokyo, fifty miles away. The sky was a deep blue, speckled with tinges of purple and green. The occasional floating cloud offered little protection from the scorching sun. The single road provided the only access in and out of New London. A dozen similar roads, and rail lines, would be needed to turn the transport network into something sustainable.

The faint sound of wolves baying in the distance reached him, presumably on the hunt. The biodomes, on the borders of the six cities, housed a mix of resurrected animals from predators to vegetarians and birds. The predators—lions, wolves, coyotes—regularly left the confines of the biodomes, but often returned to the one place where a meal was guaranteed.

Bill chose a spot five miles from New London's city limits. The predators rarely ventured farther than two miles. By staying downwind of the biodomes, they reduced the risk of the animals picking up their scent. Out here, he could also avoid the ITF listening bugs. What he had to say was off the record.

He faced the group of seven, including Caldwell and Page, directing his first question at the two officers who had almost screwed up this mission.

'Why did you two disobey my orders?'

Caldwell spoke first. 'The situation called for more action, less feelings.'

'What the hell does that mean?'

'He means doing what we were trained to do,' said Page. 'We needed to follow the alien, not just watch it.'

Bill pinched the bridge of his nose and released it. 'When I tell you to stay put, you do as you're told. Got it?' His eyes scanned the length of the group. Everybody stood at military ease, eyes forward. Except for Page and Caldwell, who looked at Bill.

'We had to make our move before the alien left,' said Page. 'You weren't going to make that call.'

'Excuse me?'

'You heard her,' muttered Caldwell.

It hadn't been Bill's call to make. Gilchrist had given observation orders only. But he didn't agree with her approach. Had Page and Caldwell made the better decision? Perhaps, if the alien showed up next week.

The rest of the group stayed silent.

'No offence, Taggart,' said Caldwell, 'but your soft leadership skills aren't the right fit for this mission. This is pursuit and catch, plain and simple. Deighton understands, and that's what we're all trained for.'

Bill felt his cheeks get hot.

Page interrupted before his anger exploded. 'Officers Wilson and Garrett carried out a search of the tunnels but turned up nothing. We think it may have exited from another station, farther down the line.'

Bill suddenly wanted a hot cup of coffee and a nice piece of lasagne from his favourite restaurant. Not that vegetarian crap. The real stuff.

'We do have something new,' said Page. 'We managed to record some of the conversation.'

At least that was something. 'Make sure you include everything in your report. But apart from some trivial new facts, we still don't know what they are or, what they're planning to do next.'

'Next?' said Page.

'Yes, next. Why they are here. Why they surfaced. Why they're hunting and killing people.' Or where Isla was.

The opportunity to question one of the Indigenes about it had slipped through his fingers.

Bill waved his hand. 'We're done here. And this conversation never happened. You hear me? Return to your accommodation. I'll contact you all shortly. And Page, Caldwell, you'd better hope the alien shows up next week.'

He stalked away from the group and climbed into his automated vehicle. If the alien calling himself Stephen didn't show up, how would he explain this mess to Daphne Gilchrist?

11

How did it go?

Anton was leaning against the doorframe to Stephen's lab. Stephen had arrived back ten minutes ago. The military had chased him as far as the entrance to the New Victoria underground station. But despite his easy escape, his hands wouldn't stop shaking.

The silicone skin he'd been wearing was now under a microscope. He held a laser scalpel next to it.

Anton lunged at the skin. *What are you doing? Are you trying to destroy my invention?*

It's too thick. I wanted to remove a layer of it.

'So you ask me to fix it.' He switched to his voice. 'You don't butcher my labour of love. You don't see me coming in here and altering your experiments, do you?'

Stephen dropped the scalpel and pushed the microscope away with a sigh. 'I'm sorry. I'm just on edge. The target noticed my skin. If he did, others did too.'

Trust me. They're not as observant as you think. I've seen some strange Surface Creatures during my research trip. He shrugged. *Easy to blend in. They all look the same.*

Stephen barked a laugh. 'As we do, I'm sure.'

Anton tapped the side of his head. 'This is where we differ.' He punched Stephen on the arm. 'How did it go? You never answered me.'

Stephen didn't know what to say. 'Okay, I suppose.'

'You suppose? What happened?'

'Nothing. It was... odd. That's all.'

'It's weird the first time, but after it gets easier.'

Stephen didn't want it to get easier. He wanted someone else to go in his place.

You going again? asked Anton. Stephen nodded. *You want company?*

As weird as the experience had been, he sensed to bring a second would scare the child and change the dynamics of their conversation. The boy didn't look like he trusted too many people. Besides, this was his mission. His target. He would see it through.

Thanks, but I've got this.

Anton folded his arms. His casual stance reminded him of how the Surface Creatures stood. Maybe Anton had spent too much time on the surface.

'In that case, Pierre wants to talk to you,' Anton said.

Stephen eyed his microscope and the piece of silicone Anton had yet to reclaim. 'Now?'

'Yes, now.' As though he read his thoughts, his friend plucked up the remaining skin. 'I'll take the skin back to my lab and work on it. How long before you need it again?'

'A week.'

He cradled his invention like a baby. 'I'll see what I can do.'

Stephen left his lab and walked through the low-lit tunnels of District Three. The rough walls hummed with the different moods of the Indigenes. Sadness, elation, irritation. He felt it all through his fingers as they grazed the rock capable of absorbing moods. A slight tension rippled down his arm and with it he sensed Elise's worry. If one of the elders was worried, then that meant Pierre was too. It wouldn't take long for their worry to filter down through the rest of the district.

Not all understood the dangers that lay above, but most had some experience of the silent war that had hit thirty years ago. A cascade of bombs had rained down on their habitats, nearly wiping the Indigenes from existence. But an adaptable species could not be killed. The Surface Creatures would find that out soon enough.

He quickened his step, keen to get his talk with Pierre over. While Pierre had pushed to learn more about the enemy, it had been Stephen's idea to target the boy.

He ran the rest of the way through the tunnels and past curious Indigenes, to arrive at the Council Chambers. This was where Pierre lived when he worked, which was most of the time.

The heavy door was shut. He pulled on a rope that rang a bell inside. Pierre liked secrecy. Elise, his wife, did not.

The door opened. Stephen was surprised to see both elders inside.

Stephen, said Elise with a smile. *You're here. Come in.*

He entered the chambers—a decent-sized room that had been excavated out of the rock. It looked similar to all the other rough-hewn spaces in the district. A bookshelf filled with Indigene and Surface Creature literature divided the space in half. Beyond it was a mattress that Pierre sometimes used to sleep on when he worked late.

Both elders wore white tunic sets that covered the

near translucent and hairless skin that identified all the Indigenes. Both centenarians looked good—strong. Powerful.

Filled with nervous energy, Stephen stopped in the middle of the room. Pierre, with a book in hand, stood by the bookshelf filled with illegally gotten literature from the surface. He was reading one that Stephen couldn't identify. Elise tapped Pierre on the shoulder. He snapped the book shut and put it back on the shelf.

Elise smiled at Stephen and sent out a wave of calm —an ability all good empaths had. At one hundred and twenty, she had mastered her ability. Stephen felt his shoulders relax, but his chaotic thoughts raged on.

Pierre, not an empath, relied on instinct to read a room. The stricter elder of the pair of a similar age to Elise looked less at ease than his mate.

Stephen, I asked you here because your meeting was today. How did it go?

He didn't know where to start. *As expected.*

A warm breeze danced across his face—a physical manifestation of Elise's power. It made his skin itch.

Pierre asked, *What did you learn from the boy?*

'Not much.' He switched to his voice. 'I think he was more curious about me than I was about him.'

Pierre's gaze narrowed. 'Was the trip worth it?'

More like, was the risk worth it?

'I don't know.' Pierre's eyes widened, prompting Stephen to add, 'But I have arranged to meet the child next week. I hope to learn more then.'

Pierre turned away, his hands clasped behind his back. Elise, who'd been more open to the idea from the beginning, watched Stephen, her brow furrowed in concentration. The warm breeze continued.

'Please stop,' Stephen said to her. She looked up in

alarm. 'I apologise, elder, but my body and my brain are conflicted right now. You are only influencing one.'

I'm sorry, Stephen. I thought it would help.

He hated speaking out of turn to his elders. 'No, it's my fault. I am preoccupied.'

Because of the boy?

Her question surprised him. Not only could Elise calm a room, but she could also read thoughts better than others, if the Indigene was willing. He must have let his guard slip.

'I am curious about him, that's all.'

Pierre turned. 'Curious? Are you getting attached?'

'No, elder. It's been a long time since my parents died. I don't want to let this opportunity for us to understand the enemy better slip through my fingers.'

Pierre nodded. *I wasn't keen on you attempting this alone. Maybe you should let Anton go with you next time.*

His reasons for not bringing his friend along hadn't changed. 'I've won the boy's trust. To change the dynamic now will lose it.'

We just want you to be careful, said Elise. *Your parents' death hit you hard. We understand your feelings towards the Surface Creatures.*

She sent new waves of calm towards him; Stephen backed up a step. He needed to reassure them of his success without Elise's influence.

'I promise I'm being careful. One-on-one is working well. My strategy is drawing little attention.'

Pierre nodded. *Elise and I trust you, Stephen. Our future depends on the information you glean. Don't let us down.*

No pressure then.

I won't.

12

Jenny Waterson sat in her space craft above Earth's atmosphere with her DPad in her lap. It was Saturday morning and the team at Hartsfield-Jackson Atlanta's docking station were being overly cautious—or her friend Stuart was. The overseer at the docking station liked to throw the newer recruits in at the deep end.

'Experience takes time to develop,' he'd told her once.

But his delay to her schedule that day couldn't have come at a worse time.

Jenny shifted in her seat as the memo, received from the ESC that morning, lay open on her DPad. A review of piloting skills was underway and she'd been caught up in the latest round of bull coming from Daphne Gilchrist's office. Last month it had been an inspection of her uniform, and she had to do a damn fashion show for Gilchrist's assistant. The young man had been apologetic, so at least that was something. But this month, she sensed this new test would be harder to pass. The memo also said she must attend the HJA for a meeting after her flight—with whom she didn't know.

She radioed in from the space above the Earth's outer-perimeter force field to the observation deck, where she knew Stuart would be.

'Captain Jenny Waterson. Craft 766-C seeking permission to land.'

The communication operative replied, 'I've confirmed your identity. Please hold.'

Jenny glanced at the time. Calypso Couriers, a subsidiary under the Earth Security Centre's control, had given her a tight schedule. Any deviation from said schedule would surely get back to Gilchrist.

She sent another ping to the operative again. 'Could you let me know how long, please? I need to leave in the next five minutes if I'm going to make my deadline.'

The operative said, 'Won't be long now.'

She heard a clap of hands and a 'Hurry up.' *Stuart.*

His newbies. Her schedule. This was bad. The operative kept her on the line.

She heard Stuart shouting in the background, 'What's your status?'

'Just a few more seconds,' said a male. Probably the trainee controlling her fate.

Ten seconds passed and Jenny couldn't take the pressure. She asked, 'Craft 766-C. Am I clear to land?'

Stuart's voice crackled in the distance. 'Hurry up. What's the word?'

'Just one more second,' replied a young-sounding man. 'I'm almost there.'

'For Christ's sake, the captain hasn't got all day,' said Stuart.

She was glad he realised that.

Then, 'About bloody time.' From Stuart. 'My heart isn't able for this shit anymore.'

'Craft 766-C, you are clear to land,' the operative

said. 'Dock Twelve is available. Set down on the port side of the hold.'

'Roger that.'

Her deep sigh did little to calm her.

Jenny ordered the on-board computer to establish outgoing radio silence. She kept the incoming audio link with HJA active in case they ordered her to divert. The computer beeped once.

She checked the time.

'Damn it.'

It was already five minutes past her scheduled drop time. That left no room for error on the way down. She ran a shaky hand through her tightly cut platinum-blonde hair. 'Okay, Jenny. You've got this. Who cares if your skills are under review? You know how to fly.' Her focus switched to her craft as she readied for the next step of the descent.

She engaged the autopilot and attempted to loosen up her rigid posture. Her pulse pounded, as it always did before a descent. The second memo had rattled her. People had been fired for lesser things. Jenny at seventy five, and with twenty years working as a pilot, was becoming an expensive liability.

She pulled her seatbelt tight and checked her descent numbers. If they wanted her gone, they'd have to do more than look at her impeccable flight record.

The operative spoke to her through the communications system. 'Strong winds at vertical eighty miles. Be on alert. Looks like a hurricane is building.'

She reactivated the outgoing link and confirmed receipt before resuming radio silence. A little gust of wind wasn't going to stop her. Jenny shook away all distractions and concentrated on getting this rust bucket to the magnetic landing plate at the docking station. She dried her palms on her military-green uniform, feeling her usual pre-flight jitters surface before the fall.

The craft remained in orbit over the landing coordinates at the docking station. Jenny engaged the thrusters sporadically, realigning the vessel as it tried to pull in a different direction. Then it began its descent, dropping into the non-existent atmosphere and through the deactivated force field. The thrusters blasted again to maintain the correct position. She monitored the increase in atmospheric density through her screen as the computer relayed progress through the audio channel.

'Density at ninety per cent, ninety-five, ninety-eight...'

She braced herself for the imminent drop.

'One hundred per cent density achieved.'

A sudden jolt and a sharp push downwards knocked her against her seat belt as the thrusters forced the craft into a computer-guided free fall. Thrusters disengaged and acceleration increased as everything dropped towards the surface. A minute passed and the vessel had reached one hundred and eighty miles above the docking station—the edge of the storm.

Winds twisted violently around the craft, attempting to push her off course. Jenny yanked hard on the straps keeping her upright. The computer corrected the vessel's position realignment to compensate for the violent winds. Jenny concentrated on the screen, the same one showing the craft's tilt variance as it lurched left, then right. She poised her hands over the controls. One touch would transfer the power back to manual. But during free fall, it was safer out of her hands.

The craft continued to rock from side to side, creaking and moaning as the computer adjusted for the motion.

Then it hit the inner circle of the storm.

A mass of blackened clouds swirled one way, then another, taking repeated shots at the exterior. She fought against instincts to grab the controls and switch back to manual piloting. Sweat soaked her skin. The craft's tilt variance remained on the edge of the danger zone for three whole minutes.

'Come on Jenny, you can do this. You've done this a hundred times.' She doubted every action made that, without a memo from Gilchrist's office, would have been instinctive.

The vessel rocked and rolled. Jenny's hands hooked in a claw-like poise over the controls. Her erratic breathing eased, but a new panic tightened her chest again. For the first time in twenty years as a pilot, she prayed to a god she didn't believe in. Earth had gone to hell. What God would let that happen?

The craft dropped below the black mass and into the grey, toxic atmosphere that hung over the cities. A laugh bubbled into her throat as the weather turned instantly calm. The only wind fifty miles above the docking station was the one created by her small ship.

The tension in her body was the last thing to break. Dizziness followed, and the full effects of the rocking motion and the vertical drop hit her. Maybe it was a good thing she'd eaten little for the last six hours. While in the training room, Jenny had been shoved vertically, horizontally and exposed to the greatest G-force in cockpit simulations. She still wasn't used to it.

The craft's motion evened out and settled her stomach. The descent continued in a controlled, smooth manner. A minute later, she arrived at the landing plate at Dock Twelve.

A nervous breath skittered across her lips as she listened to the *clink clunk* of magnetic levitation kicking in. The blocks on the underside of the craft took on a positive charge, opposite to the negative charge of the landing plate. The vessel jerked upwards; the force field surrounding it absorbed some of the sharpness, but not all. A deep shudder knocked her about as the magnets fought against each other.

At twenty feet, polarisation switched to the lowest levels. The craft hovered metres above the landing plate. Jenny regained control of her cockpit and engaged the thrusters. She switched off the magnetic field and guided 766-C into the hangar bay, setting it down on the port side. Disengaging the thrusters and force field, she stood and peeled her sweat-soaked uniform away from her back and legs.

At the exit, she scanned her security chip on the touch pad. The exit door released and she stumbled out.

A thin docking station attendant in his early thirties walked towards her, DPad in hand. Jenny recognised him —an overachieving pompous ass, if she remembered correctly.

She checked the time.

Damn.

Could her day get any worse?

He offered his hand. 'Welcome to the HJA docking station. Is this your first time?'

She closed her eyes and drew in a deep breath. When she opened them a bemused looking attendant watched her.

'Bumpy trip. I need a moment.'

What she needed was a stiff drink and a different attendant. Jenny was certain her time infringement would not go unnoticed.

The attendant withdrew his hand, muttering something about older pilots not having the stomach for it.

With one hand he motioned her closer, and used his other to comb through his oily hair.

He flipped the DPad around to face her. 'Place your thumb here.' She did; the computer scanned her chip and the words "Captain Jennifer Waterson, Grade 4 Pilot" flashed up on the screen. Her photo appeared beside her name.

The attendant glanced between it and Jenny. 'The photo doesn't match.'

She ran a hand over her cropped, platinum-blonde hair. 'I recently cut my hair and changed the colour. We had this discussion the last time I was here.' The photo on file showed her with a brown, shoulder-length style. Her face was younger than her age. Training kept her body lean and she was physically strong.

'I see. Ms Waterson. I should warn you, you're late by ten minutes with your drop. Can you verify your cargo on board, please?'

'Captain Waterson,' she corrected. 'I'm returning from Saturn with xenon compound.'

Earth's atmosphere contained minute amounts of stable noble gases—helium, neon, argon, krypton and xenon—and traces of the radioactive noble gas radon. In 2087 the World Government discovered that xenon existed abundantly in compound form within Saturn's recently uncovered supply of water. Xenon compound was primarily used as a propellant for the large passenger ships travelling to Exilon 5, but also in laser technology.

'Ah, yes, I have you here now,' he said, wirelessly scanning the on-board content through his DPad. 'Well, I guess there's just the time infraction to record.' He hit the screen with his finger.

Her heart thudded. 'About that. I hit a bad storm on the way down. It knocked the craft off course, twice.

Could you let it slide this time? I promise it won't happen again.'

The attendant smirked at her. 'If I did that for every pilot, I'd lose my job.'

'I'm not asking you to do it for everyone, just me. Just this one time. Because of the storm I mentioned.'

She eyed his finger, poised over the DPad.

'It's not my problem if you can't keep to schedule. Maybe you should consider a different job.'

Doing what? Piloting was all she knew.

Jenny forced a smile. 'You look like a reasonable man.'

The attendant smirked again. 'I guess I can overlook it this one time.'

It took all her strength not to wipe the smug look off his face. He flicked something on the screen then gave the ground staff the thumbs up to proceed. When his back was turned, a few gave him the finger. Jenny almost choked on a laugh.

'Something funny?'

She straightened her mouth. 'Still a little giddy after the flight, I guess.'

He rolled his eyes. 'How soon will you be flying again?'

'In three hours. I'm delivering cargo to the ESC in Sydney.'

He turned and walked away. 'Next time, ma'am, how about you try to make it here on time, okay?'

His words sent a shiver through her. Through gritted teeth she mumbled, 'Don't call me ma'am.' She was only seventy-five.

But the attendant was right. She couldn't afford to be late again. Except, this time the delay hadn't been her fault. It had been Stuart and his little protégé's.

13

At 6am, Bill Taggart crawled out of bed after another sleepless night. The day of the second meeting between the Indigene and Ben Watson had arrived. Last week, his team on the ground had tracked the alien to one of the underground station entrances before they lost it.

He flung his legs over the side of the bed, sick of the same routine. Sick of the feeling his body belonged to someone else.

Somehow he made it to the bathroom, where he splashed icy cold water on his face; the drastic temperature change shocked his sluggish system back into life. His reflection showed a man who lived life on the edge. Two years of sleep deprivation, and counting, and a manic diet was to blame for that. Both had left him with permanent black circles under his eyes. The Glamour package of age-reversing genetic treatments could fix his problems, but there was enough fake in the world without adding his face to the mix. Besides, Isla preferred the natural look.

'A little skin lift turns into a telomere injection,' she'd said once. 'Before you know it, you've turned back time so much you're a teenager again.'

Genesis Code

In the last century, scientists had isolated the gene that controlled the body's natural aging process. The telomeres within the body's chromosomes naturally shortened, but the genetic manipulation clinics could lengthen them by injecting a growth hormone into the telomere. This halted the ageing process and reversed the outward signs of those advancing years.

'Try to look past the exterior, Bill,' Isla told him. 'So many people still judge others by how they look. Complexities lie beneath the surface, not on them.'

Her words brought Charles Deighton to mind and he had to agree with her.

In the six months before her disappearance, Isla's personality had changed drastically. After one of her trips to Exilon 5, she had become suspicious about everything and had lost her carefree attitude. When Bill had tried to talk to her about it, she became defensive.

'Why can't you leave well enough alone? Why are you trying to mess up things that don't concern you?'

He raised an eyebrow. 'Is that aimed at me specifically?'

'Not specifically. Well, yes. Maybe.' Isla sighed.

'Love, what are you talking about?'

'Just leave it, Bill. I can't talk about it.' She turned away then back, with a serious expression that worried Bill. 'Don't jump to obvious conclusions. It's an easy out. Never stop searching for the truth.'

He hadn't thought too much about it at the time, but when she disappeared Bill combed through every conversation they'd had.

He stayed at the mirror as he remembered other cryptic conversations they'd had.

'Have you ever heard of Morse code?' Isla had asked him one evening over dinner in their apartment.

Bill picked up a replicated chicken leg and tore at it with his teeth. 'Can't say I have.' Juices ran down his hand. He licked his thumb and forefinger clean.

'Dad uses it. He once told me that he can listen in on any conversation in the world.' Her father worked for the communications section of the World Government.

That piqued his interest. 'How?'

'Through the equipment we use every day. It acts as a relay, bounces the sound around and comes through as an echo on the line. The echo is clear enough to make out conversations.'

He dropped the chicken leg on his plate. The thought of another person spying on him agitated him. 'Is he listening in now?'

Isla smiled and shook her head. 'No. He gave me a sound interrupter. We can't hear it, but it disrupts the sound enough so it plays back as gobbledygook.'

Bill relaxed a little.

'He says he doesn't listen in, but my father was sure others did, at the request of the World Government. Before he went on his last mission, he gave me the sound interrupter and told me to leave it on permanently. It's the reason he uses Morse code to communicate.'

'Morse code? How does that work?'

'It's a series of beeps or clicks, each linked to a letter, word or phrase. You can talk to another person this way.'

A vision of Isla's father banging out the code while another patron did the same made him smile.

'I know, I know. It's impractical,' she said, almost reading his thoughts. 'But there has to be a better way to communicate without being *seen* to communicate.'

She shared something she read recently. 'Back when Ireland was ruled by the English, Irish was still the primary language of the country up to the eighteenth century. But the nineteenth century saw Irish decline as a first language in favour of English. Why? Two things: because of the Great Famine and because the English prohibited its teaching in schools. Many Irish leaders also viewed the Irish language as being too backward and pushed for the more progressive English language. They were right to in the end, but Irish people felt their heritage was being stripped away by English rule, so they continued to teach the language to their children in secret. When the struggle for independence began in the late nineteenth century, the soldiers communicated back and forth in Irish because the English couldn't understand them. A secret language.'

'I like the idea, Isla. Because knowing others could be listening in at any time disturbs me. You're suggesting we develop our own language?'

'Why not? Doesn't have to be a spoken language. I haven't thought much beyond that, but I will.'

Isla said the chats with her father had pushed her to search for a solution of how to converse safely in public. He'd expected her to bring it up again, but when she didn't he assumed she'd given up on the idea. His brow creased at the memories, in particular the conversation about the secret language. What had she meant by it?

He had to let it go. Deciphering a riddle without all the parts would drive him insane. His priority was to find her.

Bill ran a hand over his two-day-old stubble. 'Grooming will have to wait, Isla.' She'd always hated the start of a beard because of how it scratched her face. He'd always made a special effort to be clean-shaven for her.

He threw on a clean shirt and pair of trousers and went to the kitchen. Making a fresh pot of coffee, he filled his mug to the brim and rooted through the almost-bare cupboards for something to eat. He settled on a box of replicated cereal flakes and munched on dry handfuls of the stuff. As he ate and drank, he stifled a yawn. Using Actigen to skip sleep was one of his more dangerous habits; he could feel his body and mind fighting against the effects. But he didn't know how else to operate, how else to function. Sleep was for the dead. While he lived and breathed he would skip it, until he got answers.

Bill reviewed the field reports from the previous week, noting the Indigene's plans to meet with Ben Watson that morning at Belgrave Square Gardens. He still didn't know if Caldwell and Page's pursuit of the alien had ruined this second meeting. If it hadn't, he would be relying on Ben Watson to bring the teddy bear with him.

The audio and visual equipment inside the bear would give them more than they had. One government file showed the capture of a young alien, a year ago. The male, similar in age to a twelve-year-old boy, had died from breathing complications. Bill had only skimmed over the report. There had been a video to go with it, but he hadn't watched it yet. Before that, there had been no reported sightings of the nocturnal Indigenes.

Nocturnal no more.

Isla had been reported missing a full year before the alien footage even emerged. There had to be a connection between the species living here and her disappearance.

Caldwell had recorded footage of the meeting the previous week. The one called Stephen had sat too stiffly on the bench to be comfortable. The alien had even smiled on occasion. Such a human act. He'd expected to feel hatred, but he'd been more surprised to see the alien walk and talk like a human.

Bill shook his head. What did it matter what the

alien looked like? Chances were high this creature knew where Isla was. That's all that mattered. He didn't care about Gilchrist and Deighton's interest in the race.

He sipped on his cooled coffee; the vile taste made him shudder. A shot of hot coffee turned the cold liquid into a lukewarm fusion and made it tolerable.

The time read six fifteen, not long before the proposed meeting time. His nerves jangled. This was it. His last chance to do something.

Caldwell was an asshole for ignoring his orders last week, but he'd done what Bill should have. At least it hadn't been a total disaster. He activated the recording equipment in the bear. The images were grainy.

While he waited for the video and audio to sync, he scrolled through news articles and official reports from the World Government and Earth Security Centre. Some were about the initial move to Exilon 5. The reports triggered a memory of when Isla had changed careers, about two and a half years ago. Bored in her teaching role, she'd expressed an interest in helping the newest residents to settle on Exilon 5.

'The population is going through these changes and I'm stuck in this classroom. I need to do something constructive, satisfy my altruistic side.'

He laughed. 'You're not being altruistic if you're satisfying your own needs.'

She counteracted with one of her witty retorts. For the life of him, he couldn't remember what she'd said.

Isla had become a Task Force soldier soon after, working for the ITF's military outfit. At the time the Indigenes weren't a threat to humans and ground patrol duties had been light.

It was around the same time—three months before her disappearance—that Isla had made another drastic change.

He stared at her. 'What have you done?'

'What? It's my hair. I'll do what I want with it.'

'But... it's all gone.' Isla had been wearing her military uniform and steel-toe boots. Her hair had been cut so short it altered the very angles of her face.

'You never liked it anyway,' she snapped. 'It's a frivolous thing to hold on to when we face an uncertain future on this world.'

'But you love your hair. It's a part of you. And I never said I hated it.'

'Like I said, Bill, it's not important.'

The World Government hadn't been able to confirm that Isla was dead—there was no body. Deighton could only confirm she'd disappeared after confronting one of the Indigenes near the city border of New Copenhagen. But Bill had one small issue with the World Government's version of events. He knew his wife better than they did, and he couldn't imagine her confronting an Indigene. More likely, she had tried to make contact. Her personality may have altered during her stint on Exilon 5, but her core beliefs would have remained the same.

He checked the time and shifted nervously in his chair. With minutes to go before the meeting, he closed all files and opened the communications channel on the DPad.

Bill tested the connection and located the unique signature code, although the sound was muffled and images were still grainy. He reasoned the bear must still be inside the boy's backpack.

To centre the investigation on an eight-year-old boy with trust issues was a stupid, risky move. But Bill needed answers: the location of the Indigenes' hideout for one and why they'd suddenly come out of hiding. He picked up a tiny earpiece and wedged it into his ear.

Stephen. Why had the alien given itself a human name? Was it the easiest way to blend in?

He scooted his chair over to the window and used a pair of magnification glasses to watch. Was it luck that the ITF had rented this very apartment that overlooked Belgrave Square Gardens? But even with the glasses, he couldn't see past the trees to the bench and the location of the meeting.

He'd sent his team out a second time to monitor events on the ground. Caldwell and Page were under strict instructions to stay put. As was he. The recording device inside the bear would act as his eyes and ears that day. Surely the Indigene would not suspect an innocent toy?

He checked in with his team, who remained on standby near the bench where the meeting was due occur. With moments to go, the images changed from grainy to clear. He hit the record button on his DPad and leaned forward, staring at the screen.

14

From behind a cluster of large trees, Stephen watched Ben skip to the bench where they'd arranged to meet. A bout of empathy for the loner boy hit him out of nowhere. He shook it off and evoked images of his dead parents, to remind him of why he hated the Surface Creatures. Last night Pierre had told him to keep an open mind about this invading race, and that not all were bad.

Easier said than done.

His doubt had led him to question his leader. 'How can you be so sure?'

Pierre had smiled. 'Someone told me once to look past the exterior.'

Stephen shifted his body on the spot to give the appearance of invisibility. The Surface Creatures could not process images at certain speeds. Nobody seemed to notice him when he performed this action.

Two military figures lingered close to their meeting place. Their musky scents settled in his nose. But he didn't fear them, knowing he could outrun them.

Stephen's covered skin prickled with heat as the rising sun warmed the cool morning air. Anton had reduced the thickness of the skin, but not by much. The protective lenses shifted against his eyes. His air filtration device felt bulky in his nose and throat. With a deep breath, Stephen tried to calm down. He could do with some of Elise's ability right now.

'Everything will be fine if you stick to the time limit.' Those had been Anton's last words to him before he surfaced.

The area close to the bench where Ben sat was too crowded. Maybe he'd made a mistake picking this spot. He waited for the area to empty a little. While maintaining his invisibility, he recalled the Surface Creatures' earliest attack on Exilon 5, thirty years ago. The attack had altered the way the Indigenes lived forever. The tunnels, colder than the surface, had protected his race from the severity of the blasts, but living underground was only supposed to be temporary until the worst of the airborne chemicals had dissipated.

At age six, he'd observed the changes that followed through the actions of others. The explosions had tainted the surface air, but with those changes came a hope that the air would soon be breathable again. He had watched the first of the exploratory groups swap the air-controlled environment for the surface, but their venture had been short lived.

'The air is still poisonous. Nothing remains,' one reported with a raspy cough.

'Everything is covered in a thick dust,' said another.

Their cities, their homes—the places where they once socially gathered, discussed, meditated—no longer existed. The atmosphere, polluted with harsh chemicals, burned their throats. Most adapted, some did not. But they'd created a new home underground. Those with a heightened spatial awareness sped up the excavation by analysing the rock's composition and finding its weak spots.

Throughout the years, Stephen kept his own notes about the conditions of the surface as seen through others' eyes. If the scientists' and his own calculations were correct, then the last of the chemicals should have been absorbed by the land. Excitement and expectation followed, but what happened next shocked them.

From the chemical haze, a new atmosphere emerged. This one contained high levels of oxygen and some nitrogen—a mix too corrosive for them to breathe. Pierre and Elise followed this news with an order to hermetically seal all entrance points to District Three. The elders of other districts followed that same plan. Scientists rushed to design a synthetic protein for long-term use, to replace their main food source.

Then, strange patterns started to appear in the weather. Yellow and orange hues filtered through light shafts in the district. Pierre ordered the shafts to be sealed when the tunnels began to heat up. Soon after, the Surface Creatures arrived.

It was yet another sunny day in the city called New London, so different to those times. The trees gave Stephen a reprieve from the harsh temperatures. He missed the atmosphere of old: cool air and grey skies with only glints of sunlight peeking through.

But what he missed most was hunting. It was in his blood.

His chest heaved with the memories of better days. But his attention drew to the boy who had removed an object from his bag and placed it beside him. With the area quieter than before, Stephen released his body from its invisibility. Gasps from the military followed his run to the bench, where he sat down.

The black-haired boy jumped with fright. His eyes were wide. 'You scared me. Where did you come from?'

Stephen vaguely pointed somewhere. 'Just over there.'

'Well, don't scare me like that again. I'm not supposed to be here. If my mum finds out...'

'I forgot you don't move at the same speed. That was a natural pace for me.'

Ben narrowed his gaze. 'How fast can you move?'

'Five, six times as fast as you.' He wanted the military to know he was a threat.

'Cool.'

Stephen looked at the object between them. 'What's that?'

Ben's face lit up. He held the bear up high. 'It's a teddy bear. You can't get them anymore, but this one was a present. His name is Snuffles, because his nose looks funny. Kinda upturned. Do you like him?'

'Present from whom?'

The boy hesitated. 'My Dad.'

Stephen looked into the reflective black eyes of the toy. He brushed his hand lightly across the furry exterior, surprised at how soft it felt.

Ben sat the bear on his lap, angling it so it looked at Stephen. 'How long have you been here for? Were you waiting for me by the trees?'

'No, I arrived moments before you did,' Stephen lied.

'This is really early,' said Ben. 'Why are we meeting in these gardens instead of at the bus stop? Why did you want to meet at seven in the morning? I know why I'm out this early. It's so my mum doesn't know where I've been. She doesn't like me going out. I don't know why. She barely knows I exist—'

Stephen sat rigidly as the boy chattered on. He fixed his gaze on a statue of a woman holding a child and used his peripheral vision to scan his surroundings. When it seemed like there was no end to the boy's chatter, Stephen forced himself to relax.

Ben looked up at him. 'I asked you why you wanted to meet this early.'

'I prefer this time as there are fewer of you about. Also, we met at the same time last week, if you remember.' He delivered the line smoothly. Speaking at their slower pace was getting easier.

Ben laughed. 'Oh, yeah. I forgot.'

A silence lingered between them. The boy narrowed his eyes at Stephen.

'Why's the skin on your face a different colour to your arm?'

'I told you, I'm wearing a special covering to protect my skin from the sun, and to blend in.'

'Why? What's wrong with it? Why would you need to blend in?'

Stephen answered only one of those questions. 'There is nothing wrong with it.'

'Why do you need to protect your skin? It's not even ten degrees yet. It's not warm.'

'I prefer a cooler climate and little to no sun.'

Ben's eyes flicked from Stephen's covered face and neck to his patchy arm, where the artificial skin had lost its pigmentation. 'Your skin looks weird. In parts it looks see-through, like on your arm.'

'My skin looks translucent, but it is not.'

The boy's eyes widened. 'If you ate something, would I be able to see it go into your stomach?'

Stephen shook his head. 'It's an illusion, that's all.'

The boy sighed. 'That would be much cooler if you

could.'

Stephen wondered about the differences between their species. How breakable was the boy's skin? 'Your skin appears to be thinner than mine. Is it waterproof?'

Ben shrugged and squeezed the bear's stomach with his fingers. 'I don't know.'

Stephen reached into a waste-bin at his end of the bench and fished out a half-empty bottle of water. He unscrewed the cap with one hand and extended the other to Ben.

'May I?'

Ben shrugged again and held out his arm.

Stephen limited his contact with the child. The tips of his fingers tingled when they brushed off Ben's warm skin. He tipped the water over the child's arm; it beaded and rolled off.

'That's interesting,' he said releasing Ben's wrist. Then he nicked him.

'Ow!'

A drop of red blood leaked onto the boy's trousers from where he'd scratched him.

'Apologies.'

Ben huffed out a breath. 'S'okay.' He rubbed away the blood. With a yawn he said, 'Do you live in a house?'

'No, I don't.'

'Well where do you live, then?'

'Near the Maglev train station.'

He screwed up his face. 'Really? You live underground where it's dark and cold? Why don't you live up here with everyone else?'

'Because we cannot survive in this atmosphere.'

'Which station? New Charing Cross or New Waterloo? Because I've been to both, and I guess I could visit you there sometimes.'

'I don't live in the station itself.'

An all-female group entered the park and performed warm-up exercises against a nearby tree. As they began their walk, the oldest female's gaze lingered on Stephen and Ben. Stephen tugged on his hat, pulling it down over his eyes. The female gasped when his partly covered arm fell into her view. She looked ahead and increased her pace to catch up with the group. He readied himself to leave, in case they doubled back. But to his relief, they disappeared into the trees.

A movement under his left elbow broke his concentration. Ben had opened his backpack and was pulling out a sandwich wrapped in plastic. He placed it on his lap and tore at the packaging. The smell made Stephen gag.

Ben picked up one half and took a bite. He held out the part he had slobbered over. 'Want some?'

Stephen covered his mouth. 'No, please, take it away.'

'You don't like jam?' He took another bite.

'I can't... eat that.'

'My mum says I can't drink milk because I'm allergic. Is it the same as that?'

'My stomach cannot process a lot of the foods you easily consume.' A breeze caught the smell and swept it away. His stomach settled.

'What do you eat, then?' Ben licked off a blob of jam that had dropped on his thumb.

Stephen averted his eyes and stared at the nearby sculpture. 'We survive mostly on the blood, and sometimes meat, of animals. We need large amounts of iron in our diets.'

'Are you a vampire?' he whispered. 'They drink human blood, though, not animals. I don't want you to eat me, please. My mum would kill me if I got myself killed.'

Stephen was vaguely familiar with the stories from the Surface Creatures' literature. The images of the sharp fangs amused him. 'No, I am not a vampire. We eat animals as your species did during early civilisation periods. We just don't alter the meat's composition with heat, as your stomachs prefer. We hunt without tools. Our physical strength can overpower any animal.' Stephen hoped the military were listening. And that they wouldn't test out his hunting skills today.

'Oh. My mum buys meat pies sometimes. There's animal in those. I could bring you one if you'd like. Then you wouldn't have to kill any.'

The beginning of a laugh bubbled up into his throat. 'That won't be necessary.' He suppressed it, reminding himself as to why he'd risked his life a second time: to get answers.

Ben finished his sandwich and pulled out a container filled with an orange liquid. He drank some and pulled up his legs onto the bench.

'Why do you eat iron? Is it like the stuff you get in a scrap yard? I wouldn't think that tastes nice.'

'My body does not produce many red blood cells because I don't live in an oxygen-rich atmosphere. We require less oxygen to breathe and because of our bodies' low levels of haemoglobin, we are naturally deficient in iron. Our stomachs absorb the iron directly from the blood. It gives us strength.'

The boy seemed to relax. Soon, it would be Stephen's turn to ask his questions.

'We breathe a different composition of gases. That's why it's difficult for us to stay up here. Where we live, we can control the air we breathe.' He waited for Ben to digest the information.

'If you can't survive here, then how are you breathing the air?'

Stephen smiled at the boy's intelligence. 'I use a device that helps me to breathe. Naturally, to all appearances.' With the disappearance of one of their young Evolvers a year ago, he was sure the military knew all about their air filtration devices.

He had broken many rules, not least his plan to keep an emotional distance from the boy. He'd shared a wealth of information with the military who were probably listening. But this mission would be the last one. From this moment on, he was certain the military would set traps for the Indigenes, possibly tagging the food source to uncover the location of their districts. He had to make this meeting count.

Stephen asked Ben about the Surface Creatures' physiology, the foods and drinks they enjoyed. He moved on to forms of entertainment: what they liked to do, where they liked to go. A pattern emerged that showed alarming similarities between the two races. Stephen would never accept their similarities.

He still had one question left, the one reason he'd risked his life to come to the surface: Who were the Surface Creatures?

'I asked you last week what you call yourselves. Do you remember what you said?'

'I told you, I'm English.'

Stephen shook his head. 'Perhaps I need to be clearer with my question. What does your species call itself? We only know you as Surface Creatures.'

He waited, acutely aware of his depleting air supply. Suddenly, the child smiled. 'Oh, you mean human?'

'Ah, human,' said Stephen, nodding. 'Thank you.'

A cold fear ran through him. His heart fluttered in

his chest. Every part of him strained against the temptation to flee.

Human. It was the last thing he'd expected the boy to say. Philosophers, dreamers, people—that was how Pierre's books described them.

He sensed the military's murderous eyes on him again, preparing to track him as they'd attempted to the week before. They'd seen how fast he could move. But he hadn't even scratched the surface of his top speed.

Human.

The boy's eyes grew large when Stephen stood. This time he offered no explanation for his leaving. This time he ignored the boy's pleas for him to stay. He raced towards the exit, close to where the military had stationed themselves.

'Where are you going?' the boy shouted after him. 'What did I say wrong?'

Everything.

You are human.

Stephen's mind raced faster than he ran. This changed everything.

The time for gentle talks was over. The elders needed a better plan than to do nothing. And it involved the Indigenes fighting back.

15

'We're going after the target,' said Caldwell into his earpiece.

Bill growled into the comms device that connected all of his team. 'No, stay put!' The audio and visual inside the teddy bear was still operational. 'That goes for all of you.'

'Bullshit, Taggart. Sitting around isn't going to help.'

'You have your orders, Caldwell.'

Bill clicked off and strode to the window. A flash of something exiting the left side of Belgrave Square Gardens caught his eye.

'To hell with it.' He defied his own orders and left his apartment, taking the stairs two at a time to the ground floor. One of his neighbours was coming in the entrance. Bill pushed past him.

'Excuse you!'

Bill didn't stop to apologise. He couldn't. The New Victoria station wasn't far. It was also rush hour, and he prayed a dense crowd there would slow his target down.

Adrenaline pumped through his body. His beating

heart roared in his ear. Someone spoke through the comms device, but he couldn't hear what they said.

His focus narrowed in on the path ahead as Bill searched for signs of the Indigene. He caught a figure dressed in brown making his way through the crowds, slower than Bill knew he could travel. Bill injected new pace into his pursuit.

Caldwell came through his earpiece. 'I thought you said no pursuit, Taggart.' He sounded out of breath, like he was running.

'I changed my mind. Keep off this channel and out of sight.'

Speed was working to the alien's advantage, but not the unfamiliar terrain in New Westminster. The alien stumbled where the crowds had forced him to slow down.

Bill heard the rumble of the Maglev train beneath his feet, heading towards New Victoria station. He had to reach the alien before he made it inside. Despite the blaze in his lungs willing him to stop, he pushed on.

One turn brought the station into sight and the rush-hour traffic Bill had hoped for. Up ahead, the dense crowds had slowed the Indigene's pace down to a walk.

Bill sped up on the downhill section. Then the alien disappeared from sight.

'Shit.'

Caldwell arrived at his shoulder. 'It's up ahead. I can catch it.'

Having his officer there angered Bill. 'Follow me if you have to, but I take the lead on this, got it?'

Caldwell mock saluted.

Bill searched for the Indigene again. 'Can you see it?'

Caldwell pointed to a group of people outside the station who were looking irritated. 'There.'

Bill raced ahead to the entrance where alarms shrilled and people yelled. He pushed through the crowds and made it inside the station. Ahead of him he saw his target heading for the stairs that would lead him down.

A queue had formed at the gate. Bill flashed his ITF badge and leapt over the turnstile. He kept running, despite his chest feeling like it might burst open.

Breathless and desperate for a break, he kept going. The stairs led him to an almost-empty platform. A train had just passed and the passengers were heading up and out. The Indigene hesitated at the edge of the platform.

He caught up to the alien just as he leapt off the end. Bill did the same, landing awkwardly on the rail.

He shouted, 'Wait!'

The Indigene turned, as shocked by his presence as Bill was to see him up close.

Strange brown eyes stared at him. Bill lost his voice for a moment.

He managed, 'I just want to talk.'

His target said nothing and did nothing. Then he turned and ran.

'Son of a bitch...'

Bill set off after him, barely seeing where his foot landed in the dark underground tunnel. Up ahead a bright light dazzled him, followed by a loud humming noise. Bill squealed and jumped into a worker's alcove. The train whizzed past him, stopping at the station he'd just left.

His heart was firmly in his mouth now, but his adrenaline kept his mind on the task. Bill stepped out of the alcove and resumed his pursuit of the Indigene. He arrived at a split in the tunnel, unsure as to which way the alien had gone.

Bill looked down the new track that was plunged into darkness, seeing nothing.

16

Stephen couldn't believe he'd been so stupid. The news of what the Surface Creatures were had thrown him for a loop. He'd allowed one of the military to catch up with him. Worse, they'd found part of his way in and out of the city.

The man with salt and pepper hair stood on the empty track.

'Wait! I just want to talk.'

Stephen froze. The man had his hands outstretched, but Stephen sensed anger and desperation rolling off him. The air filtration device pulled at his lungs uncomfortably. He had to go. Yet, his legs wouldn't move. He'd never been this close to an adult before. And this human looked familiar.

It clicked into place. He'd seen this man before, from Anton's restaurant recording. That couldn't be a coincidence. How long had he been tracking him?

His breaths shortened until they became painful. He had to go.

Stephen turned and ran into the tunnels. The military man might know one way of how he surfaced inside the city, but he would never find the entrance to the district.

He heard the man curse, his breaths shortening as he followed him. Up ahead a train approached. Stephen applied more power to his legs to reach the split in the tunnel before the train did. The air kicked up with the arrival of the train. Stephen darted down the left tunnel. Behind him he heard another curse.

Stephen ran for two miles in the dark, stopping finally at a wall. Markers identified the entrance to the way home, visible only to those with superior sight. He felt around for the opening he couldn't see with the stupid brown lenses in his eyes.

There.

He squeezed through one of many narrow entry points the Indigenes had created across the railway network. He popped both lenses out and placed them in his pocket.

That's better.

The way home took on a sharper look. The subtle markers popped in the series of linked passageways that would lead him to his district. False walls slid back and closed behind him. His chest tightened in the low oxygen and pitch-black environment where only small insects survived. But at least the military man hadn't seen his route inside.

Pain in his lungs forced Stephen to slow down. He stumbled along the narrow passageway while the time on his device blinked red. Anton's warnings had not been for nothing, and he'd spent too long talking to the boy. If Stephen didn't hurry, he would suffocate.

Stumbling over familiar terrain, his breaths shortened to a fine painful point. New markers appeared and he took left and right turns. False doors closed behind him to hide his route. He wasn't far now, but it might as well have been miles away.

The device continued to blink red—a reminder of his poor judgment.

He dropped to his knees in relief when the door to the sealed district came into view, and scrabbled the last few feet. Recognition software scanned his genetic code and authorised his entry. The door slid back into the rock face. He crawled inside a vestibule.

The outer door sealed shut; a smaller one leading into the inner sanctum remained closed. He willed the whirring air pumps to work faster and clear the contaminated air. Out of air, Stephen slumped on the floor. He felt himself slipping into unconsciousness.

The inner door released suddenly and one last effort pushed him over the threshold. Strong arms dragged him inside.

What did I tell you about the time limit? I was about to go after you.

It was Anton. He sounded mad. His friend pulled the air filtration pieces out of Stephen's throat and nose. Stephen snatched at new air and it eased the pain.

Anton got him to his feet. *I'm taking you to the infirmary.*

No, I need to see Pierre and Elise.
Why, what's wrong?
He stared at his friend. *Everything.*

17

'Jenny!'

Stuart's loud voice carried across the observation deck.

Standing at the entrance with her bag on one shoulder, she ignored her friend and looked around the room. Several domed sections made of high-density glass formed the roofline, giving the Air and Space Traffic Control Observation Deck the best three-sixty views of the city. What a view that must have been in the old days. But all Jenny saw was a broken city that went on for miles, choked by low-lying black and grey clouds.

Wall panels containing computer visualisation screens each displayed different images: space debris, planets in the solar system, and the area immediately above Earth. All facilitated by satellites orbiting the Earth. The almost-imperceptible beeps of fingers gliding over monitors at workstations filled the room. Three of Stuart's team stood in front of the visualisation screens, traversing the entire galaxy with a flick of their wrists. One flustered young man checked the outlying areas of space where the passenger ships could run into debris. The trainee, Jenny assumed. An older woman monitored his work.

Not closely enough, it would seem.

Stuart walked over to her. 'I was calling you just now.'

She blinked. 'I didn't hear you.'

Stuart steered her towards his office with a view overlooking the deck. 'How was your flight?'

'Fine.'

He went ahead and opened the door. The room had a desk and two chairs, and barely enough room to stand. She squeezed in beside the desk and folded her arms. Stuart shuffled to his chair and sat down. He gestured for her to do the same.

'I'm not staying.'

Stuart stood up. 'Something wrong?'

'What the hell were you thinking, putting a kid on my schedule?'

He frowned. 'You made it, didn't you?'

'Ten minutes late.'

He winced. 'I'm sorry, Jenny. Galen, he's... conscientious. But a good worker. I think he'll do well here.' Jenny's foot tapped out a rhythm on the floor. 'But that's no excuse and I shouldn't have delayed you. What's the big deal anyway? You've been late before.'

She uncrossed her arms. 'I got a memo from Gilchrist's office. I'm under review again.'

Stuart's eyes widened. 'Again?'

She hadn't told him about the first review. 'Yeah, last month it was an issue with my uniform. This month they are reviewing my "piloting skills".' She air quoted the words and sighed. 'It's all bull. I know what they're trying to do.'

He walked around to her side. 'Come on, it's not that bad. They're just crunching numbers. It doesn't mean they're trying to get rid of you.'

She hadn't told him everything. 'I have a meeting with someone from Gilchrist's office now.'

Stuart actually flinched. That didn't settle her nerves one bit. 'I'll talk to them, explain the time infraction was my fault.'

'No need. The attendant overlooked it. I'll be fine. Besides, I don't want to mess up your clean streak.' The HJA docking station, under Stuart's direction for the last ten years, had an infraction-free sheet. She guessed her friend wanted to keep it that way.

That appeared to relax Stuart. 'Lunch after?'

'We'll see.' She pulled her DPad out of her bag and read the memo again. 'Now, where can I find room 15?'

☼

Jenny followed Stuart's instructions down two flights of stairs into a basement and along a corridor that smelled of damp. She stopped outside an unremarkable door with the number fifteen printed on the outside. The light overhead flickered off, then on.

Who in their right mind came down here?

She knocked on the door and heard a faint 'Enter.' She opened it to see a familiar young man wearing the grey uniform of the Earth Security Centre.

He proffered his hand, but the shake in it told her he was nervous. 'Tim, from Gilchrist's office. Nice to see you again.'

Gilchrist's assistant. The one she'd done the fashion show for. She shook it and sat down.

The man no older than twenty five sat opposite her, his lips drawn thin and white. His eyes were focused on a DPad in front of him.

'Jenny Waterson?' He glanced at her and she nodded. 'Please state your credentials.'

'Captain. Grade Four.'

Tim looked between the pad and her. 'And how long have you been at that grade?'

'A year.' She twisted her hands together on her lap. 'Is there a problem?'

His fingers glided over the DPad as though he were rearranging data. 'No, just updating the details on here.'

'Am I your first meeting today?'

Gilchrist's assistant glanced up at her and smiled nervously. That made her nervous. 'No. I've seen seven other pilots before you.'

She couldn't stand not knowing. 'Please, what is the purpose of this review? Have I done something wrong?'

He put the DPad down and clasped his hands together on the table. 'Ms Gilchrist is asking me to speak with all the grade four pilots. She wants an assessment of skills, to ensure our pilots are fit to fly.'

Or not fit, and cleared to be fired.

She gestured to the idle DPad in front of Tim. 'If you look at my history you'll see I have an exemplary record.'

Tim's mouth thinned. 'Yes, until today.'

'Excuse me?'

'You were late.'

'I was not.' The attendant had told her he wouldn't record her infraction.

'Except that you were. The attendant confirmed it in a report to me.'

That lying... 'Why would he?' She blinked once. 'What did he say?'

'That you missed your scheduled drop by ten minutes.'

She peered at the blackened screen of the DPad, wondering if she should take Stuart up on his offer to explain. 'Did he also tell you it wasn't my fault?'

The DPad sprang into life and Tim shielded the screen from her. 'Oh, how so?'

His finger was poised, ready to record her answer probably.

Stuart had delayed her, or rather his trainee had. But trainee or not, Stuart had been in charge. 'There was a storm. It knocked me off course. The craft battled to regain course for a few minutes.'

That's when she saw the red light, indicating Tim was recording their session.

'For the record you were late, and you lied about it?'

'I didn't say that.' Except she had. Jenny huffed. 'Look, it was one time. It won't happen again.'

Tim leaned forward, nerves forgotten, as he settled into his role. He had Jenny on the back foot, and that would look good when Gilchrist reviewed the data.

'Ms Waterson, I didn't ask you here to frighten you.'

She suppressed a laugh that any twenty something could frighten her. But these days, they held more power than she did.

'So why am I here? Is this a warning?'

'Yes. I'm meeting with all the grade four pilots, as mentioned. Please don't take this the wrong way, but we've noticed that efficiency levels drop when pilots reach a certain age.'

How else was she supposed to take it? 'There's nothing wrong with my skills. As I said before, I had a good reason for being late.'

'Yes, but you also made a judgment call to keep the

craft in autopilot rather than take control and make up for lost time.'

She laughed once. 'You weren't up there. The winds were violent. It was safer to keep the autopilot on.'

Gilchrist's assistant nodded, but kept his expression neutral. People who sat on the fence, who refused to use common sense, irritated Jenny.

He said, 'Sure, but it still doesn't change the fact you were late.'

She had no comeback.

Jenny slumped back in her chair. 'What now?'

Tim hit something on his DPad. 'Now, I record it. Ms Gilchrist doesn't like infractions.' He stood up. 'Consider this your first warning. Make sure this doesn't happen again.'

18

Laura spent the afternoon sorting through a snapshot of the world's most boring crime: tax evasion. With another thirteen hours left of her shift, she didn't see how she'd get through the steady stream of documentation hitting her monitor.

Spread the work out, take regular breaks from the screen.

Her mantra worked most days, even when the light-starved office triggered a bout of depression that a shot of vitamin D couldn't fix.

Before his death, her father had suffered from regular depression, but Laura's own was triggered by seasonal changes. With a never-changing season, her darker thoughts often spoiled her happier ones. Most times the vitamin D shot worked to keep her thoughts on track. While she had never considered ending her life, the termination rooms provided by the World Government gave an easy out to a population that could live to one hundred and sixty.

After legalising what had once been a criminal practice, termination rooms could now be found everywhere. Her great-grandfather had used one and Laura and her mother had been with him at the end. Her father hadn't been well enough able to face it. While it wasn't a bad way to end life, surrounded by loved ones, Laura wasn't ready to check out just yet.

Those had been better times when she and her mother used to have actual conversations. Her father's suicide a few years later had turned her mother into a recluse—not to mention a handful.

Laura blamed herself for her father's death. And her mother? She blamed Laura for it too. She'd thought about talking it over with someone, but Chris and Janine were the only friends she had. They were not people she trusted with her weaknesses.

She shook the negative thoughts from her mind and stood up from her workstation. Feeling stiff and like she needed to move, she walked a few laps of the room. After, she stopped at Janine's workstation, her cheeks flushed.

'Having fun, are we?' Janine wore a strange expression; something split between humour and jealousy.

'If I don't move, I won't make it to the end of my shift.'

'Just take another Actigen then.'

'Can't. I'm at my limit of four this week. Plus, they aren't working anymore.'

'Look, I've got work to do and you're disturbing me,' said Janine.

'And there it is,' said Chris, with one eye on Laura.

'What?' snapped Janine.

'The inner bitch.'

'Piss off, Chris.'

'I've made my point and you've just proven it. So what if she's exercising? I for one am enjoying the distraction.'

'You just want to get into her pants,' said Janine.

'So? What man wouldn't?'

Laura blushed. 'Stop talking about me like I'm not here. And Chris, watch your mouth.'

Chris sounded offended. 'Fine. Sit down then and stop wiggling your hips.'

'I need to clear my head first. I'll feel better in a moment.'

'You're wasting your time, you know,' said Chris. 'You'll only feel worse, especially with Actigen in your system.'

'Exercise helps me in other ways.' She wanted to explain about her Seasonal Affective Disorder, how distractions helped with the lack of control. 'You wouldn't understand.'

Chris wiggled his eyebrows. 'Besides there's only one type of exercise I like to do.'

Janine pulled a face. 'Oh, keep your thoughts to yourself, for once. Please.'

Keen to move the focus away from her, Laura said, 'Chris, any word from your friend on the lottery's next hit after Perth?'

'You're not going to like it. Melbourne next, then Europe.'

'Europe? Shit.' She thought they'd circle back and hit Sydney again.

'Why do you want to go so badly anyway?' Janine's gaze narrowed.

'I don't,' Laura replied too fast. 'I'm just interested, that's all.'

'Well, seems to me like it's more than that. What does your family think about it?'

Her pulse raced as they inched closer to the topic of her dysfunctional family. 'My mother will probably end up coming with me.'

Janine swept her hand around the room. 'And leave all this behind? You'll never get a job as good as this on Exilon 5. You'll probably have to work as a cleaner for crap pay.'

'Janine, what the hell crawled up your butt today?' said Chris.

'Nothing. I'm just enquiring about Ms O'Halloran's eagerness to leave Earth, that's all. She gets so excited every time the lottery sniffs near Haymarket.'

Laura had her fill of Janine and her petty sniping. Beneath all the bravado, Janine was insecure and lacked personal ambition.

Laura rubbed her tired eyes and began the short walk back to her desk.

'Is that it?' said Chris. 'No more bending over to show us your perfect ass?'

'Bite me.'

'Don't mind if I do.'

'Would you two stop with the sick flirting already and let me tell you what I've heard,' said Janine. Heads lifted up from workstations. Janine was a sure thing for the gossip and she flirted with every male in the building to get it. Her powers of persuasion had proven to be useful. She usually heard news before the other floors.

Janine twirled a few strands of her long brown hair between her fingers while she waited for everyone's attention.

'There's a massive meeting happening in Gilchrist's office today. All the security heads will be there. Tom from Level One heard it from Julie, who knows someone who works near Suzanne Brett's office.' Brett was the overseer for Level Five and directly under Gilchrist's command.

A low whisper carried around the room. 'Yeah, I saw Daphne Gilchrist in the lobby this morning, flanked by her minions.'

'That woman puts the frighteners up me,' said Chris.

'All women scare you,' said Laura. 'Any of those who have a bit of power, that is.'

'Not all women, just the ball breakers. She has the power to castrate men with her stare.'

'Exaggerate much?' said Janine.

'I speak the truth,' said Chris. 'Did you know her voice gets so loud during meetings it shatters unbreakable glass?'

'You are so full of shit.'

The room exploded into peals of laughter.

Another worker cut in. 'Does anyone know why they're meeting? I can't remember the last time all security heads were in one room.'

'Since when are we ever told about anything in this place?' said another. 'I barely know what the replicated specials are in the cafeteria, let alone important business that might actually concern us.'

While everyone guessed what the meeting was about, Laura stayed silent. She didn't remember there ever being a security meeting during her three years at ESC.

She couldn't shake the feeling that something bad was coming down the line.

19

Daphne Gilchrist paced at the top of the large meeting room adjoining her ESC office on Level Seven. A huge oval-shaped walnut table sat on a circular cream-and-black rug. Twelve hand-carved oak chairs hugged the table's edge. A painting with a concentric pattern of rings in black and charcoal grey hung on one wall, representing the force fields that protected levels five through to nine.

She hated this room. The concentric circle design reminded her of being trapped, a feeling she'd struggled with for the last few months. Things were bad on Earth, but little was being done to rectify it. Her future hung in the balance and she was certain Charles Deighton would have the last say.

Daphne blinked and refocused on the nine representatives for the ITF security branches ranging from London to Bangladesh sat around the table. They each had power in their respective roles, but here Daphne was in charge. Suzanne Brett, overseer for Level Five, sat to her right, someone she could trust to toe the line when needed. Right now, she needed people on her side. Her assistant Tim sat to her left, back from his meeting in the HJA station.

She motioned for him to leave. He did so reluctantly.

'Everyone, what is the plan?' she asked as soon as the door closed. Daphne checked her grey trouser suit for lint.

The reps stayed silent. She had called them in early to coincide with the alien's planned meeting. They'd been sitting in the room for an hour now.

She locked eyes with Simon Shaw, the rep for the London ITF office, where Bill Taggart was stationed. He flicked his eyes away from her penetrating stare. Daphne knew she wasn't an easy person to deal with, but one thing she despised most was displays of weakness.

Her father had been a strong, domineering character, ruling her weak-willed mother with an iron fist. Daphne had learned how to use the same tactics in the boardroom. All her mother had taught her was that she would never become a doormat.

She sat down at the head of the table and tapped her nail on its lacquered surface.

'It appears from Bill Taggart's preliminary report that we face a serious problem with these Indigenes. They have the advantage and Deighton isn't happy. What I need are solutions. Raise your hand if you want to speak.'

She liked formality and structure. Structure allowed her to predict what was coming.

Simon Shaw, head of the London ITF office, raised his hand.

He cleared his throat. 'Bill Taggart is the best investigator to come out of my office. His performance on other missions has been exemplary and I am confide—'

'I know exactly where he came from, Shaw,' said Daphne. 'I placed him there myself, if you recall. I don't need you to recite his credentials. If that's all you have to say—'

'No! I mean, we should wait to hear Taggart out, get his thoughts on it. Knowing him, he'll have come up with another solution to track down the Indigenes.'

She locked her eyes on Shaw's thin face and grey eyes. He wasn't much older than Taggart. He'd be more likeable if he wasn't so weak willed. Deighton ate types like him for breakfast.

'We can't lose the progress made so far. It's our job to determine the next steps in this investigation, not him. What happened after the meeting was no mistake. Officer Page said Bill Taggart followed the alien to the underground station ten minutes ago and lost it. He is a hothead and not ready to lead the investigation.'

That was also Deighton's opinion of him. She still didn't understand why the investigator had been allowed to head up the team in the first place. She suspected it had more to do with Deighton's history with the Taggarts. Was this entire charade to teach Bill Taggart a lesson?

'I'm not saying he's perfect, but—' Shaw continued.

She snapped her fingers at the room. 'Someone else who is not part of the London office, please.'

Shaw sat back in his chair, eyes blazing.

Emotions had no place in Daphne's world. Emotions got people killed, or worse, fired. Twenty years as CEO of the Earth Security Centre had taught her how to play the game the way the men did.

The representative from the Bangladesh office raised his hand. Daphne nodded at him to proceed. 'Was there an issue with the military personnel Taggart had been assigned?' he said. 'Two of the officers followed the alien after last week's meeting.'

Yes, Caldwell and Page had done the exact same thing Taggart had. But it was Taggart's job to keep them under control.

'Nothing more than usual with those beefed-up military types,' said Daphne. 'I'm looking for real suggestions, people.'

The rep from the Tokyo office stood up and bowed to his host. 'Please, Ms Gilchrist-san. How much does Taggart know about our situation?'

Junsuke Sato was the only rep that Daphne could tolerate. It had been ingrained in her to show respect to the Japanese man.

'Konnichiwa, Sato-san,' she responded with a brief respectful bow. 'Other than the basics, nothing. Shaw, care to elaborate?'

'He still thinks he's on a fact-finding mission. He knows little about the Indigenes or where they came from. As you instructed, I fed him the false background files.'

The files had come from the World Government; some propaganda ones, most of them real. Deighton wanted Taggart to know what he faced, but not why. She was also a little fuzzy on the why.

'Good. I'm ordering Taggart to return on the next passenger ship leaving Exilon 5 tomorrow. We will speak to him then.'

'But what about his wife?' asked Sato. 'After two years, he is still obsessed with finding her. What does he know about her fate?'

'He still thinks the Indigenes took her. I don't plan on correcting that.' She couldn't if she tried. Deighton had never shared more than the basics with her. She went missing during a routine mission. That was how Deighton had explained it. 'He's more useful fighting against the Indigenes than with them.'

'Is he a risk?' said Sato.

Daphne shook her head. 'He is manageable. Shaw will see to that.'

'But what if he finds out about her?'

She smiled. 'I really don't see how that's possible. He doesn't have access to that information and I'm not about to tell him, are you?'

Sato shook his head and sat down.

The Bangladesh rep spoke again. 'What exactly do the Indigenes know about us?'

'Very little, if Taggart's observations are anything to go by. Although the revelation about what we are must have come as a shock to this "Stephen" character. The boy, Ben Watson, had no idea what he was saying, and to whom.'

'Have the files from the investigation been processed yet?' asked the San Francisco rep.

Daphne slid her eyes to her number one. 'Brett?'

'Not yet,' said Suzanne. 'We're sending them down to Level Five now. They will be processed later on this afternoon.'

'Brief me straight away when that's done,' said Daphne.

Sato stood, still looking concerned. Daphne released a soft sigh.

'Forgive me for my worry, but we know not what information the Indigenes have on us,' he said. 'Do we know what they plan next?'

'No, we don't.' She offered him a smile. 'But I can assure you, we have put in place the proper measures to make sure no harm comes to us. The meeting with Ben Watson was innocent enough. I don't think the Indigenes will act on their new findings, at least not straight away. I'm still looking for suggestions from the table.'

They had a rogue investigator about to be recalled, a bunch of files from the investigation that were most likely useless, and a race on Exilon 5 that still needed controlling. Not many people knew about the Indigenes, and that's how Deighton wanted it.

No suggestions were put forward. That disappointed Daphne. She'd wanted some new ideas that might remove some of Deighton's control.

She stood and brushed down her suit. 'Let's reconvene when we've given this situation more thought. Next time, I want one idea from everybody.'

'On a related matter,' said Suzanne. 'We're short of people in Level Five. With the extra work coming our way, we'll need an extra body to pick up the slack.'

Daphne snapped her fingers. 'Who do you have as replacement?'

'I have some options available in Document Control and Storage,' said Suzanne. 'But the specific person I recommend is Laura O'Halloran.'

Daphne's interest piqued. The girl from the lobby, the one Daphne had made a spectacle of.

'What can you tell me about her?'

'Three years on the job. Lives alone. Only child. Has a mother she doesn't visit often. Father is dead. No friends outside of work. She volunteers for extra shifts when they arise.'

Everything she already knew about the girl. But when the time came for Daphne to choose her own fate, she'd need people on her side. People who would know a truth she was not permitted to divulge.

'Sounds like a controllable candidate. Inform her of the promotion, effective immediately, and make her swear to all-out confidentiality. The last thing we need is for the human population to get wind of an alien race occupying their saviour planet. Deighton and the board members need the transfer to Exilon 5 to go ahead as planned. Thank you everyone.'

Suzanne nodded and headed for the door.

Daphne motioned for her to wait. The room cleared until it was just the two of them. 'Make sure her clearance is restricted,' said Daphne. 'I don't want her getting access to Level Six information unless I give the order. Taggart's files should be clean enough. Need-to-know only. Got it?'

Suzanne nodded. 'Understood.'

'Will she be a problem?'

'Not if I tell Chuck to keep her in line.'

The worker in booth ten on Level Five. A creepy fellow with a stick up his backside.

'Good. As soon as she's settled and you have them ready, give her Taggart's files for processing.'

'Are you sure?' said Suzanne. 'She has no experience at this level. We have twenty-two other operators with better experience.'

'It's exactly for that reason she's getting them. If anything should go wrong, if the news about the Indigenes gets out, we'll need someone to blame.'

20

It had taken years for Bill to build up trust, but now it hung in the balance. He had almost guaranteed Gilchrist and Deighton a result from the day's operation—an alien to question, at a minimum. He'd even assured the pair the Indigene wouldn't be expecting them at the second meeting.

Bill walked back to the platform where Caldwell waited.

'What did you see?' he asked.

'Nothing.'

'I thought we weren't supposed to follow them.'

Bill couldn't stand Caldwell, a stocky-built asshole with a problem following directions. He made it outside without telling him as much. Voices from his team buzzed in his ear. He thought he heard Officer Page mention something about Gilchrist. The idea of doing a debriefing with the team now made his stomach churn. He'd just broken the one rule he'd told them all to follow.

'We should meet to discuss this,' said Caldwell.

Bill pinched the bridge of his nose. 'Not yet.'

'When?'

Bill waved his hand at him. 'I'll let you know.'

He walked the three miles from New Victoria station to Cantaloupe. All that chasing had given him an appetite, but his foolish actions had killed it again. What he needed now was time to think.

Bill idled outside Cantaloupe, knowing results like today's ones wouldn't stay quiet for long. He needed to get ahead of the news. He was sure Caldwell would phone this in if he didn't first. He ducked down an alleyway and called Gilchrist back on Earth, a connection made possible by the interstellar wave. Pacing the alley, his gut twisted with nerves. The connection rang and rang.

Eventually someone answered. 'Hello?'

Bill released a breath, recognising the voice of Gilchrist's assistant. 'Yes, can you put me through please?'

'I'm sorry, Ms Gilchrist is in a meeting.'

'Well tell her it's Bill Taggart. She's going to want to speak to me.'

'Her instructions were clear. I can't make an exception.'

Bill ground his fists into his legs. 'Well, when is she due to be out of it?'

'I'm not sure. I'll make sure to tell her you called.' The connection ended abruptly.

'Fuck!' Bill yelled. A couple of passersby slowed and stared at him.

He stared back. 'What?'

Hands on hips, he doubled over and released his anger in a loud grunt. Then he marched to the restaurant.

The bell on Cantaloupe's door rattled overhead. It was early enough in the day that his usual seat by the window was free. He ordered lasagne from the menu, earning him a curious look from the waitress.

'I skipped breakfast,' he growled at her.

Bill slumped back in his seat and waited for his food to arrive. It didn't take long for his thoughts to comb over that morning's events.

How could he be so stupid? The alien had been right there. He'd faced off against him in the tunnels. His arrival had even caught the alien off guard. It had been the perfect time to ask about Isla. But he'd stood frozen in place, unable to move let alone demand answers.

Had he scared off the alien now? Would Stephen risk meeting Ben Watson a third time?

Bill shook his head and smiled. No he wouldn't.

At least he had a recording of the meeting. Audio and visual. Maybe he could learn something new from the footage.

His irritation set his mind to race faster than it already was. The way forward refused to come to him. He'd messed everything up.

Bill buried his face in his hands. 'I shouldn't have gone after him.'

The waitress startled him as she arrived with a plate of lasagne, a side order of bread and a cup of strong black coffee. He looked up and muttered a quick thanks at her.

The smell made his mouth water; he shoved his first mouthful down. He ignored the burn and the fact his overuse of Actigen had killed his taste buds. A few minutes later, he mopped up the remaining tomato sauce with a slice of bread.

Bill sat back with his coffee. The food tempered his frayed nerves and left him feeling drained. He was certain his actions had driven the Indigene away for good.

But something about the alien seemed off.

Feral, wild. Known to kill on sight.

Official reports harped on about how these feral

Indigenes lacked real intelligence. Who the hell had compiled that data? The filtration device, the artificial skin, the ability to communicate? It all pointed to intelligence. But whatever had the aliens running scared, it didn't give them the right to threaten humans.

What would Isla have done? How would she have handled this situation?

He knew the answer. She'd have tried to understand the Indigenes. For the first time since this began, Bill wondered about Stephen and his story.

Sipping on his coffee, he watched the people of New London on the streets outside. The transfer numbers had eased off, but as far as he knew the progamme was still on track. The World Government had done well to ease the residents into a new life of clean air and no overcrowding. A tacky neon sign caught his eye, welcoming people inside the only digital library in New London. These days, people showed little interest in libraries, and so few knew the history of how humans had ended up on Exilon 5.

Time had been short to find an exoplanet with the same density as Earth that could support human life.

When he was a child, Bill's father had told him how the newer ship designs would facilitate their discovery of a suitable planet. The first of the people-carrying ships had been in operation since 2115, a few years before he was born. Professor Tessa Gogarty, a propulsion engineer and lecturer in Astrophysics in Trinity College Dublin, had designed the hyper drive. Her contributions had helped to revolutionise space travel.

Years later Exilon 5 was discovered, just as the Gogarty Hyper Drive 8.0 was implemented in the newer ships. The new hyper drive shortened the travel time between Earth and Exilon 5 to two weeks.

A noise jolted Bill out of his thoughts. His communication device shrilled in his ear. The unique tone identified a call from the Earth Security Centre. Heart thumping, he activated his earpiece.

'Bill, is that you?' said Daphne Gilchrist.

'Yeah.' When he'd called her earlier, he had a speech prepared. But now? He wasn't ready to have this conversation.

'I heard that you called. Charles Deighton also asked that I contact you directly. You should know Caldwell and Page contacted me separately and told me what happened.' *Assholes!* 'I'm reading through Caldwell's recount of events. Not looking good, is it?'

In the half-full restaurant, he kept his voice low. 'There were problems with the personnel I was assigned. They disobeyed a direct order.' That much was true. He included himself in that mix.

'This was your operation, Bill. You were in charge and you promised results. Deighton and I can only consider this mission to be a failure.'

Bill couldn't have agreed more. 'Our investigations did produce some extra data on the Indigene that could be worth analysing. I will send that on to you shortly.'

He pictured her nodding. 'Send it in the next hour. We'll put our Level Five team on it.'

A brief silence followed and Bill tried to think of something else to say.

Gilchrist saved him the trouble. 'From Caldwell's report, there appears to be new information about the way the Indigenes move around the city. I assume your specific target's location is still unknown?'

'I followed the alien to one of the train tracks before it disappeared into New Victoria's tunnels. We think he exited from another station.'

'*He?*' Gilchrist barked a laugh. 'How soon will the alien reappear? Or did your impromptu chase scare *him* off completely?'

Bill cringed at his inability to follow his own instructions. 'Slim, I would think. The alien knows we were watching.' A clue he should have picked up on earlier.

'There's a passenger ship leaving for Earth tomorrow. Be on it. I'll send a car for you then. I'll see you at the ESC for a debriefing in two weeks. Out.'

Gilchrist severed the connection.

'Shit.' Bill pulled the earpiece out and tossed it on the table. An order to return home meant he was off the case.

The waitress caught his eye and held up a pot of coffee. He waved her away and stared out the window. He couldn't do anything from Earth. Somehow he would need to convince Gilchrist to keep him on the investigation, so he could continue his search for Isla.

But right now with the Indigene gone, returning to Earth looked like his only option.

☼

Back at his apartment, Bill prepared the video and audio files of the meeting for the ESC, and tossed his meagre possessions into his suitcase. Today's result had been a massive setback, both professionally and personally. He should have controlled his team better. It was his fault he was going home.

His eyes drooped with exhaustion, but his body was too wired to sleep. Dizziness made his head swim; he shook off the feeling long enough to finish his packing and set his suitcase down by the door. For the next hour, he combed through the recording from that morning's meeting. Maybe there was a clue that he'd overlooked. Nothing.

He kicked the coffee table and fired off the results to the ESC using an encrypted channel, via interstellar wave.

Bill paced the room. An order to return home meant returning to the apartment he and Isla owned and possibly facing up to the fact she was gone.

He wasn't ready to let her go.

Isla was out there somewhere. And he was sure the Indigene, Stephen, knew exactly where.

21

A low murmur ran around the Gathering Room, the meeting place for the Central Council and the Indigene representatives. Constructed out of omicron rock, the room's natural sound-insulating properties kept the discussion private.

Fifty Indigenes from the other nine districts, and representing their elders, stood inside the room. From Stephen's elevated platform position, he watched their concern shift to anger and fear as he relayed the information from Ben Watson. He'd already given the same information to Pierre, Elise and Anton an hour ago. They'd discussed plans of what to do next, but everyone had been too stunned to come up with solutions.

Pierre and Elise had insisted he repeat the information to the representatives who had been meeting with Pierre in District Three on other matters.

'We have to get ahead of this story before it gets out of control,' Elise had said.

'Maybe they can help,' Pierre added.

Stephen struggled to keep calm as he shared his conversation with Ben Watson. The atmosphere shifted again, this time to shock, when he revealed the true identity of the Surface Creatures.

Stephen searched the sea of faces and found one, Anton's, staring back at him. He snatched his eyes away and focused on the representatives.

'Please, everybody needs to calm down,' Pierre said as the group's agitation increased.

The elders stood alongside him. Elise leaned in closer to Pierre and whispered something. If she was trying to calm the room, she had her work cut out for her. A rush of questions followed.

'What does this mean for us?'

'What will happen if the humans discover our districts? How will we protect ourselves?'

Pierre fanned his hands. 'Please, we won't help matters by panicking. We will arrive at a solution together, I promise you. We aren't in any immediate danger and I urge you all to calm down.'

Elise added, 'We have an advantage. They don't know what we are, and their interest in us appears to be low at this stage. That gives us time to discuss a strategy.'

'Stephen,' whispered Pierre. 'Elise and I must speak with you and Anton privately. We need to discuss this further. I will ask Leon to join us.' Anton's father.

Pierre's reasons for excluding the representatives were sound. This was too big an issue to get group agreement on, and one that was likely to spawn vigilante groups. Pierre had to keep control of this mess.

His elder addressed the room again. 'I urge the districts not to act alone. Please do not share this information beyond your elders until we can come up with a collective strategy. We must protect ourselves, and right now we appear to have the upper hand.' The group mumbled their agreement. 'I assure you we will keep all representatives apprised of any developments.'

The reps nodded, buying Pierre's lie.

☼

Fifteen minutes later, Stephen stood in Council Chambers alongside Pierre, Elise, Anton, and Leon. Anton's pacing did little to settle Stephen's nerves. Elise and Pierre's stillness in the middle of the room didn't help either. His skin grew warm suddenly, and he knew Elise had something to do with it.

Leon, a trusted friend of the elders and Anton's father, watched his son pace. But Anton looked more nervous than stressed.

So this news only troubled Stephen?

Pierre nodded at him to share the details he was asked to keep from the representatives.

Stephen kicked off the discussion with a deep sigh.

What do they call their planet? said Leon.

Earth.

And this is the human's home planet, where they originated from?

As I understand it, said Stephen.

Elise switched to her voice. 'Why do we share the same name? What are we to them?'

Stephen had no clue. 'I don't know. Distant cousins?'

'Our species has existed for thousands of years on Exilon 5,' Pierre said. 'Something must have happened to separate us from them.'

'But that doesn't explain why they've come here to destroy us,' said Leon. 'Did you learn about their intentions, Stephen?'

He pressed his hands together to stop the shake in

them. 'I'm sorry, Leon.'

With a nod Pierre said, 'We won't make any hasty decisions today. First we must understand their motives. To learn all we can about them may be our only defence.'

Stephen glanced at the bookshelves. 'Information on them is limited.' He'd gotten more out of a brief conversation with an eight year old than he had from the stolen human literature.

Anton stopped pacing, his energy less nervous and more excited now. 'I say we visit this planet Earth, see what we can learn about them there.'

'Settle down, Anton,' said Elise touching his arm. 'We'll probably need to discuss this a little more.'

Thick warm air enveloped the space, relaxing Stephen's body but not his mind. Anton's eyes glazed over. Elise let go.

'Anton might have a point,' said Pierre. 'We're on the back foot here. All we know is the military was watching Stephen and the child, but not why. This latest meeting will only feed their curiosity.'

'Apart from Anton, we all remember the day when the explosions happened,' said Leon. 'Distant cousins or not, their species can't be trusted.'

Stephen had witnessed the explosions on the surface that wiped out two-thirds of the Indigene population. The aftermath had killed his parents. 'I wish I could say for certain they're all the same. It would be easier to hate them all. But I sense that some are different.'

Pierre's eyes brightened. 'What do you mean?'

'I sensed no malice from the child, only curiosity.' He recalled the Evolver who had been kidnapped after a hunting trip, never to return. 'Yet, the older humans murder innocents.'

'Stephen, your senses rarely fail you,' said Pierre.

'Do you believe there is more to this story?'

He caught the change in the elder's tone. From day one, Pierre had been all for his idea to meet with the boy. 'Why do you keep pushing me to accept them?'

'I just want you to consider all the options, that there may be other reasons behind their actions.'

What an odd thing to say.

He held the elder's gaze. 'Like what?'

Pierre next words rushed out of him. 'Nothing specific. I want to float Anton's idea about travelling to their home world. It would be the fastest way to learn more about them.'

Despite his reservations, Stephen had arrived at the same conclusion. He wanted to understand the enemy better. He hadn't mentioned his encounter with the military man in the tunnel.

'I agree.'

Anton smiled and paced the room again. Elise's calming effect must have worn off.

The second elder didn't look as enthusiastic about the plans as her husband. 'It's too dangerous.'

'I'm sorry, wife,' said Pierre. 'But we must be proactive. We have been backed into a corner by the humans. Our actions will not only give us control of the situation but allow us to control the message being fed to the districts. If we do nothing, I'm certain new vigilantes will fix that. Stephen and Anton must go before this turns into a bigger problem.'

'You want to risk the lives of our best two?' said Elise.

'It's because they're the best that I'm considering this. It will work.'

'I agree with Pierre. We don't have a choice.' Leon gripped Anton's shoulder. 'Stephen, Anton, are you both up to the task?'

His friend grinned at him. Stephen nodded. 'Yes, I think so.'

'Good,' said Pierre. 'We've been watching the docking stations for a while and we know a passenger ship is scheduled to leave orbit tomorrow for their home planet.'

Elise grabbed his arm. *At least send a back-up group with them, Pierre.* She turned to Leon. *Why are you allowing them to travel alone? They won't be able to protect each other if something happens.*

But if we send too many, they'll be noticed, said Pierre.

Stephen agreed with his reasoning.

Leon smiled at the elder. *They'll be fine, Elise. They know how to look after themselves.*

She shook her head. 'You're fine with risking your son's life?'

'Amelia and I raised our son to think for himself. I will not tell him what to do.'

But that did not satisfy Elise. She stared at the bookshelf. Pierre placed a hand on her shoulder; she shucked it off.

'Stephen, Anton, what do you two think?' he said.

'It will be safer if we do this alone,' said Stephen. 'There'll be less chance of triggering an alarm. If they find us, they might just think it's a solo mission, rather than an organised attack on humans.'

'Anton?'

'I say we give these humans a taste of their own medicine.'

'This is not an attack,' said Pierre. 'You're to add to the knowledge of what we already know about their species. That is all. No risks. Is that clear?'

Anton nodded.

There were many intelligent Indigenes, but none with his friend's ability to create and adapt technology. Anton was by far the youngest of their technological protégés and his talents had been publicly and privately lauded. His friend buzzed with enthusiasm; the difficulty lay in curbing it. But in any life or death situation, Stephen wanted no other Indigene watching his back.

When Elise grabbed a book and pretended to read, Pierre flipped his attention to the finer details of the trip. 'Anton, how about you give us an update on how you're progressing.'

Anton beamed; he loved to talk about his inventions.

'Well, thanks to Stephen's meeting last week, I was able to thin out the artificial skin and improve its pigmentation. I've updated the existing air filtration device to work for two full days on a single charge. I've devised mobile recharging units that we can carry with us. They should give us an indefinite filtered air supply.'

'What about getting on the ship?' asked Leon. 'Don't you need identity chips to board?'

Anton nodded. 'Have them. I asked one of the recent hunting parties to bring back identity chips. They also brought me a security chip from a worker whose thumb had been accidentally cut off.' Elise turned, book in hand. Both she and Pierre stared at Anton. He waved his hand at their concern. 'Don't worry he was dead at the time. Besides, there's a black market for this technology and crime of this sort is common.'

Pierre blinked. 'Continue, Anton.'

'I've made a decent clone of their security chip that should work as a replacement for theirs. I've temporarily re-routed the tracking device embedded in the one we borrowed. It links to a central command. The chips are wired to self-destruct if they can't verify the unique bio signature of the original host. Presumably, the unit will use the tracking device to locate the chip—which it won't be able to because of my reroute—to arrest whoever tampered with it. So we need it gone before it destroys itself and breaks the tracking reroute.'

Anton switched to telepathy. *You're going to have to run fast, my friend.*

Well, you'd better hurry up.

Elise put the book back on the shelf and rejoined the conversation. 'Why do you also need the identity chips? Won't the security one be enough?'

'Both chips are present in human bodies,' said Anton. 'Their age or skill level determines whether their security chip is activated but we know both chips are scanned when humans leave the planet. The computer checks for bio compatibility and that they haven't been tampered with. I designed a generic identity chip that the mission group used to replace the ones they took. In theory, the workers they removed them from shouldn't notice any difference, unless they try to leave the planet.'

'Is that a likely occurrence?' said Leon.

Anton shrugged. 'I hope to have returned home before they find out. We have to take the risk.'

'I agree,' said Stephen. 'Where do the chips go?'

'The identity chips go in our left thumbs, same as the humans.' Stephen recalled the automated bus from his meeting with Ben Watson and the passengers tagging on. 'My fake security chips should fool the system as long as the other chip is an original. Stephen will be known as "Bob Harris", an underground station operations manager, and I will be "Colin Stipple", road maintenance worker. That's the information that came back when I scanned the originals into our systems. That's how the logs will know us when we attempt to board.'

Leon looked happier after Anton's explanation.

'Good job, Anton,' said Pierre.

'As much as I'd like to take all the credit, I had a little help from my team.'

'Please try not to get killed out there,' said Elise.

'That isn't part of the plan,' said Stephen.

Pierre lightly gripped his wife's shoulder, as if to reassure her. 'When does the ship leave for Earth?'

'Tomorrow at noon,' said Stephen. 'That will also be the hottest and most dangerous time of the day. We'll need to keep our bodies covered. That's bound to attract unwanted attention.'

'I have cooling packs that we can wear inside our coats,' said Anton. 'We should be fine until we get on board. Oh, I forgot to mention, we need to inject our food directly into our stomachs. We won't be able to eat with our filtration devices in place. I've already made modifications to the synthesised protein packs, so there should be minimal side effects.'

Stephen grimaced at the idea. 'Sounds challenging.'

'What will we tell the representatives about this trip?' asked Elise

'Nothing, for now,' said Pierre. 'The less they know the better.'

In the meantime... Anton removed the security chip from his pocket and dropped it into Stephen's hand. *Get rid of this, will you?*

22

Laura looked up when Suzanne Brett burst into Document Control and Storage, followed closely by the overseer for Level Four. Work ground to an immediate halt as dozens of pairs of eyes watched them.

'Carry on with your work,' said Brett.

'Yes, carry on everyone.' The overseer mimicked Suzanne's order, as he ran to catch up with her.

Laura stared at her screen so hard the letters blurred. Brett's uniform made a swishing sound as she walked. Why was she here? Who was she here for? Laura had only met Suzanne Brett once before, back when she had started work. She hadn't warmed to the woman's chilly desk-side manner and her black hair and thin lips had given her the name "the ice queen". Laura knew better than to cross the women who occupied the top positions in the ESC.

Her intense study of the screen made her dizzy. The swishing sounds abated causing her to tense up.

A tap on her shoulder startled her. She wheeled round, face flushed, to see Brett standing behind her. The room fell silent. Brett's cold eyes bored into her while the overseer hovered uneasily in the background.

'Laura O'Halloran?'

'Yes?'

'You are being relocated as a matter of priority. Get your things.'

'What? Where?'

She glanced at her overseer who nodded it was time to go. She stood up and gathered together her meagre possessions that included her DPad and a framed picture of her parents. 'Where am I going?'

Brett took the lead. The overseer for Level Four followed behind Laura as Brett walked her to the exit. Her panic grew.

She saw curiosity on her colleagues' faces. Janine mimicked a call sign and mouthed 'later'. No doubt Janine would be talking about her as soon as she left.

When would "later" even be?

Brett led her to the turbo lift and called it.

'Where are you taking me? Have I done something wrong?'

The lift arrived and Brett entered first. The overseer for Level Four shoved Laura inside.

'Thanks for your help, Phil,' said Brett. She placed a hand on the overseer's chest, preventing him from following. 'I'll take it from here.' As the doors closed, Laura saw Phil mouth the word 'bitch'.

'One floor down,' said Brett.

At first Laura thought it was a command for the lift. But then her heart battered against her ribs when she realised where she was headed.

'Why?'

'Hold out your right thumb.'

Laura complied and Brett jabbed her with a pointy-tipped instrument. Laura winced, but didn't pull away her thumb while Brett upgraded her security chip access.

The lift doors opened. 'That will give you access to Level Five,' said Brett. 'Gilchrist's orders. But before I can take you there, you need to come with me.'

Gilchrist?

They stepped out into an unremarkable corridor of grey walls and matching carpet. If it hadn't been for the number five flashing like a beacon in the turbo lift, Laura wouldn't have known what floor she was on. Brett ushered her into a small room two doors down from the lift. A stern looking man wearing the familiar purple uniform of Level Five was sitting at a table in one of two chairs. The man's uniform was adorned with almost as many accolades as Brett's. Clearly, he was somebody important in the ESC.

He pointed to the second chair. 'Please, take a seat.'

She sat down and looked around her. The door sucked shut, trapping her. Brett remained inside the room, standing in one corner.

The purple-clad man thrust a DPad at her. 'Read this out loud, so I know you understand it.'

Laura shakily read the full text of the document.

CONFIDENTIALITY AGREEMENT

You are entering into an area which contains highly sensitive documentation.

You may not discuss the information you see with anyone.

You must only divulge information to an employee of a higher rank than you.

If you do anything that is in direct

violation of this agreement, you will be severely reprimanded.

Place your security chip at the bottom of the screen if you comply with this agreement.

What reprimand? Perhaps she'd find out at her induction programme later.

Laura's excitement and shock pushed her towards the promotion, but her mind pulled her back. This was all happening too fast. She wasn't scheduled for promotion for another two years and hadn't heard of anyone being fast-tracked. Gilchrist had ordered her promotion? Was that good or bad?

Had her recent run in with Gilchrist had anything to do with it?

What do you care, Laura? This is what you wanted, to get on Gilchrist's radar.

'I suppose.'

'Excuse me?' asked the man.

Laura blinked at him. 'Oh, nothing.'

The transfer list to Exilon 5. That's all that mattered.

Laura placed her right thumb on the marker below the text and took a leap of faith unto the unknown.

23

The midday sun was as hot as Stephen had predicted. The humans in the queue were getting too close. His efforts to avoid contact with them were in vain as the humans repeatedly encroached on his space. Anton, standing next to him, was studying his thumb where he'd inserted one of the chips last night.

Ahead was New London's docking station, a large prefabricated cabin between the waiting passengers and the area where the spacecraft docked on the other side. At least a large white tarpaulin covering was shielding them from the midday sun. Stephen bounced on his feet. Once he boarded the space craft taking him to the passenger ship in orbit, there would be no turning back.

A short man to his front spoke to the tall man beside him. 'Definitely could have stayed for a lot longer. Going home again is the worst.'

'Yeah, I know what you mean,' said the taller man. 'Guaranteed sunshine during daylight hours? To be able to breathe without wearing those stupid masks? Remind me why we're going back there?'

'If we don't, the damn gov'ment will track us down.

We'll be blackballed from ever returning here. Better we don't give them a reason to leave us behind—'

A man charged up the outside of the queue suddenly, knocking the short man's arm as he passed. Stephen drew up to full height when he sensed Anton's agitation, like a quivering down his spine. A young officer at the head of the line blocked the man's path. Stephen couldn't see the man's face.

The short man grumbled. 'What the hell... He just pushed me. Someone thinks he's more important than the rest of us.'

An argument unfolded between the officer and the queue-cutting man. Stephen listened while Anton chewed on his thumb.

'Where do you think you're going?' said the officer. 'Didn't you see the queue behind you?'

The man reached inside his shirt pocket and pulled out some sort of identification. He held it inches from the young man's face. 'I am a high-level employee of the World Government.' He nodded towards the waiting craft. 'I'm scheduled to travel today on the passenger ship.'

His voice sounded familiar.

The short man in front of him straightened up with a new interest. 'Looks like a fight's about to happen.' He stood on tip toes. 'What's he saying now, Gerry? I can't hear 'em all the way back here.'

Even his taller friend looked to struggle to hear anything.

Anton helped him out. 'The man is telling the officer that he's not going to queue and he wants to pass now.'

Stephen shot Anton an angry look.

Anton shrugged. *Sorry, they were irritating me.*

The shorter of the men turned around. He gawked at

Anton's appearance. 'Er, thanks.'

The argument up ahead picked up steam, pulling the man's focus off Anton.

'There's still a queue, and these people were here first,' said the officer to the man. 'Everyone's been waiting for at least two hours.'

'Look, I don't really give a shit...' The man pinched the bridge of his nose. 'What's your name, soldier?'

'Uh, Officer Ridge.'

'Well, Officer Ridge, I have orders from Gilchrist and Deighton to return to Earth today. Would you prefer if I call one of them? Have them confirm this?'

The officer pressed his lips together and studied his DPad.

An eerie silence descended through the crowd. Stephen sensed agitation from the queue-cutting man. Something about him, about the way he stood, nagged at him.

The taller man craned his neck towards the front. 'Looks like the kid's about to crap himself.'

The shorter man tried to make himself taller. 'What's happenin' Ger?'

The officer fumbled with his DPad. 'No need to call Ms Gilchrist.'

The crowd groaned with disappointment.

'Ah, it's all over. The officer backed down already.'

The short man returned to normal height. 'Without a fight? People got no backbone anymore.'

The officer's finger shook as he ran it down the passenger manifest. He turned the DPad around. 'You're on the list. Place both thumbs here.'

The man obliged.

'Investigator William Taggart, International Task Force,' the officer read out loud. 'Ah, it seems you should be in the 'Other' queue, over there.' He pointed to a large white tent, where just ten people waited, and called the next person forward.

The man walked away and the officer sighed with relief.

A new shiver caught Stephen, caused by Anton's agitation.

What is it?

Anton nodded at the investigator, who was making a new fuss at the second queue. *I think I recognise him, from the restaurant. He was sitting at the table by the window when I recorded those scenes for you. He looked at me twice.*

Stephen stilled. He'd seen him before. In the tunnels.

Why was he returning to Earth? The investigator was following orders from a Gilchrist and a Deighton. Hearing one of those names had clearly rattled the officer.

Do you think he might recognise you now? asked Stephen.

Anton shook his head. *He didn't pay me much attention. Seemed distracted by something. Do you think he could be involved in the surveillance on us?*

He is. Anton frowned at him. *He followed me into the tunnels after the second meeting.*

Anton switched to his voice. 'What?'

He shushed his friend when the pair ahead of them turned around, eyes narrowed. Anton smiled at them sweetly until they turned back.

What did the officer say his name was? said Stephen.

Investigator William Taggart.

He committed the name to memory. Who was the investigator, and what instructions had he been given by Gilchrist and Deighton?

24

The driver called him to say his car was waiting outside, but Bill had spent a moment longer in his ITF apartment. The half empty place had been his life for the last year—barely an existence while he'd searched for his wife. That morning, the fog from his brain still had not lifted. Nor had it delivered a creative way to convince Gilchrist to keep him on.

Bill tossed his suitcase into the waiting vehicle and climbed in beside it. The driver commanded the vehicle to drive to the nearest docking station, located fifteen miles outside New London's border.

While it followed the only road out of New London, Bill watched couples laughing beneath the warm sun. City parks hummed with the sound of squealing children. Chatty parents carried picnic baskets. He rolled down the window and dangled out one arm, to absorb the last goodness this planet had to offer. The warmth on his skin pushed away his anxiety. He needed this city.

He also felt closer to Isla here.

The vehicle trundled along a dirt road before pulling up next to the docking station. Ahead of him was his dreaded return to Earth, looming over him like a dark and dingy threat. It was where all his problems had started. A year was a long time to be away.

He glanced down at his carry-on bag containing his DPad. A two-week trip home would give him time to catch up on what he'd missed while away. Developments on Exilon 5 had stalled in tandem with the transfer programme, but what was happening back on Earth?

He wasn't done here; the alien's appearance confirmed they were at the start of something huge. What didn't make sense to him was Deighton and Gilchrist taking him off the hottest investigation the ITF had ever started.

After a run-in with an officer for the wrong queue, Bill boarded the correct craft that held just twenty other World Government employees. None of them looked familiar. Not surprising. He wasn't exactly the get-to-know-you type.

Bill slumped into the first available seat and pulled the restraints tight across his body, in anticipation of the rough flight ahead.

The craft pushed off, assisted by magnetic polarisation that gave the craft a swift sharp shove. Bill's stomach lurched forward then up. The craft passed through the planet's shield to reach the passenger ship orbiting fifty miles above it. With a groan, Bill tried to control his queasiness. Others, not as successful, lunged for the sick bags and filled them up.

He stared out the window at the ship measuring a mile high from base to tip and two miles long; a tubular core ran through its length. Circumnavigating the core was a trio of wheel-like structures, attached via interconnecting tubes or "spokes". Powered by a Faster Than Light drive, the ship used the natural magnetic fields between planets

Genesis Code

to navigate a path home.

The spacecraft docked inside the main hold of the ship. Feeling like he was on a different kind of ship, Bill gripped the railing to stop his world from spinning. Gingerly, he joined the others in the hold and waited in line. A push and pull of dwindling energy made it hard to focus on much. All he wanted were two things: an easy registration process and a place to store his personal items.

A female officer waited up ahead as the high-level officials formed a queue. She hummed a tune as she ran a finger down a list. 'Not too many on board, I see. We're already off to a good start.' She smiled at the waiting group. 'Looks like I got the easy list. I'm assuming everybody has been on-board a passenger ship before?'

They nodded.

'Good. But I should run through everything once more. Protocol.' Looking up from her DPad, she launched into the rules and regulations from memory.

'The journey takes two weeks. There are two accommodation options available to you. Option one, you can stay in normal mode, during which you will be provided with sleeping quarters and have access to a stocked kitchen. You will be charged for your stay and board. Option two, you can avail of one of our sleeping pods. You will be sedated and sleep-suspended until you arrive at your destination. You will be revived and administered with a nutrient pack upon arrival. Naturally, the cost of option two is cheaper than option one. All expenses will be recorded on your identity chip. Is everyone clear?' The group nodded again. 'Please line up on the left-hand side, and when you reach me, state your accommodation requirements.'

Bill kept his eyes on the ground as he moved forward. When it was his turn, he placed his thumb on the

DPad and picked the only option he could live with. 'Sleeping quarters.'

'That's what I would have picked too.' The officer wrinkled her nose. 'I hate giving up control to the machines.'

For a second Bill forgot himself and smiled back.

But a new feeling overcame him, and he felt himself sway.

She grabbed his arm. 'Are you all right, sir?'

'Yes, I'm fine. Just need sleep.'

The officer nodded. 'Don't worry about it, sir. It's more common than you think. The journey can be a little disorientating. A little rest and you'll feel right in no time.' She released him and he walked towards his uncertain future.

It didn't take long to get to the sleeping quarters with a dozen individually sized units set against both walls. Bill punched in a code for one of them, climbed in, closed over the side-flap and locked it. The accommodation was no bigger than a coffin.

Aside from his fear of being under someone else's control, he had to prepare for his debriefing with Gilchrist. The only items he'd packed were his clothes, some personal items and his recollection of yesterday's events. Plus a copy of the videos he'd used to prepare for the meeting between the Indigene and Ben Watson.

Bill turned on the DPad. The brightness of the screen illuminated his coffin. He opened one of the official World Government reports about the initial move to Exilon 5.

"Grey skies, frigid temperatures and a vanishing sun; clear signs that Earth is changing. The first layer of atmosphere has strangled the sun's attempts to reach the surface. A drop in air temperature has turned the planet ice cold. We passed on four unsuitable exoplanets before we discovered Exilon 5—our last hope. The terraforming process will make it possible for plants and trees to grow there."

The ITF's initial role on Exilon 5 had been to help new transferees adjust to their new home. But the shock of living on an alien world had been too much for some people to handle. The World Government, in its pursuit of a utopian society, had separated them from the rest of the transferees.

Bill read the report.

"We intend to reintroduce technology slowly to avoid triggering addiction in those who use virtual systems as a replacement for living. Exilon 5 will give its residents new opportunities to re-learn the basics of thinking, feeling or just being, as well as accessing technology in a safe and productive way."

The undeveloped land beyond the city boundaries was known in ITF quarters as no man's land. Officers armed with Buzz Guns and Impulse Tasers patrolled the area day and night. Transport arterial routes swept outwards to connect the six cities. Criminals operated black markets in the area, taking advantage of the shortage of technology on the planet to swindle the desperate and vulnerable. No matter how often the ITF smashed the operating rings, fresh businesses would emerge unscathed in alternative places.

According to one report, it was on such a night that an officer heard an animal sound. The noise had originated inside the border limits, where the biodome animals were strictly forbidden.

Bill opened a video file containing an interview with the ITF officer who had discovered the unusual animal activity near New London's border. In his haste Bill had skimmed over this video, not finding anything useful to help him understand the Indigenes.

A yawn caught him off guard. The images turned blurry as sleep tugged on his eyelids. He blinked away his tiredness and concentrated on the video.

The officer had been the first to arrive on the scene of some reported trouble. After calling for back-up, he approached the animal alone. Sitting across from the interviewer, the officer held his hand up like a gun.

'Eyes fixed on me before looking away.' The officer's own gaze flicked from the interviewer to a spot on the wall. 'I heard the animal. It sounded like it was injured. But when I got closer, I couldn't believe what I saw.'

The interviewer frowned. 'What was it?'

The officer laughed. 'Two boys, crouching over what I think was a wolf. The smell of blood turned my stomach. There was so much of it.'

The interviewer leaned forward. 'So you're saying they killed the animal. You were right to report this illegality. The biodome animals are protected.'

The officer shook his head, whispering, 'No, you've got it all wrong...'

Bill blinked away his exhaustion a second time. The video he couldn't focus on continued to play in the background.

What would happen when he got to Earth—would he be fired? Possibly. Would he be reassigned? Even more likely.

His eyes grew too heavy and he shut off the recording. A yawning Bill vowed to find a way to return to Exilon 5 and continue in his search for Isla.

25

Yesterday morning, Laura had put in a call to her mother. It was the anniversary of the death of Laura's father. Fionnuala O'Halloran wasn't the easiest person to deal with on the best of days, but his anniversary made her impossible.

Four years after his suicide, her mother was still struggling to cope.

With the existence of termination rooms, death by hanging was a brutal way to die. It was also a novel way, and the event had attracted unwanted attention from the press. Fionnuala still harped on about the embarrassment of seeing the family name in digital print. Laura had found him. It was her name they'd printed. She was over it. But her mother would not let it go.

During their Light Box call, Laura had been forced to listen to Fionnuala's blame game.

'You should have stopped him.'

'I couldn't—'

'You should have tried to save him.'

'I did—'

'You should have tried harder.'

Laura had not only found her father that day, but also a hysterical Fionnuala curled up in one corner of the room. Her mother had found him first, but the press hadn't mentioned that. Thanks to Fionnuala's ability to twist the truth.

There wasn't much Laura could say to her mother on his anniversary. She would do what she normally did: give her mother a few days to calm down.

No matter how strained their relationship, Laura planned to take her mother to Exilon 5. Perhaps a new planet would kick them both out of their melancholy. When they'd ended yesterday's conversation on a semi-pleasant note, Laura had decided not to mention her promotion. Fionnuala would only have found something to criticise about it.

After Laura had added her signature to the confidentiality agreement, Suzanne Brett had escorted her to the door leading to Level Five. 'You're about to view sensitive information and you must never discuss it. Your work will be continually monitored while you're at the Centre. Understand?'

She nodded, her pulse thrumming with excitement as Brett opened the door. She peered inside the room to see twenty-four isolation booths facing towards the centre aisle. Twenty-two were occupied. Brett led her down the aisle and deposited her at a vacant booth. Nobody said hello.

'You can take this one. Someone will contact you shortly. For now, just sit here quietly.'

Those had been Suzanne's last words before she marched out the door like her backside was on fire. Laura had stared at her blank monitor, unsure of what she was supposed to do. A few hours later, she'd received orders to go home and rest.

The next day, and after her mother's call, Laura arrived into work with a new attitude and ready to get started. But her excitement about her new promotion waned when lunch came and went without a congratulatory word from her former colleagues, Chris and Janine. Suzanne Brett's chilling warning the day before reminded her of the confidentiality agreement she'd signed.

'Listen up, everyone,' said a short man with black beady eyes who occupied booth ten. 'Brett says some important files are on their way. We need to process them fast and get them into the central computer.'

Laura flexed her fingers and waited for her monitor to spring to life. She listened to the soft sound of fingers gliding across screens as the others got to work. But two hours later, her screen remained blank and she felt the cabin fever set in.

Bored, she got up and explored the room that was half the size of the one on Level Four. Beyond the twenty-four booths was a water station, a bulletin board that displayed a different motivational quote each day, and a vacuum tube with a sign that read: "Gilchrist's office".

The bulletin board message read: *We are the sum of our counterparts.*

Laura turned her back on the confusing message and walked along the central aisle. A new irritation bloomed in her chest as the bad thoughts she'd kept at bay tried to worm their way in.

Even though her new colleagues on Level Five were ignoring her, she stopped at the first booth.

'Hey, I'm Laura,' she said. The woman didn't look up. Laura moved on to the next booth and rattled out the same line, to no response. She worked through six more people with none showing her any interest.

A voice boomed from behind as she moved away. 'Hey! New girl.'

Laura turned. The man from booth ten stood and motioned her over. Reluctantly, she went.

'Since you are clearly unfamiliar with the way this place operates, let me enlighten you,' he said. She looked around. The other workers ignored their interaction. 'Don't bother getting to know anyone here. Nobody is interested in you or your story. Have you been briefed yet?'

Laura nodded.

'They are serious when it comes to this floor. You will be monitored like they said, and if you have to take breaks, make sure they're sanctioned ones.'

Laura could do with a break right now.

He continued. 'The information we see is extremely confidential and highly sensitive. What we learn puts a target on our backs. And your worst enemies are the people in his room.'

Her lips parted. Her eyes grazed the heads in the room. Nobody was laughing.

Laura attempted to lighten the heavy mood. 'Picking on the new girl. Ha ha. Very funny.'

The man glowered at her. 'I'm just like you. I came from another floor, but I've learned to survive here. When you stepped through that door, your old life ceased to exist. So, honey? Learn the rules fast.'

'What rules? Are there more I should know about?' Laura had no idea what her job even was.

'You've got brains? Figure it out. But know this, they're always watching. So instead of bothering everyone, return to your booth like a good girl and wait until they send your work programme to your monitor.'

The man broke off his stare and sat down.

Who was watching, Gilchrist? Laura stumbled back

to her booth and her chair. Her racing heart, aggravated by the man's words, refused to settle.

While Brett had warned her already, this new advice only confirmed the warning.

Her stomach growled just as her monitor sprung into life.

Finally.

She put aside her reservations about Level Five and read to herself the instructions that appeared on her monitor:

> *Worker. Welcome to the High Level Data Storage Facility.*
>
> *The information stored here is confidential. When the high-level files are decrypted upon arrival at the Security Centre, the outward tagging system, that indicates the level of security on the file, is stripped.*
>
> *This is done to prevent the supercomputer from automatically storing the file in the central database, which requires twenty-four hours notice for retrieval. It is an automatic security measure for all files with clearance levels of Five and above.*
>
> *The Level Five and higher files sent to this location require investigation by the Data Analysis Unit on Level Six, before they are sent for storage to the central database on Nine. All files of this nature must be accessible at any time, day or*

night.

You must process each file as it comes into the waiting area. The security level is printed in the file. You must re-tag each one before a new encryption code is embedded. If you receive Level Six files by mistake, please redirect to booth sixteen immediately. Or you can create a blind copy of the information using one of the spare discs and deposit it into the vacuum tube on the wall.

You must never discuss the sensitive contents with a rank lower than yours. Please place your right thumb at the bottom of the screen before continuing.

Laura blinked back tears. 'What the hell...?' A separate message flashed up asking for confirmation before she could continue. She complied. The screen flipped over to a pooled list of waiting files.

The list looked remarkably similar to the same work she'd been doing on Level Four. She hadn't endured three years of hell to wind up in the same place as before. Not even the purple uniform and extra accolade could make up for this move.

Her lips trembled as she sucked in new air. Her anger that refused to settle... she buried it deep, deep down. Away from her long-term plans to transfer to Exilon 5.

Gilchrist had noticed her. She had to find some way to use that attention to her advantage.

Scooting the chair closer to the desk, Laura focused

on the monitor before her. Some files disappeared from view. Booth numbers flashed up beside random files, as they were processed: sixteen, nine, eighteen.

But despite her new confidence, she couldn't muster up enough interest to do a job the super computer could do better. *A lesson in character building.* That's what Chris had called their jobs.

Maybe she should just go back to Level Four. Tears stung the corners of her eyes. She couldn't. They had her locked in through contractual agreements. Through blurred vision, she opened the first file that hadn't already been claimed by another booth.

Another three years of doing this work? 'Give it a chance, Laura. You haven't even started and already you're quitting.' Her crazy moods said she wouldn't make it.

It was a memo from the World Government to Head of Operations, Suzanne Brett, about a staff member at the Centre. It read:

> *Dear Ms Brett,*
>
> *A member of your staff has leaked confidential information to a person or persons outside the Centre about the status of various bank accounts and their details, presumably to access the funds.*
>
> *This matter was brought to our attention by our insider, who had been offered the information in return for stolen goods. We will allow you to deal with this staff member.*

However, if storage-bound information is leaked again, we will take the appropriate measures.

Sincerely,
Tom Billings

Overseer for Security Matters
World Government

She noted the clearance level at the top of the document—Five—and closed the file. Then she tagged it and ran it through the re-encryption program placed as a shortcut on her monitor.

She picked another random document marked as confidential. It was another memo from the World Government to Suzanne Brett.

Dear Ms Brett,

We have reports that one of your workers may have accessed certain security areas within the Centre during the recent temporary power outage. The rooms were unsecured at the time and recorded nothing more than a bio signature to indicate someone had been there. Their identity is unknown.

Find the worker responsible and deliver them to us.

Sincerely,
Tom Billings

Overseer for Security Matters
World Government

It was marked with that day's date and had been sent within the last ten minutes. 'Don't piss off the World Government, got it.'

She tagged it as Level Five and ran it through the re-encryption file, same as the last one.

Only five minutes had passed and already Laura was getting antsy about her new role.

The ESC had trapped her. Worse, she'd allowed it to happen.

26

It had been a week since Jenny's meeting with Gilchrist's assistant, where he told her she was on review. Jenny had ignored Stuart's offer to get lunch after. Despite several calls from Stuart asking how the meeting went, and offering another apology about making her late, she still hadn't gotten back to him.

The latest report, delivered a few days, ago sat open on her DPad. It contained an official warning about her time delay last week and a new one, citing her lack of judgment to keep the autopilot on. She wore a new pattern in the carpet of her apartment, wondering if Gilchrist had added the extra warning.

But the addendum, 'Three strikes and you're out,' rattled her the most. She popped her thumb out of her mouth where she'd been chewing on it. Stopping the ESC from firing her seemed like an impossible task now. Jenny cost too much and someone higher up than Gilchrist wanted her to know it.

Her scheduled trip to Hartsfield-Jackson Atlanta went off without a hitch. She even arrived early with one minute to spare. The attendant didn't look happy about it

Genesis Code

as he recorded her latest cargo.

Jenny exited the hold and headed to the HJA's cafeteria. Her growling stomach flipped her thoughts over to food. She didn't like to eat much while flying, not when her stomach lurched after each flight. But she'd eaten little over the last twenty-four hours for another reason. Her nerves before this flight—and probably every one, going forward—were all over the place.

She arrived at one of HJA's four self-service canteens, nestled in the eastern part of the station. The long room with enough space for eight hundred seated workers was divided up into several rows of black tables and white chairs. Jenny grabbed a tray and joined the shortest queue for dozens of silver-and-black replication machines set along one wall.

Her order to the machine kept growing: beans on toast, with a side order of sausage, a chicken pot pie, two black coffees and three pieces of chocolate cake. She could eat twice that amount and it wouldn't matter; all replicator food was calorie controlled. Finding a quiet spot, she slumped into a seat. Her hectic flying schedule, plus her efforts to stay off Gilchrist's list, was killing her. Other pilots used Actigen to stay awake, but it made Jenny nauseous to take it.

She barely paused between bites, wolfing down just enough food to satiate her. She sipped on her coffee, hoping it would give her a boost of energy to finish her shift. One last run to Sydney then she could sleep. At least the journey from Sydney to Brisbane and her riverfront apartment would take only forty minutes by high-speed Maglev train. There, she would put her eight hours off to good use and banish all thoughts of warnings, strikes and infractions.

Stuart sauntered into the canteen and she felt last

week's irritation with him return, but with food in her stomach it didn't feel as venomous. The man with chestnut-brown hair, blue eyes, and a face no genetic manipulation clinic had touched, spotted her and made his way over. Jenny had no such reservations about using the Glamour package. It had turned back her looks by twenty years. Sometimes a girl needed a little help.

She and Stuart went way back to when they'd both worked as controllers in the docking station at Auckland, New Zealand. After a divorce and raising her only child, Jenny had enlisted at the Air and Space Control Academy to pursue her passion for flying. At fifty-five, she began her training as a pilot, after having completed just four years as a controller. Stuart had stayed put, eventually being offered the role of Operations Overseer in Auckland. He'd worked in HJA for nearly ten years now.

She glanced up as Stuart reached the table. 'I see you found me then.'

'Not hard in this place,' he said, holding up both thumbs where their chips—both identity and security—were located. 'Our very own tracking devices.' He sat down opposite her. 'What happened to you last week? I thought we were doing lunch?'

Jenny brushed her fingers across the nape of her neck. 'I didn't feel like chatting. I'm still pissed off with you, by the way. '

He raised a brow. 'I can't imagine why.' Several dishes of uneaten food separated them. Stuart eyed one plate with a piece of chocolate cake on it. 'How did the meeting go?'

'I've got two strikes.' She sighed and pinched her fingers together. 'I'm this close to getting another. One more and I'm out.'

'Another? What happened?'

'According to them, I made poor decisions during the flight.'

Stuart checked behind him. Jenny saw what he was looking for: a roving camera hovering over a group of trainees in one corner of the room. It turned around to look in their direction.

He turned back around and leaned forward. 'I saw some memos the other day. Apparently, Charles Deighton is looking closely at budgets and pilots of a certain age. I didn't think that included you.'

What she'd suspected.

She sipped on her coffee; the caffeine did little to improve her mood. 'I knew the risks when I reached Grade Four, but now it's like I have an actual target on my back. That no matter what I do, I can't change the outcome.'

'I'm sorry, Jen, I didn't know things were that bad.'

His apology soothed the rough edges of her mood.

The roving camera focused on the trainees again. Several bodies shifted nervously in their seats; others tried to act brazen, as if the camera's presence wasn't an issue.

'Why couldn't you have given me Maria?'

'I did. She was supervising Galen. Look, it wouldn't have mattered by the sounds of it. Deighton and Gilchrist are assholes and you don't need their drama. Why don't you go out on your own again? You still have that rust-bucket in storage, don't you?'

Yes, her old spacecraft. It had been too long since she'd done freelance piloting work—it was how she'd started in the industry after getting her pilot's licence. But giving up a steady monthly wage didn't appeal to her, not at her age.

'I don't know, Stuart. Seems like a lot of hassle.'

He grabbed her hands. 'If they're going to fire you anyway, then quit first. You deserve better.' He let go.

She did, but it wasn't easy to go it alone in an industry the World Government and Earth Security Centre dominated.

Jenny stabbed a piece of chocolate cake with her fork and shoved it into her mouth. It had the texture of sponge but tasted more like dirt sprinkled with cocoa powder. She'd tasted real chocolate cake once, in Cantaloupe restaurant. But the memory only made eating this replicated mess a lot harder. Places like Cantaloupe weren't for people like her, surviving on a pilot's income. Replicated food only reminded her of what she may never have again.

'I'm sorry, Jenny. I have an obligation to let my trainees loose. But I promise not to put him on your schedule again.'

'Thank you.'

He pushed one plate closer to her. 'Now, eat your food.' She moved the plate off to the side. 'Take a few days off, more than the eight-hour layovers they give you. Things might look brighter at the end of it.'

Jenny eyed him. 'Time off?'

'I'm just saying Deighton and Gilchrist don't give a shit about you. You need to think about what you want.'

Jenny agreed but she couldn't see a way out. If she survived this latest Deighton-driven cull, she had another twenty years to give to the job. The alternative to working was living off World Government replicator rations and living in a communal property she was sure she'd hate.

'I might as well hand in my resignation. Time off is not an option, I'm afraid.'

The camera turned around again, seeking them out.

Stuart glanced at it and switched subjects. 'How's your daughter?'

'Eleanor's doing well.' Jenny pushed her mug of

coffee away. Her appetite was gone. 'She's thinking of starting another course in college, decided to change career paths from law to politics. She can't sit still for five minutes, that one. So like her father. How about you? Any decent women made an honest man of you yet?'

'Never going to happen. I've had my fill of wives, ex-wives, the lot. I'm planning on living out the rest of my life alone.' Stuart remained stubbornly single after his last wife had almost bankrupted him. He'd been married three times before that and was still paying for his mistakes. At least he had no kids.

'When's your last shift?' asked Stuart.

She yawned. 'One last run to Sydney now followed by a layover for eight hours.'

Stuart shook his head. 'Wow, they really know how to look after their old-age employees.'

'Hey! Less of the old, please. Seventy-five is the new forty in this genetic age of ours.'

He pulled the plate with cake towards him. 'Bastards. They wouldn't recognise talent and experience if it bit them in the ass.'

They recognised it. They just didn't want to pay for it.

He raised an imaginary glass. 'Here's to you-know-who burning in hell.'

She grinned and clinked her mug against his fake glass. 'I'll drink to that.'

27

Working at the Earth Security Centre had earned Daphne Gilchrist the respect she'd craved all her life. But twenty years at the wheel of an organisation that was losing direction was taking its toll. She blamed Deighton and the board members for that. In her office, her male assistant sat across from her. She barely listened while Tim rattled off her schedule for the coming week. Meetings to discuss who should be fired were low-brow tasks for the ESC.

It didn't help that the transfer programme had stalled for now, thanks to the Indigenes. Deighton—meaning the board members—had been hunting for their location for the last two years. While everyone who mattered had known about their existence on Exilon 5, it had not stopped ambitious plans to transfer twenty billion people to the new planet.

Until recently.

She had sensed the change in direction, even though Deighton had only hinted at the existence of a new plan. Daphne was no idiot; she'd seen it coming. Deighton, an overachiever like her father, liked to play games. And now he was using her the same way she was using O'Halloran.

Genesis Code

Her ridiculous itinerary had pulled Daphne's focus away from other matters. Bill Taggart's files for one. Because of it, the O'Halloran girl had yet to receive any confidential material. It was clear the girl's interest in the new job had begun to wane. Now might be a good time to call her in and remind O'Halloran of her loyalties to the ESC.

Tim droned on. Daphne insisted on the weekly face-to-face meetings, but the micro managing of her organisation, to deflect any surprises from Deighton, was starting to tire her.

'Is that it?' she asked.

Tim, a weedy fellow with a nervous twitch, looked up from his DPad. 'What? Eh, yes.'

'Fine. Set up the reminders in my diary.'

She dismissed him with a wave.

Her assistant stood up. 'Of course.'

The young man fumbled with the door handle, drawing new irritation from her, before slipping out. Alone again, she dug deep for some of that interest she used to have. But instead, her weary focus blurred the lacquered table she stared at. A new call buzzed on her monitor, one that bolted her upright in her chair.

She recognised the tone.

Pulling in new air to settle her nerves, Daphne smiled and answered the call.

'Charles!'

The CEO for the World Government came into view.

'Daphne,' he crooned, his voice crackling with age.

Cracks in Deighton's genetically treated one-hundred and nineteen-year-old face were starting to show: his skin was sagging south. His hair was full, but losing thickness. A degenerating larynx gave the raspy sound to his speech. Although he'd been scheduled to have his larynx replaced, Deighton said the sound gave him a mysterious edge. Every time he spoke, Daphne fought the urge to clear her own throat.

'To what do I owe the pleasure?'

Deighton rattled with laughter. 'Do I need a reason to chat, my dear?'

She matched his fake smile. 'Of course not. I don't normally hear from you, that's all.'

She waited for him to speak; whatever his reason would be revealed soon enough. 'Daphne, my dear, how soon before Mr Taggart reaches our shores?'

'A week, Charles. He will be coming in here for a debrief.'

'Yes, yes.' The centenarian waved his hand in the air. 'Make sure to temper his interest in the Indigenes, will you? He's been useful in dragging those degenerates out of hiding, but he's still far too emotional about his wife.'

'Of course.'

She and Deighton had already discussed Taggart's fate a week ago, on the same day he'd boarded the passenger ship. But she didn't remind him of that.

'Oh, and another thing,' he added. Daphne widened her smile; she hated Deighton's addendums. 'Laura O'Halloran.'

Somehow she managed to keep the smile in place. 'What about her?'

He clasped his hands together and leaned forward in his usual, condescending way.

'I just heard from one of the ITF reps that you promoted her to Level Five. What were you thinking, Daphne?'

That she was CEO of the ESC and it was her business who she promoted.

She shook her head softly. 'Nothing to worry about, Charles. The girl is a hard worker and we were short handed, what with the investigation wrapping up.'

Deighton stared at her; his watery blue gaze showed no emotion. 'I'm surprised, that's all. You usually run these decisions by me.'

No she didn't.

'I don't understand, Charles. The ESC has always been under my control.'

'Of course, under normal circumstances, but we are under a new threat.'

'From whom?'

He laughed and leaned back. 'The population for one. The workers, when they realise most of them won't be transferring to Exilon 5. The Indigenes. Take your pick.' He leaned in again. 'I don't want any changes right now. Status quo.'

Daphne kept her tone light. 'Of course, Charles. But I must insist she stay.'

'For what reason?'

She needed her. Laura would be her insurance policy if things turned bad.

'Well, to undo the confidentiality agreement now would be a headache.'

Deighton leaned back, resting a finger on his lips. He liked to play. Too much.

Keeping up appearances for him exhausted her.

With a clap of his hands, he said, 'What's done is done. You can keep her. But no more promotions.'

She shook her head. 'Last one, I promise.'

He clicked off suddenly. Daphne slumped back in her chair with a sigh. She knew how to keep Deighton happy, but for how much longer?

Time to bring in her insurance policy.

She called her assistant. 'Yes Ms Gilchrist?'

'Send Laura O'Halloran to the boardroom on Level Five, immediately.'

28

'Shit.'

Laura stood outside the door of a room she'd never been inside. Gilchrist's assistant had fetched her moments ago. He led her across the Level Five foyer and down a corridor that was only accessible with the right bioscan.

'Don't worry, her bark is worse than her bite,' he said with a grim smile.

Funny, his jittery disposition told her otherwise.

Laura gave him a tight nod and knocked on the door of the glass-walled room with no view inside.

'Enter!' A commanding voice boomed through the wood. She pushed the handle down and poked her head in.

'You wanted to see me?' Her voice came out as a squeak.

Gilchrist was sitting at a boardroom table. Her chair was turned away from her. All she saw was the back of her head.

As if in slow motion, the CEO swivelled round to face her. She was tapping one finger on her lip.

She gestured to the seat opposite her. 'Yes, please sit.'

Laura perched more than sat. 'Am I in trouble?'

Gilchrist stared at her for a moment; her gaze was so intense that Laura struggled to maintain eye contact. But Gilchrist wasn't looking at her. She was looking past her.

With a cough from Laura, Gilchrist snapped out of it. Her gaze remained chilly but her mouth turned up into what could be a smile. Laura had only spoken to this woman once so she had no reference point.

Gilchrist made a bridge with her hands. 'Laura O'Halloran. How are you enjoying your promotion? It's been about a week now. Are you settling in?'

A creepy man occupied booth ten. The other workers ignored her. 'Fine.'

Gilchrist crossed her legs and brought her hands down to rest on one knee. 'Ms Brett says that you're not getting through the work as fast as the others.'

Laura shifted in her chair. 'Uh, I was expecting an induction, to be honest.'

'An induction?' Gilchrist laughed lightly. 'I'm afraid we don't do those on Level Five. You've been here how long?'

'Three years.'

'Consider that your induction, Ms O'Halloran.' She uncrossed her legs. 'We're not in the habit of training up our best personnel. I chose you personally to work on Level Five because I saw potential in you.'

Laura froze. Potential?

Gilchrist smirked. 'Does that surprise you?'

'Well, yes. I didn't think anyone noticed me here.'

'I notice everyone, Ms O'Halloran, especially those who work more hours than they roster for. You love your job, and your dedication shows.'

She wouldn't say that exactly. 'I believe in the work we do at the Earth Security Centre.'

Gilchrist's lips drew thin and white. 'Yes, well I'm glad you have a good impression.'

Laura had to ask. When would she be alone with Gilchrist again?

'I was... wondering about the transfer programme to Exilon 5.'

'What about it?'

'I heard the workers on Level Five have a better chance of making the transfer list.'

Gilchrist raised a brow. 'Is that what you want?'

'Yes... Well, eventually. '

Gilchrist leaned forward. 'We are not there, Ms O'Halloran. There are more important matters we must focus on first.'

'Of course, I'm sorry. I didn't mean to imply—'

'I brought you in here because we are in the middle of an investigation. Many files from that investigation must be processed. I need you to give a hundred percent. Can you do that?'

Laura twisted her hands together on her lap. 'Of course.'

Gilchrist leaned back, her eyes narrowed. 'What matters to you most Ms O'Halloran?'

'What? Um, doing a good job for you, Ms Gilchrist.'

'But not to transfer to Exilon 5 with your mother?'

Laura widened her eyes. 'Well, yes, but you said it wasn't important right now—'

'Make no trouble and I'll make sure you're on the list for Exilon 5.'

'Really? That would be great. I won't let you down.'

Gilchrist held up her hand. 'See that you don't. There are important files on their way to Level Five. I want you to keep what you read to yourself. Do you understand?'

Laura nodded, not caring what she promised. Her dream to transfer to Exilon 5 was still alive.

'You can count on me.'

29

Bill wandered the passenger ship's empty corridor, calling out. An eerie silence filled the ship. The hairs on his arm stood to attention. He forced one foot in front of the other, moving silently along the dark, tube-shaped passageway. Where the hell was everyone?

The ship's overhead lights illuminated each step. Was he the only one on-board? His trust issues kept him hidden from others, but in that moment he needed to know he wasn't alone.

He moved his tightly coiled body forward; every new step plunged his last one into darkness.

The ship felt unfamiliar, even though it had become his second home for the last week. He'd memorised every inch of it so he could stay off the radar.

But his skin tingled with worry.

The air turned thicker, tightening his chest and making it hard to breathe. He clawed at his throat, trying to push new air into his lungs. Bill dropped to his knees, weak.

A male figure stood in the corridor before him, weak light illuminating his tall shape. 'Let me help you.'

The tension in Bill's body melted away. The tightness lifted from his throat. But his heart slammed against his ribcage when the dark shape glided towards him.

Bill scrambled back. 'Who are you?'

The figure, dressed in a long trench coat and fedora hat, stopped a foot away. He recognised him as the alien he'd been tracking.

'What are you?' He got to his feet.

The male didn't reply. Instead, he removed his hat to reveal a face void of features and expression.

Bill reached out and touched the shape in front of him. His hand sliced through the wispy cloud that instantly reformed into a solid mass. Fascinated, he let go of his inhibitions. Was this real or a dream? It felt real enough.

That's when the alien stepped closer. Bill caught sight of a shiny object in his hand. He tensed up a second too late as the knife sliced across his throat.

☼

Bill woke with a start and drenched in sweat. His throat tightened, like someone had a hand around it.

The lack of air pinched at his lungs. Resistance on his arms and legs shocked him into action. Remembering where he was, he stopped struggling.

Bill groped in the dark for the lock on the sleeping pod. His mouth searched for new air. He found the lock and smashed it with his fist, but it wouldn't release. His efforts sapped what little strength he had. Light-headedness made his head swim.

'What the fu—'

His eyes squeezed shut when new pain bloomed in

his lungs. He felt for the lock a second time, using his elbow next to try to open it.

A pain blazed through his bone when it connected with the hard surface. 'Christ—'

He continued to pound on the lock, softer now.

'Please open...' Panic gripped him first, followed by a strange calm. This was the end.

He turned on his side and closed his eyes, resigning to his fate.

Isla shouted at him to 'Get up!'

Bill tried, even though he had no strength left. Nothing but a feeling that his lungs might implode any second. A tear landed on his hot cheek. He left it there.

A blast of cool air revived him. He sucked in a new breath, like he was reclaiming his soul.

Somebody pulled him free from his unit.

His head hit the floor with a thud. He barely felt the sting as he swallowed another lungful of sweet, oxygen-rich air. In the dark of the sleeping quarters, a figure stood over him. Cool fingers rested on his neck. The man spoke low to another in the room.

'His pulse is strong. They all seem fine now.'

Bill blinked to focus better on the men's faces. But when he opened his eyes again, in that short moment, they were gone.

He sat up slowly, fighting against the new throb in his head. That's when he saw the others—nine, he counted —lying on the floor.

The wall propped him up. He looked around the room trying to make sense of what had just happened. Bill crawled forward and checked each body for a pulse. They were all alive.

One man was staring up at the ceiling.

'What happened?' Bill asked him.

'I couldn't breathe. The lock was stuck. If it hadn't been for those two men—' He closed his eyes and breathed out slowly.

When enough dizziness subsided, Bill walked the halls in search of someone in charge. He found a senior officer and flashed his World Government credentials. The officer rushed to explain the situation, with obvious embarrassment.

'I'm sorry, sir. There was a power failure in Section Seven, where your unit and fifty others are located. The situation is now under control.'

'How the hell does a ship this size get power failures?' Bill winced when he touched the golf ball-sized lump on his head.

'Normally the back-up power supply takes over, sir, but because it didn't engage immediately, the computer shut off the oxygen levels to that area.'

'Surely the computer detects when someone is occupying the sleeping quarters.'

The officer's face reddened. 'Normally, sir, but the computers on board this ship are designed to save power, not to detect life on-board.'

'So, when the computer knocked out the oxygen to that section, the sensors locked the units so we couldn't escape?'

'Not quite, sir. The sensors assumed they were unoccupied and initiated lockdown to prevent tampering with unused units, sir.'

Bill shook his head. 'Well, if it wasn't for your officers, we would have all suffocated in there. Please thank them for me. I didn't get a good look at their faces.'

'Sir?'

'Your officers,' said Bill.

The man stared at him. Then he answered in his best

military tone. 'Of course, sir. Immediately.'

A stab of pain shot through his tenderised elbow and he winced.

'Do you need medical help, sir?'

Bill began the walk back to his sleeping quarters. 'No, I'll be fine.' He trusted doctors as much as he trusted Charles Deighton.

He returned to his room to see the floor was clear and his sleeping pod was still open. He shuddered at the sight of it.

His weird dream moments before he woke came back to him. Something about it and his near-death experience made him want to review the last video he'd watched. After snatching up his DPad and kicking the door closed, he sat on the floor with his back against the wall.

Bill started with the video he'd begun watching a week ago, but had lost interest in. It was the one of the officer being interviewed about an animal disturbance near New London's border. He hit play, skipping over the parts that were still fresh.

'Eyes fixed on me before looking away.' The officer stared at the wall behind the interviewer. 'I heard the animal. It sounded like it was injured. But when I got closer, I couldn't believe what I saw.'

The interviewer asked, 'What was it?'

'Two boys, crouching over what I think was a wolf. The smell of blood turned my stomach. There was so much of it.'

'So you're saying they killed the animal. You were right to report this illegality. The biodome animals are protected.'

The officer shook his head and whispered. 'No, you've got it all wrong. They didn't just kill it, they were eating it.' He drank from a cup of water in front of him. 'I thought the attacker might have been another animal because of its body contortion, its reflective eyes, and its interest in the wolf. I couldn't retrieve my Buzz Gun without attracting attention to myself. While I waited for back-up to arrive, I moved in closer to try to corner it and make the catch a little easier? But that's when I saw something that chilled me.' He swallowed hard.

'Saw what, exactly?'

'It looked at me and smiled. *Smiled*, for God's sake! I mean what kind of animal was it? What creature of God's making looks and acts like a wild animal, then takes time out of its killing spree to flash its pearly whites at me?'

The interviewer sat back in his chair.

The officer continued. 'I felt a rush of cool air pass right by my face. We caught one bastard but the second one escaped.'

'They caught one of them. That's good.'

But the officer was shaking his head. 'There's nothing good about this. Have you even seen what these vile creatures can do?' He closed his eyes. 'I never want to find out.'

The video stopped. Bill stared at the floor.

Why had he overlooked this crucial piece of information? The government had caught one of the Indigenes before. He checked the time stamp. The interview was a year old.

Why? Because his obsession with finding Isla had blinkered him. All Bill had cared about was finding her. Tracking the Indigene, confronting him, learning of her location.

He'd done all that and he was no closer to the truth.

Bill should have been looking for clues to the aliens' behaviours and mannerisms. His job was to profile criminals—learn their habits so he could trap them. Well here was the information, right under his nose. He searched for another file he'd skimmed over. It was one that followed soon after the creature had been captured. A video called *Initial Examination of Species 31*.

Dr Frank Jameson, a physician working for Bio Technologies according to the accompanying notes, took the lead in the video. Bio Tech was listed as a World Government subsidiary on Earth specialising in genetic manipulation therapy and disease control.

The doctor was using a roving camera to record events through subject motion-tracking. While the laboratory's interior appeared sparse, a file note said the New London-based laboratory had been kitted out with high-end equipment just before the examination. The request had been approved by Charles Deighton.

Dr Jameson looked into the camera as two colleagues entered the room. All three wore white boiler-suits. He flipped up the hood and pulled the drawstrings closed until it puckered around his face.

Bill felt the palpable excitement on video as Dr Jameson introduced Doctors White and Henshall. To the left was a small workstation where one of two assistants sat at a research monitor. A stainless-steel shelf ran almost the full length of the back wall. A large sink took up almost a quarter of its length. To the right was a tray with various cutting tools, including a laser scalpel. Off to one side, Bill saw what looked to be a flexible membrane containment unit, with an examination table inside.

Dr Jameson gestured at the unit. 'We are able to control the containment unit's gaseous composition through our workstations. For the purpose of explanation, we can pass through safely without breaking the seal or compromising the atmospheric configuration inside. The membrane has tiny memory particles scan our security chips to allow entry and exit from the unit. Mostly used for infection cases and detainees, today we will use the containment unit for both.'

Moments later, one assistant wheeled in a young male Indigene inside the containment unit. Dr Jameson entered first followed by the two doctors. The roving camera hovered above the examination table. Bill zoomed in for a closer look.

Dr Jameson spoke. 'Species 31 will remain sedated until we are ready to wake it. We haven't altered the gaseous composition inside the membrane, as it seems the alien can breathe our air. We will wake the alien soon, but we don't know if it can understand us, or whether it speaks any language. How useful the information will be from Species 31 is anyone's guess.'

Bill studied the separate 3D body scan of the Indigene, which compared physically to that of a twelve-year-old boy.

When the roving camera focused on the young Indigene, a flicker of movement caught Bill's eye. It wasn't until the Indigene's breathing pattern changed—from long even breaths to short sporadic bursts—that the doctors also noticed.

Jameson turned to Dr White; the camera mirrored his movement. 'How much sedative did you give him?' White threw out some numbers, to which Jameson nodded. He spoke into the camera, but his eyes were on the alien. 'We have given Species 31 a dose designed for a human, but we can't tell if it's too much or too little.' Jameson turned to Henshall. 'I think we should wake it.'

The female doctor prepared a syringe filled with liquid. The roving camera focused in on her nervous face. She explained, 'This solution will counteract the administered sedative.'

White monitored the young Indigene's heartbeat, which registered at thirty five beats per minute, according to him. It continued to breathe in uneven, short breaths.

Dr Henshall tied a piece of rubber around the upper part of the Indigene's arm and pulled it tight. She slapped the arm in several places.

Her wide eyes found Jameson. 'I can't find a vein.'

'Just use the same one as before,' he said.

She examined the arm and pulled in an extra source of light to help. 'There's no evidence of the original entry point.'

'Then just guess.' Jameson tapped his finger in the crease of his elbow. 'Insert it here.'

Bill zoomed out just as Henshall made her attempt. The titanium needle broke twice. On the third attempt, she pierced the skin. It took less than a minute for the young Indigene to stir from its drug-induced sleep. He blinked its eyes open, but squeezed them shut just as fast, straining against the harsh lights.

'Dim the lights by two-thirds. Now!' Jameson was breathing hard. That made Bill nervous.

The laboratory plunged into near-darkness and took on a more sinister look. Bill zoomed in on the young Indigene. He opened his eyes again, this time appearing more comfortable with the lower level of light. He looked around in confusion.

'The alien's eyes seem to be photosensitive. See the lack of pigment here?' The roving camera nose-dived for a better look.

The Indigene, trapped beneath multiple restraints, panicked and twisted until one arm broke free from its wrist clamp. White, Jameson and the assistant rushed to restrain the alien while Henshall struggled to strap down the rogue arm.

Jameson yanked the hood off his head. A breath rushed out of him as he pushed hair out of his eyes. 'We are attempting to place further restraints on Species 31. It seems to have broken... Shit, this thing is strong... I need help over here.' He trailed off and protected his face as the young Indigene's free arm smacked him.

A low guttural snarl escaped from the alien. The twisting and thrashing gave way to violent convulsions directly beneath the doctors' grip. They let go and backed away from the table. Jameson shot a look at Henshall.

She shook her head and stared down at the Indigene. 'That wasn't me.'

Jameson attempted to restrain it once more. 'White, help me hold it down. Give it the anti-convulsion drug, quickly.'

Henshall picked up another liquid-filled syringe and quickly pushed it into the alien's arm. The needle bent again, but the skin yielded to her urgency.

When the convulsions stopped, all four stood back from the table.

Jameson was silent. His mouth opened but he didn't explain what had just happened.

Bill turned off the video and released a long breath. Had Isla disturbed one of these Indigene feeding frenzies? Had they attacked her because of it?

He swallowed hard and opened a new recording. The same three doctors came into view, more composed than before.

The young Indigene lay motionless on the table. Bed sheets and bandages littered the floor; cutting instruments previously placed neatly on the tray were now tossed around.

Jameson clicked his fingers at the assistants when he

noticed the camera was still recording. They cleared the debris out of shot.

The lack of blood and incisions on the Indigene surprised Bill.

Jameson cleared his throat and pushed his hair back. 'At first we thought the epidermis was translucent in colour, but on closer inspection it was actually opaque and not as delicate as we first expected. It's several times more durable than human skin. The laser scalpel had trouble penetrating the outer layer. Skin pigmentation is not visible. I'm not even sure there are melanocytes present in the toughened layer. Species 31 is capable of regeneration. We cut the male several times but he healed in less than a minute, even in posthumous conditions.' He touched the Indigene's face. 'The eyes lack pigmentation, which probably explains the photosensitivity. This species can see better in the dark than we can.'

Bill had read about a case in the early twenty-first century: children in East Asia and South America were recorded as being able to see in the dark. Doctors had attributed the mystery to leukoderma, a rare condition which strips pigmentation or melanin production in random areas of the skin, leaving white patches. But where it affected the eyes it would cause blindness, not improve vision. The medical world turned its attention towards hemeralopia—or the inability to see in bright light—to explain the increase of these nocturnal-children cases. The story lost momentum when nothing beyond hemeralopia could explain the condition.

Bill tuned in again to Dr Jameson.

'There is no visible hair on Species 31's body. We also found low levels of red blood cells in its body, other than trace remnants in the digestive system.' He sighed. 'Human blood accounts for seven per cent of bodily fluids.

In Species 31, it accounts for less than one per cent. When we sliced the skin open, a clear fluid secreted out. It's what gives the alien an almost-translucent appearance.'

Dr White picked up three items and showed them to the camera. 'We discovered these, in the alien's nasal cavities and in the back of its throat. We think it's an air filtration device. It would explain the scarring we found on the male's lungs. Species 31 didn't die because of anything we did. He died because of too much oxygen to the brain.'

Bill turned off the video and stared at the ceiling. He tried to erase the disturbing image of the panicky young Indigene from his mind. That's all it had been; panic. Not aggression. A young Indigene had been separated from his friend and the government had experimented on him.

Bill thought of Stephen and his targeting of Ben Watson. Hunting was instinctual for these creatures. The interview with the officer had said as much. But animals appeared to be their preferred diet. Not humans. That made the alien less of a threat than Gilchrist had implied.

If the Indigenes were more passive than the reports suggested, what the hell had happened to Isla?

30

Tucked into a darkened doorway, Stephen and Anton watched the exchange unfold between the official and Bill Taggart.

A week of life on board an oxygen-rich ship had given Stephen a headache.

Why do you hate the humans? asked Anton.

Stephen stared after the investigator as he walked away. He switched to his voice; his head hurt less when he talked out loud. 'Because they are killers.'

'I'm glad you decided to help those people in the end.'

'I came close to ignoring their screams.'

'I don't believe you would have let them die. You're nothing like the vigilantes trying to make trouble for the elders.'

The vigilantes blamed the humans for everything.

'Maybe they have a point.' But he was tired of despising a race that had killed his parents and almost wiped the Indigenes from existence.

Yet, that hate had become a part of him.

Anton's brow creased. 'Pierre's opinion of the

humans seems to differ.'

'Pierre is practical. He prefers the option with the least carnage.'

'Maybe we should make our own mind up about them.'

Stephen smirked. 'You sound like Pierre.'

'He's not an elder for nothing.'

'The fact that they are also called "human" bothers me.'

'No matter what they claim to be, we can't immediately assume they're enemies. A sentence without trial would make us just like them.'

'But we *are* like them. That's the problem.' Stephen sighed. 'Maybe not physically, but in other ways.'

Anton gestured after the investigator. 'He's alone. Why don't we just approach him? Demand answers about why they're investigating us? Why he followed you into the tunnel?'

'I'm not ready for that yet.' The thought of getting close to any human terrified him. 'Besides, this Gilchrist and Deighton character appear to run things on Earth. I don't want to tip them off about our arrival. We should wait until we get to Earth before we strike.'

His answer didn't appear to satisfy Anton. 'But what if we lose him after we disembark? We don't know where he's headed.'

'It will be fine. When we reach their planet we can turn the tables and track him.'

Stephen remembered back to the event a year ago that had claimed the life of one of their Evolvers. The pair had been hunting away from the main party. It had been on that same night the humans had discovered the existence of the Indigenes.

Stephen had been out that night too, in a hunting

party of six. The cries of the trapped wolf had alerted them to the danger, but the activity had also attracted the attention of the military patrolling the borders of their cities. Seeing the young pair trapped that night, Stephen had tried to help them. But a new source of light had frozen him to the spot.

The wolf put up a good fight. The young pair teased the wolf. One danced as a distraction, while the other fixed his eyes on the prey. But closing in fast on their location was a military human who stopped as soon as his light exposed the truth. When he surrounded the first Evolver, Stephen grabbed the second one and ran.

His ragged breathing broke him out of the memory. Stephen tilted his head back and pulled out the three sections of the filtration device, wiped them down and placed each in the recharger unit that hung from his belt. He grabbed a spare set and adjusted the larger part at the back of his throat with his finger.

He would not allow the humans to gain the upper hand this time. He and Anton would be one step ahead.

When the air filtration unit felt comfortable, Stephen asked, 'Will the chips work at the exit point?'

'In theory. Disembarkation should be straight forward enough,' said Anton. 'As for getting around the planet, I haven't figured out that part yet.'

31

A seemingly endless list of documents appeared on Laura's monitor, including various memos sent between the World Government and its subsidiaries about security matters. While some issues were minor enough, others looked more serious. Gilchrist's warning to not make trouble stuck with her. That meant forgetting about the crappy work and working hard.

She could do that.

A blinking folder appeared on her monitor. She ignored it and concentrated on clearing the backlog from the main list that was growing by the second. Booth numbers and names flashed up beside files and disappeared: booth one, her frenemy in booth ten, booth sixteen. Nobody claimed the blinking folder sitting separately to the main list. Laura grabbed her next file from the shared pool that she'd been told to work from.

Twenty minutes of reading through complaints about tax evasion and snippy memos between the World Government and the ESC left her with a headache. She massaged her temples to ease the pressure. Something on screen winked at her. It was that damn folder icon again.

Genesis Code

Gilchrist had promised to get her on the transfer list, but only if she played by the rules. Was the new folder a test, to see if Laura could toe the line? Of course she could. She'd been doing just that for the last three years.

She tried to ignore the folder, but it called to her to open it. Laura raised her head and looked around the office. Dozens of heads, low and impassive, continued to work. She listened to the sounds of fingers gliding over touch-activated monitors. Asking about the folder would go against the rule of not speaking to others. But what if she was supposed to open it?

She stood, tugging at the suddenly tight neckline of her uniform. The man from booth ten flicked his eyes to her as she logged a bathroom break through her monitor. A clock flashed up on screen and a two-minute countdown commenced.

In the bathroom down the hall, she splashed cold water on her face, allowing it to drip down her neck where it soaked into her collar. The steel-top counter chilled her hands. She stared at the stranger in the mirror. Her green eyes were missing their usual sparkle. Her pale skin looked even more so under the harsh lights. Laura took down her messy blonde ponytail and redid it. Her loose and baggy uniform couldn't hide the weight she'd lost recently.

Laura leaned in closer, searching for the girl she used to be, for the one who'd wanted to work at the ESC. But all she found was a woman with a set of dreams hinging on how compliant she could be. She dragged her weary thoughts from work to the transfer to Exilon 5. She needed it, more than she had admitted to Gilchrist. The longer she stayed on Earth the more she risked losing herself. Usually a vitamin D shot pulled her out of her funk, but these days it barely glossed over the edges of her pain.

After patting her face dry with her sleeve, she returned to her workstation to find the folder was still there, unclaimed. Laura chose files from the common list that populated faster than the team could claim them.

But the ominous folder continued to flash.

Ah, what the hell. She was stuck here, no matter what she did.

Her finger grazed the folder icon; her thrumming heart set her nerves on a new edge. A new screen showed a second folder labelled 'Private'. It opened to reveal nine documents, all with the security tag 732-554-ITF-TGT. Several had the prefix "to be re-filed" attached.

A breath rushed out of her. It was just another set of files waiting to be processed. Odd that it had been kept separate from the main pool. Why hadn't anyone else opened the folder?

Maybe it had only been sent to her monitor. The thought pushed her on.

She opened the first document and scanned the contents; the name Bill Taggart repeated throughout. She guessed the TGT on the security tag stood for his name. ITF, it explained in the document, stood for International Task Force. She read on. Words like "Exilon 5", "investigation" and "meeting" caught her attention as she scoured the document for the clearance level. The document appeared to be a preliminary report sent a week ago. About two-thirds in, she found the hidden clearance level. She closed the file, tagged it and ran it through re-encryption.

Laura opened the files sequentially. The documents labelled "for re-filing" contained both video recordings and notes. Unsure of how to file a document with more than one element, she broke the cardinal rule.

'Video and text together in the same file,' she said to nobody in particular. 'Do I tag together or separately?' Her pulse raced at her deliberate infraction.

The room fell silent. She pushed up from the desk and looked around her. The woman from booth sixteen who handled Level Six information stared at her.

'Together,' she said.

'Thanks.' Laura dropped into her seat. She found the clearance attached to the video file, simply titled "Examination", and tagged the two files without bothering to read the text.

It wasn't until she had opened the sixth document in the list of nine—labelled "to be re-filed – 732-554-ITF-TGT"—that she paid closer attention. Inside, the file had a different name: "Autopsy of Species 31".

Her breath caught in her throat as she read on. The words "Exilon 5", "investigator" and "meeting" developed context, but she was unsure of how "meeting" connected with anything. A meeting with whom? Species 31, perhaps? Did the alien autopsy pre-empt a meeting? What if the meeting hadn't gone according to plan?

She speed-read the document, tempted to labour over its contents, but she didn't want to attract Brett's attention, or Gilchrist's if she was watching. Key phrases caught her eye: "translucent skin", "photosensitive eyes", "discovery of object lodged in back of throat and nasal cavity".

What the hell is this?

She straightened up in her chair and looked over the top of her booth. The woman from booth sixteen was watching her. Laura's skin flushed and she quickly concentrated on her monitor.

Another species living on Exilon 5? This information couldn't be public—Janine would have told her about it. Maybe this had to do with the investigation Gilchrist had told her about. Her chest tightened as Gilchrist's warning not to make trouble made her skin itch.

Had the CEO meant her to see these files?

Relax, Laura. She gave you the Taggart files to process. You're supposed to see them.

Still, her inner voice warned her to be careful. She ignored it and opened the remaining files.

32

Daphne Gilchrist sat in her office on Level Seven. She had her back to the glass wall with the privacy settings set to view out only. The face of a female doctor stationed on Exilon 5 filled her screen. Daphne leaned forward in her leather chair and examined the close-ups of a replicated identity chip, small enough to fit under the skin of one's thumb. Stellar wave technology facilitated a clear line between Earth and Exilon 5, making it feel as though the doctor were in the next room.

'As you can see, Daphne, it is a highly advanced design.'

She balked at the doctor's use of her first name. Only Deighton addressed her in that way, and that was because she was too scared to correct him.

'That's Ms Gilchrist, doctor.'

The doctor looked amused.

Daphne seethed at the lack of respect being shown to her. It wasn't that she despised women, but women knew how to be manipulative. And Daphne didn't trust people she couldn't control. Her strict, and sometimes violent, home life had made her fear the unknown. She liked knowing what was coming.

The doctor continued. 'If you examined an original chip and a security chip side by side, you would see they both have an inbuilt communication thread, allowing them to talk to each other.' She tapped the active thread on the replica chip with a minuscule pointer. The thread squirmed in the enlarged image as if alive. 'This replica is mirrored after an identity chip. The thread here is composed of nerve receptor molecules, which normally receive signals from a cell. The security chip's thread has the same molecular structure, except it has extra molecules called ligands that act as agonists. The agonists stimulate the receptor to send signal information, using the cells as a go-between.'

Daphne combed her fingers through her hair, mostly to settle her irritation. It wasn't the doctor's fault that she was in a bad mood. Deighton had called her again last night to remind her of Taggart's arrival, as though she were incapable of remembering on her own. But this new problem on the screen needed her immediate attention.

The doctor's soft tone irritated her. Her dark hair was tied into a loose bun. Blue eyes that placed her high up the genetic transfer list complemented her oval face. The doctor reminded Daphne of Isla Taggart, before she'd cut her hair.

The doctor waited. 'Shall I continue, Ms Gilchrist?'

Daphne waved her hand to proceed.

'The original and security chips can also work independently of each other. The identity chip is implanted at birth, but the communication thread remains dormant until the recipient receives a security chip. Once that happens their connection is live. Equally, if you remove one, they both revert to their original state and can work as single units. But without two original chips present, they can't be activated together, as the unique connection no longer exists. Unfortunately, you need to activate a pair simultaneously to see if the connection has been severed.'

'Did the host try to leave the planet? Is that how the replicated chip was discovered?'

'No. Bob Harris presented with an infection yesterday.'

Naming her patient made the doctor too emotional. Caring about the Indigenes' plight was why Isla Taggart had failed in Deighton's eyes. If only she'd left well enough alone.

She shook away her thoughts and refocused on the doctor. 'Did he try to remove it?'

'He swears he didn't. The chip is developed out of his DNA and becomes part of his body, compatible in every way. Mostly, it remains inert. He said he hadn't tried tampering with it, either. Apart from updates to record changes in his work status and living arrangements, he'd forgotten he even had it, until a month ago.' The doctor paused before continuing. 'He was in a lot of discomfort, poor guy. Didn't see it coming.'

There it was again: the emotional response that made people weak and controllable.

Daphne rolled her hand. 'And?' She had something important to do after.

'Well, the microchip is an integrated circuit device encased in a polymer compound. The compound is created by taking a DNA sample from a baby, then mixing it with the liquid solution. The identity chip is then inserted under the skin of the left thumb. As the human body grows, the chip adapts to the host. The silicone breaks down over time, releasing a compound that partially solidifies the saline, holding the chip in place. Over time, the DNA polymer and saline fuse, providing the final housing over the circuitry. It's entirely natural and identity chips never need replacing, just updating, which can be done with a simple tweak.'

Daphne sat back and released a discreet sigh. Someone else was listening in on the call. She had to sound interested. 'And?'

'The security chip is developed from a section of the identity chip. You see, it's the DNA marker that makes them unique. If one or both chips were ever removed from a host, they wouldn't work in another human. They're worthless on the black market, but the public's lack of knowledge keeps the market lucrative and their sale active.'

'So, it was stolen?'

'Yes, but it doesn't make sense to replace it with something else. The chip is tamper-proof and will eventually destroy itself if physically removed. In theory, replacements shouldn't work. That's why this replication model is so amazing.' The doctor produced side-by-side images of an original and replicated chip. Daphne saw no difference.

'It even has a similar thread like the original one,' said the doctor. 'And it works. Can you believe it? Whoever designed this knows a lot about genetronics.'

'What about the replicated chip? How was it discovered?'

'The replication is superb,' said the doctor, her eyes widening slightly. 'Aside from being able to attach itself to the host's DNA, it works as if it's the real chip. As I've already explained, the originals must be activated simultaneously to see the problem. Fortunately for us, Bob Harris has a rare condition.'

'How is that fortunate?'

'Bob has a super-charged immune system that

rejects the presence of foreign matter. He will never get sick. Only a handful of humans have this affliction.'

'Knowing your area of expertise, Doctor, I assume you cannot brief me on genetic anomalies?'

'Actually, I studied anatomy extensively before turning my attention purely to the sciences.'

Daphne waved her hand for the doctor to continue.

'His unique immune system means he's protected from the most aggressive medical conditions that still exist, rare as they are. The original chip bonded to his internal network because there was DNA present in the chip. When his DNA is removed from the equation, his system will recognise the object as foreign. That's what happened here. His body fought the invasion and turned it into an infectious mass because the chip had nowhere to go.'

'Is that how you found it?'

'His thumb had blown up to twice its normal size. I didn't notice the incision until I examined the area more closely.'

Daphne had heard enough. 'Your analogy has been helpful, Doctor. I'll be sure to pass on details of your cooperation to your superior.' She allowed the lie to surface. If anything, a damning report would follow. It was nothing personal, but the doctor needed a reminder of her place in life. 'Out.'

With a flick of her index finger, the screen changed and a new face appeared.

She forced a smile. 'Did you hear everything, Charles?'

The man controlling her future smiled back; his watery-blue gaze lacked empathy.

'Well, this is a turn up for the books,' he said. 'One of the buggers managed to fool us. I wonder how long they've known how to replicate the chips? Did Taggart know they could do this?'

One of the Indigenes was on the passenger ship, travelling under the alias: Bob Harris. Daphne was more worried about Earth's protection from this threat than how he'd managed to do it.

'What should we do?'

As though Deighton hadn't heard her, he said, 'Do you think we accelerated their cognitive function with the early testing?'

'Charles,' Daphne said softly, 'how would you like us to handle it? I can send word to the passenger ship to take the individual into custody.'

Deighton's eyes snapped up. 'Nobody is to interfere!'

She recoiled from the screen. 'Of course, Charles. I hadn't intended on sending out an order without clearing it with you first.'

Deighton regained composure. His stare unsettled her. 'The ship won't be here for another five days. We'll send a special team to meet and greet our new friend upon arrival. Don't you worry, he won't get far.'

That wasn't what worried her. It was Deighton's new obsession with the Indigenes and Taggart. A new plan appeared to be shaping in the CEO's mind. She just wished she knew what it was.

33

A few days had passed since Laura's chat with Gilchrist. She'd done everything the CEO had asked.

But now? Screw the rules.

Her new colleagues refusing to speak to her had gotten on her last nerve. She missed the banter from her old floor, even if Janine was a pain in the ass and Chris was a sexist pig.

Laura clocked off and headed to the cafeteria on Level Two for lunch. She grabbed a tray at the entrance and ordered beef stew and a glass of lemonade from one of the replicator machines. Searching the room she found the pair huddled in their usual corner, and walked towards them.

Chris noticed her first. His eyes widened in surprise, or shock—Laura wasn't sure. He leaned forward and whispered something to Janine who sat with her back to her. Laura glanced down at her purple Level Five uniform that had already attracted the attention of others in the room.

She should have gone to eat in the terminal across the road from the ESC. But her pride, hanging on by a thread, pushed her on to their table. She stopped when she caught the look Janine flashed her that barely registered above chilly. Laura ignored the woman and set her tray down. If Janine wanted her gone, she'd have to say it to her face.

'Hey,' she said.

Neither Chris nor Janine said anything. She'd been hoping for a little more interaction from the pair. Excitement at seeing their friend again, perhaps? Janine loved the gossip and Level Five had created plenty in the past. Was that jealousy in Janine's hardened eyes? Chris was staring down at his plate of food, his mouth drawn thin and white.

The tension mounted but she stayed put. She needed to hear her promotion was a good thing. She needed Chris to tell her that Haymarket was back on the transfer list.

'What's up with you two?' The pair sat at the edge, leaving no space for Laura to sit. 'You don't have room for your friend?'

'Friends?' Janine spat. 'Is that what we are?'

'Excuse me?'

She folded her arms. 'You heard me. You've been gone for a week and a half and we've been left to deal with your workload. That's right, nobody replaced you. Now you're here to what, rub your promotion in our faces? Well, congratufuckinglations.'

'Chris, Janine, I can explain...' She hadn't come here to gloat. She came to tell the pair the job was nothing special.

Chris's nose wrinkled like he'd stepped in something. 'Crawl back to your new friends, Princess.'

Movement from across the room alerted her to a new change since she'd last been here. A roving camera, glossy and golden and shaped like a ball, hovered over a group in one corner. 'Since when did they put cameras in here?'

'Since a week and a half ago,' said Chris. His gaze flicked to the camera that was on the move. He shooed her away with his hand. 'Bugger off. We can't be seen taking to you.'

But Laura refused to leave. The thoughts of returning to the silence on Level Five made her skin itch.

She leaned in and lowered her voice. 'How much trouble can we really get in? We used to work together, for Christ's sake.'

Janine refused to look at her. Laura couldn't tell if it was jealousy or fear driving her cool attitude.

'Oh, shit,' said Chris, his body stiffening. Laura turned around to see the roving camera on its way over to their table. 'See what you've done now? You'd better talk your way out of it.'

'Yeah, you're good at getting what you want, aren't you?' said Janine.

Chris glared at Laura. 'Fix this, Princess.'

She wasn't too keen on her new nickname, but the camera's arrival cut off her chance to tell Chris that. The camera that could easily fit in the palm of her hand scanned her.

An electronic voice boomed through the device. 'Laura O'Halloran, you are Level Five. Please explain why you are speaking to Level Four employees.'

She straightened up, seeing her shimmering reflection in the golden ball. She'd seen these cameras before, but usually in public spaces like the entrance to the ESC, or in the lobby on the fourth floor. Never in the cafeteria. It was also her first time being this close to one.

She cleared her throat, considering her next words. It would be so easy to drop the pair in it, to save her skin;

she owed them nothing.

Laura glanced at the pair, then looked at the camera.

'I was just asking—'

'Just asking what?' said the camera voice.

Talking to an AI camera was too weird, so she pretended she was speaking to an operator holed up in some basement room.

She glanced down at her food she'd yet to touch. 'I was asking them where the swipe cards for the machines were.' The cards reset the replication machines that ran on cycles. At the end of a cycle, the quality of the food degraded enough that the machines needed a reboot. 'My stew has this weird metallic taste to it.'

The camera scanned Chris's face, then Janine's. 'Don't you three know each other?'

'Yes,' said Laura. 'We used to work together on Level Four.'

'Workers from different levels are not supposed to fraternise. I must report this.'

Laura caught the look of fear on Chris' face. She couldn't see Janine's face but she imagined the same look.

'I only asked them *because* I know them. I don't know anyone on Level Five yet, but I promise this will be the last time.'

She meant it. She was done with the pair.

The camera made a humming noise as it continued to hover in the air. 'The cards are to the side of the machines, where they always are.'

'Sorry, I didn't see them. I'll check again.'

The camera lingered on her face a little longer—or the operator in the basement did—before moving away.

Without a backward glance at Chris or Janine, she collected up her tray and marched over to the machine. There, she reset one—it didn't matter which—and ordered another stew. To keep up the charade, she dropped the original dish in one of the waste receptacle units.

Dozens of eyes were on her as she sat down with her food. She ate but her anger at Chris and the imaginary camera operator absorbed all the flavour from the food. Mostly she was angry at herself for allowing Janine to make her feel crap about herself. In the past, her former colleagues had treated her like she was nothing. She was something, and far better than that pair.

Screw them. They could wallow in their self pity all they wanted. Laura had already met with Gilchrist and received assurances that she would be on the transfer list. Could they boast the same thing?

Despite the pep talk to herself, the last of her appetite vanished. Laura forced down another gulp of lemonade that tasted more bitter than usual, and ate a rabbit-sized bite of her average-tasting stew. After enduring all the stares she could, she abandoned her lunch and went back to her workstation.

She immersed herself in her duties. No further files appeared about Bill Taggart that day.

34

The recreation room aboard the passenger ship was quiet. A brief orientation at the start of Stephen and Anton's journey had shown them the true size of this ship. Their own exploration after, however, had revealed that not all areas were accessible. Just seven humans sat in the sparsely decorated space, with tables and chairs huddled in a room twice the size of District Three's Central Core. At busier times, Stephen guessed the numbers would be different. It settled his nerves to find it quiet that evening.

In the presence of humans, the pair sat in chairs to blend in. Despite their best efforts to look and act like those they despised, the humans kept away from them.

Our outfits are drawing more attention than I'd like, said Anton telepathically. He provided cover for Stephen while he injected a synthesised protein pack directly into his stomach cavity.

Stephen grabbed the edge of the table when the first stomach cramp hit—one of the nastier side-effects that Anton had forgotten to tell him about. He squeezed his eyes shut, concentrating on the pain to control it. But the presence of others shot his concentration to hell. He straightened up halfway, only for the spasms to double him back over.

After a few controlled breaths, the pain plateaued.

I'm sorry. The packs aren't designed for prolonged use, said Anton, keeping one eye on a group of three across the room. *The first thing I'll do when we get back to the district is correct the protein imbalance. I was under a little pressure before we left.*

A new pain hit Stephen that felt like it was ripping his body in half. *Don't worry about it, please. It will pass soon—* The pain cut him off.

Anton shook his head. *I should have done more tests. It wasn't ready.*

Stephen sucked in air through gritted teeth. *The alternative is starvation.*

Anton sat up, too alert. His focus was on two humans who were on their way over. Stephen recognised the short man and his taller friend from the queue for the space craft.

'Don't let them get too close,' growled Stephen. 'I don't want them to notice the inconsistencies in our appearances.' His stomach muscles jerked again.

The shorter man pointed. 'Hey! What's wrong with your friend? You need a doc or somethin'?'

They inched forward until just two table-lengths separated them. Anton stood and smiled. 'He's feeling sick. He doesn't like to travel.'

Stephen groaned.

Both men jerked to a halt. The shorter man said, 'Gerry here...' he elbowed his friend. 'He knows CPR and worked as a nurse for a stint. Didn't you, Gerry?'

'Eh, sure but—'

'Well, go and help him, will ya? Don't just stand there.'

'I'm not sure. I think he might need a real doctor or something.'

The short man mumbled. 'Well, you can still take a look, can't ya? You're embarrassin' me.'

'Er, sure, I guess.' His taller friend stepped hesitantly towards Stephen.

Anton blocked his path. 'That won't be necessary.'

The shorter man's gaze flicked from Stephen to Anton and back again. 'Weren't you two standing behind us in the queue for this rust-bucket?'

His friend nodded and smiled. 'Oh, yeah, I think you're right. In the queue.'

Another spasm hit. *Get rid of them...* said Stephen.

Anton smiled. 'I'm sorry, but my friend here is about to be sick, so I suggest you keep your distance.'

The shorter man made a face and backed off; his friend wasn't far behind. 'Don't do well seein' sick,' he said, holding up his hands.

'Me neither,' said the taller man.

His friend shot him an odd look. 'Whatcha talking about? You're trained for this kind of thing.'

'Only lasted a month at nursing school. Once we started the practical stuff, I was out of there.'

The short man shook his head. 'Useless.'

Both headed for the exit. A passing warning from the pair was enough to move the remaining five passengers.

Stephen sucked in a deep breath; the worst of the pain passed. 'I think we should restrict future injections to the sleeping pods.' He shook his head. 'Why did you let them get that close? We must keep under the radar more. Last thing we need is them telling everyone about the odd looking pair in the recreation room.'

'Maybe we should ditch these hats back at our

sleeping pods. And stick to only darkened areas from now on.'

With the room empty, they both dropped the pretence and stood. *Referring to them as humans will take some getting used to,* said Anton. *What are we looking for when we get to Earth?*

Answers, plain and simple. Something to explain how they exist, and why they want to destroy us. That Taggart man will be our lead.

They walked back to their sleeping quarters. On the way, Anton asked, 'Why him?'

'Who?'

'You can't stand to be near any of them but you met the boy Ben Watson twice. Why?'

Stephen shrugged. 'I saw something in him that the others didn't possess—innocence, perhaps? It was easier to be around him.' He stopped and leaned against the wall. 'I don't know, Anton. I can't explain why I feel angry at the rest, but not him.'

'Maybe you're coming round to the idea that not all of them are bad. I mean, you saved those men when they were suffocating.'

'I *saved* Taggart because we need him alive. The others just happened to be there.' Stephen made two fists. 'I let my guard down with the boy and that pair just now. It won't happen again.'

35

What Suzanne Brett described as a "hectic" period in the calendar was an understatement. Neither Laura nor her colleagues knew when the gruelling double shifts on Level Five would end, but everyone hoped it would be soon. In no position to negotiate an early release from duty, Laura accepted that Brett needed her more than Laura needed sleep.

Despite her exhaustion, Laura decided against taking a fifth Actigen pill. Twenty-four hours remained in her current double shift. She could make it without the pill. Maybe she could squeeze in an hour's sleep in the Energy Restoration room on Level Two.

Her head pounded. Just one more day, she reminded herself. Chris and Janine's behaviour a few days earlier had soured her mood, but something else played on her mind. The Taggart files.

The grey partitions encasing her isolation booth did little to ease her headache. Even her rearrangement of the items on her desk—a family photo, a fake plant and her communication device—couldn't distract her from her thoughts.

Maybe a drink of water would help.

She shuffled over to the H2O replication station at the top of the room and requested water. The woman from booth sixteen arrived, disc in hand, and deposited it in the vacuum tube connected to Gilchrist's office. The tube made a sucking noise and the disc disappeared. Sixteen returned to her seat without looking at Laura.

Laura drained the tiny cone-shaped cup and requested a second refill. But the hydration effects didn't do much for her pounding head. She returned to her workstation and sat down, sick of the pain in her head. Sick of her colleagues' indifference to her. Sick of others controlling her fate.

She closed her eyes and dreamt up other ways she could escape this planet. But the files about aliens and autopsies, and some investigator she'd never met, crept into her thoughts.

The transfer to Exilon 5 was a good thing. It would rescue the human race from an Earth past saving. But now this race called the Indigenes had shifted the World Government's focus away from the transfer programme. It wasn't clear from the files what it planned to do with the race, only that the investigation, led by Bill Taggart, appeared to be recent.

How long would Laura have to wait before Gilchrist allowed her to transfer to Exilon 5? Her Seasonal Affective Disorder needled her sanity daily. To everyone else sunshine was a luxury. To Laura it was life and death. Maybe she could explain that to Gilchrist?

No, she'd promised to pull her weight, to work hard. Making the transfer list would be her reward.

But what planet would she be heading to? One occupied by a violent Indigene race?

Two words stood out from the latter files: "Intelligence" and "Adaptability". For any race to survive, they needed both.

The image of the alien named in the files as Stephen stuck in her head, along with Bill Taggart's naturally aged face. Would she recognise either of them if they passed her on the street?

According to the files, the investigations were to gauge the threat levels of the Indigenes towards the human population. But with hundreds of millions having transferred to Exilon 5, it wasn't like they could keep this information a secret. She was certain the World Government didn't have endless resources to start again.

The government had to stay and fight. It's what Laura would do if she were in charge.

She had to make Gilchrist understand. To stay on Earth would be a death sentence for her.

Couldn't the Indigenes live separate to humans? The planet, three times the size of Earth, could easily accommodate both species. Was that the reason for the ongoing investigation, to determine the willingness of the Indigenes to share the planet? But that wasn't clear from the reports. The alien's side of the story had been omitted.

☼

Lunchtime couldn't come around soon enough. Laura clocked off from the system and headed for the cafeteria on Level Two. Chris and Janine would not scare her off. She just made sure to go at a time when she knew they wouldn't be there.

In the nearly empty cafeteria, Laura sat down and ate her lunch of grilled chicken and potatoes. She ignored the slight jolt when someone sat down beside her, just one seat away. Glancing up, she half-expected to see Chris or Janine there to offer an apology. A breath caught in her throat when she saw it was the dark-haired woman from booth sixteen. The woman who handled level-six information.

Sixteen scooped food onto her fork and stuffed it in her mouth. Laura stared at the woman in her mid sixties. Her shoulders were rounded, as though she carried a heavy weight.

'Eyes down,' growled Sixteen looking ahead.

Laura stared down at her food. A new burst of adrenaline had ruined her appetite. She picked up her coffee mug, hoping to settle her stomach, and took measured sips.

In a hushed whisper the woman said, 'You've been told lies. The ESC appears to work for the good of the people, but it doesn't. Things are going on here... things I'm not allowed to speak about.' Laura searched for the roving camera. 'They are using you. So far, they've only shown you things they want you to see.'

What things? What was she talking about?

The woman continued, 'You think you know why you were promoted. Gilchrist said she saw potential in you, correct? That's what she says to everyone, but we're not needed to do this work. They're using us to further their own cause.' She shifted in her seat. 'I know you were sent the Taggart files. Have you wondered why?'

Yes she had. Laura glanced around her, relieved to see the camera at a table farther away, interrogating some young woman from Level One. She coughed into her fist to disguise her next question. 'Why *did* they give me the files?'

'I don't know, but Gilchrist doesn't home in on someone unless they can help her. I'm guessing it's because you're new and less likely to cause trouble.'

That's what Gilchrist had said: Don't make trouble.

Sixteen forced more food into her mouth. She chewed and spoke again. 'You're the first person in a while to grab Gilchrist's attention. That's why I'm giving you these.'

She pulled out three folded envelopes; one had a tiny micro file taped to the front. 'You've seen some files already, but they're nothing compared to these. Be careful, or Gilchrist will keep pulling your strings, making you dance.' Her words were barely audible now. Or maybe the thudding in Laura's ears had killed off her ability to hear. Sixteen shoved the envelopes into her sweaty shaking palm. 'These will tell you what's really going on. Maybe you'll do the right thing, maybe you won't. But I can't sit on this information any longer.'

Laura resisted the urge to look at Sixteen, to see the truth—or the lies—in her eyes. Keeping her eyes down, she slipped the envelopes into the waistband of her trousers. The adrenaline agitated her body to the point where she couldn't sit still. Her head told her to calm the hell down.

Her hand trembled as she brought her mug to her lips. 'What are they?' She took a sip and put the mug down, feeling more alert than she'd done all week.

Sixteen finished her meal. 'Try not to get caught with them.'

'But I still don't understand. Why me?'

Sixteen picked up her tray. 'Because Gilchrist likes you.' She stood up and headed for the exit, depositing her tray along the way.

Laura's heart fluttered, in its vain attempt to return to a normal rhythm. If her experiences over the last week were anything to go by, then getting caught talking to anyone—including her Level Five colleagues—would be bad. She hoped the authorities would view Sixteen's proximity as an oversight rather than a deliberate attempt to make contact.

The envelopes in her waistband stuck to her skin.

She resisted the urge to take them out and look at them. All eyes were on her. That's what she'd been told. Despite wanting to run, she stayed put for a further five agonising minutes before leaving the cafeteria.

On her way back to Level Five, she slipped into the bathroom and into one cubicle, locking the door behind her. She removed the envelopes from her waistband and peeled away the micro file. It measured the size of an old Australian two-dollar coin, with a tiny wire-feed extruding from one end. This was meant to be viewed through a monitor. No way could she risk hooking it up to her workstation. Any deviation from her regular tasks would surely raise the alarm.

The same tickle in her chest that drove her to open the folder with Taggart's files was back. She had to know what was on the file and in the envelopes. Why would Sixteen risk giving them to her if they weren't important?

An idea hit her. The hardware control unit for the Light Box in her apartment could accept micro files like this. She had no way of knowing if they were monitoring her activity at home. It would be risky.

Laura shrugged off her jacket and unbuttoned her blouse. She ripped a small hole in the fabric of her bra and slipped the micro file between the padding, then folded and tucked the envelopes into the back of her underwear where they wouldn't slip down her leg. She washed her hands and tidied her appearance last. Sucking in a new breath, she hoped it would settle her nerves. It didn't.

Returning to work feeling the way she did took guts. Sixteen was in her cubicle and focusing on her monitor. Laura slid into her own cubicle and resumed her shift, wondering how the hell to act normal anymore.

36

Bill stood at the window looking out as the ship tore through space. The stars in the black night's sky melded into one blur of white light. He liked the simplicity of the sky, of space, of the untroubled planets far removed from Earth's mess; anything that suggested life could exist without complications.

His life was far from simple.

The ship rode the magnetic slipstream between the planets, passing by what looked like two moons. The light changed from white to grey, then back to white again. A moon, that's what Earth looked like now; the dense weather formation over the entire planet had altered its appearance. Long gone was the luminous blue-and-white sphere depicted in old photos. How had two generations managed to ruin something so magnificent?

It was close to midnight, the time when Bill knew the last of the passengers had retired to their sleeping pods. Nearly two weeks had passed since he'd left Exilon 5, and while he'd managed some sleep it had done little to stave off his exhaustion. The one time he'd succumbed, Bill had almost suffocated in his sleeping pod. The Actigen in his system would make sure he'd never get caught out like that again. Every day he thanked the timely arrival of those two men.

But their faceless silhouettes with bright burning eyes continued to haunt him. Who were they? Others continued to praise their efforts, but nobody stepped forward to claim the hero status. It was like the pair had vanished off the ship.

The videos of the child Indigene showing physical similarities between their two species still bothered Bill days after he'd watched them. But they hadn't shed new light on what had happened to his wife. The only way to get answers would be to return to Exilon 5 and catch one of the Indigenes.

Like he'd been trying to do.

But the Indigenes' fight against oppression reminded him of human struggles, past and present. Those thoughts had forced him to see Stephen in a new light.

He shook his thoughts away and leaned against the wall.

Almost two weeks on the ship had given him too much time to think. Something about the investigation he'd been asked to head up bothered him. What had Gilchrist and Deighton wanted Bill to do exactly? He'd managed to corner Stephen in New Victoria's underground tunnels. Okay, not cornered exactly, but if he'd sent a team down there he was certain they would have found Stephen's entry and exit points. Now Gilchrist was demanding his return? The videos proved she and Deighton knew plenty about the Indigenes. Why were his orders to watch the creature only? Then there was Deighton's call to him before the start of the first meeting.

Deighton never called anyone.

After a year on Exilon 5, Bill was returning to Earth

a failure. Except he wasn't. This mission wasn't over. There had been plenty more to do.

His abuse of Actigen left his head feeling heavy. He hated feeling so out of control on it. He hated the paranoia, his inability to trust anyone. Were his suspicions about the investigation real or to do with his Actigen abuse?

Bill trekked down one of the tubular passageways that connected the wheel rim to the hub of the ship. With each heavy step, he fought against his chemically-maintained consciousness. It was no way to live, permanently awake, but he refused to let go of control until he reached Earth.

His paranoia moved him fast. Each step illuminated a new section and plunged the previous part into darkness, just like in his dream. He zigzagged along the horizontal tubes that connected to the vertical spokes. If someone was following, he wouldn't make it easy for them.

Bill arrived at an empty recreation room. The door at the back of the room caught his attention, and not for the first time. He'd seen officers accessing parts of the ship that were off limits using their security chip. He trudged over to it. An access control panel sat to the right of the door. He pressed his thumb against it. The panel flashed red.

Bill turned away—a little too fast. A bout of dizziness hit him. He stumbled forward, caught in the grip of one of Actigen's side effects.

His legs buckled inches away from a table and chair, and sent him crashing to the floor. With a grunt, Bill groped for the edge of the seat but he lost his grip.

A breath rushed out of him when he hit the floor a second time. He stared up at the ceiling as a new panic flared in his chest. He couldn't have picked a worse time to be alone.

His arms refused to work; his legs felt like they had atrophy. With a grunt, he rolled to one side and crawled forward. The cold floor chilled him as he felt around for the seat.

Another bout of dizziness hit him. He hauled himself up fast before he fell to the floor a third time. Secure in the seat, Bill slumped forward. It took all his concentration to stay put.

His eyes drooped, as did his head. It slammed against the table. The hard knock kicked him back to consciousness. Bill blinked away his exhaustion, but his eyes closed against his wishes.

☼

Bill jerked awake and looked around the black space. Where was he? Feeling for clues, he found the sleek rounded shape of his coffin. The rest of his sleeping pod slowly came into focus. How did he get here? He shook his head, remembering passing out at the table, but not much more. His head throbbed from where it had hit a hard surface.

Then what? In his unconscious state, he'd crawled back to his sleeping pod and climbed up the ladder?

Bullshit. He knew how Actigen worked. And also how it didn't.

Panic and fear gripped hold of him.

In the dark he whispered, 'Who brought me back here?'

37

The unopened envelopes haunted her. The micro file, hidden between the fabrics of her bra, reminded her of her betrayal. Laura hadn't looked at anything yet. No crime had been committed.

She tossed and turned in her apartment in Haymarket, Sydney. The time projection on the wall read midday; she'd arrived home from her shift three hours ago. Now she lay in bed, unsure if she should look at the contents of the micro file. She should be dead on her feet, but her body pinged with nervous energy.

What harm could it do to look? It might turn out to be nothing. For the last three hours she'd imagined the worst, whether ESC were remotely monitoring her Light Box, or if Gilchrist had ordered someone to follow her home. She scrapped the last idea on the basis that nobody had shown up. As for the idea of someone monitoring the Light Box, she couldn't know for sure.

Laura ran her fingers across the unopened envelopes on her bedside table, the ones addressed to Bill Taggart. She brought the paper up to her nose, smelling faint perfume. The handwriting was feminine. She desperately wanted to rip them open and read the letters inside, but instead she looked and wondered. They weren't meant for her and she sensed they were personal.

Viewing the contents of the micro file didn't feel as personal, but Sixteen's warning repeated in her head.

'These will tell you what's really going on. Maybe you'll do the right thing, maybe you won't.'

She'd never promised to *do* anything.

For too long she'd listened to Chris and Janine stir up gossip about the terrible things the ESC had done. Laura had chalked that gossip up to boredom, but what if they had been telling the truth? What if she had actual proof of foul play? To look at the micro file would mean no going back, no pretending things were okay. Her chance of a transfer was on the line. But her curiosity ran deeper than whatever punishment Gilchrist might throw at her.

Laura pulled the covers over her head. Maybe if she stayed in bed long enough, her mind would quiet down.

Yeah, right. With a sigh, she got up.

Her apartment on the tenth floor had a clear view of the street below. She checked both the street and the block opposite her, where the rooms were dark and she could see nothing. Laura decreased the tint on her window to the lowest level.

Slipping her robe on, she tied the straps securely around her waist, as though the action might protect her more. She retrieved the micro file from its hiding place and studied it in her palm.

How could something so small be so dangerous?

The Light Box's virtual display hummed into life when Laura stepped into the living room. It waited for a first command. She prised open the cover to the hardware control unit, below the virtual display, and inserted the file's tendril into one of six openings. The opening swallowed it and the two temporarily merged into one. The display changed and a new screen filled the wall, illuminating her apartment. On the left-hand side, a yellow icon flashed.

'Open icon,' said Laura, and the screen listed the contents of the micro file. There were ten documents, each one identifiable by a security code, followed by the date; the files were arranged in chronological order. The information spanned across several years. Nothing hinted as to what was in each document.

'Open first document'.

Her heart thumped in her ears as she spoke. She would start at the beginning and work her way through to the last.

The display changed and a report filled the screen. Laura checked over her shoulder—a new habit. She perched on the edge of her dining chair. Its lacquered edge bit into her skin, reminding her not to get too comfortable.

The on-screen report had been issued from Daphne Gilchrist to Charles Deighton. At the time of correspondence, Gilchrist was Head of Operations at the ESC—a position that Suzanne Brett now filled—and was in charge of Level Five. The document centred around the indigenous species on Exilon 5, the same species Laura had read about in one of Bill Taggart's reports. The report had been written twenty-five years earlier, five years after the controlled explosions that had transformed Exilon 5 into its current state.

Bill Taggart's reports, containing information about the same events of thirty years ago, had given her a base understanding of what was being discussed. She ventured further into the new report that mentioned experiments on the indigenous race. It wasn't clear when humans had carried them out exactly, but she assumed it was after they'd discovered the race.

The contents forced her to stop. Nausea made her stomach dance. 'What the hell is this?'

She looked away from the photos of Indigenes as young as seven receiving shock therapy, and adults, red-eyed and teary, being subjected to bright lights. Her curiosity won out and she turned her attention back to the screen. As she read more, the details of how humans had interfered in the lives of the Indigenes were laid bare for her to see. The recent World Government experiments on them, the planned terraforming, the knowledge of their underground tunnels, but not the precise location.

But something confused her. The photos showing torture were from fifty years ago, before knowledge of Exilon 5 had even been reported.

With a shaky hand, Laura waved the first document closed.

Was this even real? Had the government known about the existence of the Indigenes before the discovery of Exilon 5? If so, the torture would have taken place on Earth. In Earth labs. By Earth doctors.

Laura forced her weak voice to issue the next command.

The second and third documents opened and she read the content. The experiments on the Indigenes weren't mentioned again until the fourth document—a recent one, just three months old. It tied in with the ongoing investigations on Exilon 5, mentioning the investigator Bill Taggart, who had headed up the mission. The story she knew so far made sense.

But she couldn't have prepared herself for what she saw next. Around three-quarters of the way into the fourth report, it outlined the reason for the World Government's obsession with the Indigenes. Enough information explained its motives and exposed its lies and secrets. Then there was the ESC's involvement. Neither organisation had carried out the experimentations to discover more about the aliens; they already knew everything about them.

Humans had not discovered this race. Humans had placed them on Exilon 5.

When Laura read the fifth document, she gasped.

Her eyes shot over to her bedroom, where she had left the unopened letters addressed to the investigator.

38

'Eleanor, love, it's great to see you.' Jenny Waterson hugged her daughter as they sat down to lunch in a local Brisbane restaurant. 'How long has it been since we last caught up in person? I can't remember.'

'About two months now, I'd say.'

That couldn't be right. Jenny shook her head. 'I can't believe how quickly time is passing these days.'

'That job of yours has you working all sorts of hours. You look tired, Mum. When was the last time you took a proper break?'

Jenny browsed the digital menu set into the table. 'I don't know. When was Christmas?'

'Be serious.'

'Okay, about two months I guess. The last time we caught up, probably.'

'How long are they giving you this time?'

Jenny hesitated before replying. 'A couple of days.' She braced herself for what came next whenever she talked about her job.

'See? That's what I'm talking about. Last time you were given a whole week off.'

'Look, love, I'm here to spend time with you. Can we change the subject?' Jenny selected chicken teriyaki with Singapore noodles and a glass of red wine. She'd been feeling good this last week. Her flights had set off and landed without a hitch. The last thing she wanted was to talk about work on her day off.

'I can't help it, Mum. The way they treat you, it's appalling. Maybe you should think about changing careers, working for people who actually show you more respect.'

Jenny stared at her. 'And do what? The only thing I know how to do is work as a pilot. If I leave, I lose all privileges and have to start at the bottom.'

Eleanor glanced at the menu. 'The bottom's not so bad.'

'But you're only a third of the way through your life cycle. Just a baby. Plenty of years ahead of you yet. I'm no spring chicken.'

'And you're not down and out.' Eleanor huffed. 'Give yourself some credit. I can't pretend I like the way the company treats you. You're nothing more than a commodity to them. It annoys me to even think about it, especially since you're the best pilot on their books.'

'You know how it works, love. It's my choice to stay.'

Eleanor rolled her eyes. 'This is exactly why I changed from law to politics. I hate the way the World Government runs things... But I'm still a qualified lawyer, so if you need someone to argue your case, you only have to ask.'

Jenny touched the back of her neck. She hated arguing, especially with her daughter. 'Sure will, love. I couldn't ask for a better lawyer. Just leave everything to me. I know what I'm doing. I'll be fine.'

'I wish there was something I could do for you.'

'There is. Keep me company while I enjoy my first day off in months.'

Eleanor conceded with a smile. 'I guess I can do that.'

Jenny's communication device shrilled, loud and persistent. It was her employers, Calypso Couriers.

Her daughter's eyes widened when Jenny touched the device. 'Don't you dare answer that.'

Maybe when she reached seventy-five, Eleanor would feel the same terror at being fired for no good reason.

'I have to, it might be important.' Jenny connected her earpiece and ignored her daughter when she mumbled something rude. 'Yes,' she said flatly.

'All personnel are required to report for duty. Report to the Hartsfield-Jackson Atlanta docking station by five pm. Deighton's orders,' said the female voice at the other end.

She checked the time. That was three hours from now. 'But you don't understand, it's my day off—'

The line clicked dead. Jenny popped the device out of her ear and tossed it on the table. If she didn't show up, it would be her third and final strike.

'I warned you not to answer it,' said Eleanor.

Jenny agreed as she stood up. 'I'm sorry, rain check?'

☼

She rushed home to change into her uniform before taking the high speed Maglev train to the Sydney docking station. An hour and a half after leaving Eleanor, she was trussed up in her space craft and ascending into the space just above the Earth. Twenty minutes later, she hurtled back to the ground amid the calmest weather she'd experienced over the last few weeks.

At least one thing was going right for her.

Her arrival at HJA's docking station was met with a strong military presence. Not for her, but they were definitely expecting someone. She released the door and exited from the craft. The thin docking station attendant was waiting for her, looking worried as ITF military swarmed the area behind him. She pictured an equally worried Stuart pacing the length of his observation deck.

Barely looking at her, the attendant stuck the DPad out for her to register her arrival. She pressed her thumb to it and walked away from him. Behind her, he yelled to someone, 'Don't touch that!'

Jenny walked fast to the double doors at the back of the hold, her heart slamming against her ribcage. During her freelance piloting days she'd carried her fair share of dodgy cargo. But transferring prisoners between prisons had not stressed her out as much as being here did. The sight of so many ITF military kept her body coiled tight.

The ESC only ever interfered in the running of the docking stations if there was a security breach, or if cuts were on the way. But Deighton had ordered her here. That meant something big was happening. Or about to.

She entered the observation deck to see four people —pilots in uniform—crammed into Stuart's tiny office. Stuart and a few of the senior staff were standing in one corner of the main room while a man with a tight crew cut, and dripping in military accolades, walked around. He stopped randomly at a few desks and observed the work over several shoulders. He wasn't alone. More military bodies serving at a lesser grade than him interrupted the operations that she knew Stuart had under tight controls. Jenny caught the glare Stuart directed at the man. But his eyes softened when he spotted Jenny.

'Captain Waterson,' he declared loudly, as if to divert the senior man's attention away from the communications operative. He strode over to Jenny and mouthed, 'Help me,' just before the senior military man arrived.

'Captain Waterson. Sergeant Briggs. We've been waiting for you.'

'We?'

He gestured to Stuart's office. 'Yes, shall we talk?' The sergeant placed his hand on her back. She walked out of his reach.

Stuart marched on ahead and opened the door to his office. Jenny shuffled in beside four others. The sergeant made it seven.

He sat down on Stuart's chair. 'We're expecting a passenger ship from Exilon 5 in the next hour. I've been informed by the ESC that there's a possible stowaway on board.'

Jenny frowned. 'Who is this mystery stowaway?'

'A man travelling under the alias of Bob Harris,' said Stuart.

The sergeant flashed him a look that told him to shut up.

'Yes, someone will be arriving that the ESC and World Government want taken into custody. We're here to facilitate that.'

One person, five pilots. Jenny didn't understand why she was here. 'What do you need us to do?' Her eyes flicked over the group of pilots who looked as unsure as she felt.

The sergeant said, 'All of you will be taking your quota of passengers from the ship and returning them to here. But we are covering our bases. We don't know which space craft the person will use to leave the ship. By briefing all of you, we are covering all our angles.'

Okay, that made sense. 'How dangerous is this individual?'

'He shouldn't make trouble for you on the way down,' said the sergeant. 'In fact, I'd be surprised if he does anything to alert us to his arrival. But under no circumstances must you engage with him. We expect this to be a simple process. Once we have our man, we'll be out of here.'

Stuart visibly relaxed. This intrusion must be killing him. He'd always hated people telling him what to do.

Jenny relaxed too. What the sergeant was asking sounded straightforward enough and unlikely to attract a penalty.

'When does the ship get here?' she asked.

'In the next two hours.' That meant the five pilots and their craft would head up to space from HJA three minutes apart. Fifteen minutes to complete the lift off and another fifteen minutes for all of them to reach space and get settled.

'Any questions?' asked the sergeant.

Jenny had none. The other pilots shook their heads. This was a simple run up to the passenger ship and back down. Not much could go wrong.

The sergeant stood and left the office. Stuart ran after him, his worry evident.

Jenny left the office and stood outside with the other four pilots. While they'd met, an extra dozen military personnel had slipped in. Nervous personnel tried to do their job while the extra military made a nuisance of themselves.

All this muscle for just one stowaway? A bit much.

One pilot said, 'We're heading to the cafeteria. You

wanna join us?'

She smiled and shook her head. 'I need to speak to the overseer about my last schedule. I'll see you soon.'

The pilots left the observation deck.

A nervous looking Stuart shadowed the military around the room. She felt for her friend. This high level of attention could have ramifications for his position. Deighton was known for being whimsical. If he got an idea into his head, it was hard to know if he would act on it or forget about it.

Stuart broke off his shadowing and marched over to her. The sergeant, she saw, paid him no attention.

'Jenny,' he said in a whisper. 'I need this to go well.'

Jenny frowned at him. 'Of course it will.'

He grabbed her arm too tight. 'I need this job. I...'

She worried for her friend's behaviour. 'What's wrong, Stuart?'

He glanced behind him. 'Remember that clean sheet I have? Well, I may have changed a few dates and numbers to keep it. Yeah, two people got fired over it, but the ESC never questioned the discrepancies at the time.'

'Shit, Stuart.'

He let go of her and combed his fingers through his hair. 'I know, and now Sergeant Dickhead and his friends are going through everything.' His eyes flashed with worry. 'Just don't let anything happen.'

'I wasn't planning on it. Besides, it will be a reflection on me, not you.'

Stuart sighed. 'I'm sorry. I just want this to go well.'

She touched his arm. 'It will. You've got this. They're not going to find anything because the discrepancies are buried.'

Stuart perked up. 'You're right, they are. They

happened three months ago. If the ESC didn't pick up on anything then, they won't find it now.'

'That's the spirit.' She saw the sergeant look their way. 'Looks like someone wants you.'

Stuart glanced behind him again. 'Ugh. When this is over, let's get drunk.'

'Deal.'

Stuart rejoined the sergeant, who was pointing at the comms operative. She heard Stuart say to him, 'Because we don't rely on technology for everything. Hearing a voice on the line calms the pilots.'

Military stood at the wall panels showing space debris, planets in the solar system, and the area immediately above Earth. Their presence rattled the controllers whose job it was to monitor space debris in the ship's path. The sergeant stood over the communications operative while he tried to speak to someone. Stuart folded his arms and sighed heavily.

'Ask the ship pilot if there were any disturbances on board,' the sergeant said to the operative.

The operative checked and replied. 'Nothing reported, sir.'

'Doesn't mean anything,' mumbled the sergeant. He turned around, startled by Stuart's proximity to him. He backed up a little. 'We'll need everybody's full cooperation until the person we're after has been safely apprehended.'

'Of course,' said Stuart. 'If there's anything at all we can do, please don't hesitate—'

'I want to speak to him myself,' said the sergeant. He grabbed the operative's shoulder and held out his other hand. The operative handed over the earpiece and the sergeant shoved it into his ear. 'Pilot of the passenger ship, you have a dangerous stowaway on board. Do not engage with your passengers under any circumstances. Proceed as normal. The military will be handling this situation on the ground.'

The sergeant nodded at what Jenny assumed was the pilot's response, then pulled the earpiece out and tossed it on the table, out of the operative's reach. It appeared the sergeant had downplayed the threat during his talk in Stuart's office.

Jenny backed out of the room. She didn't need this stress right before a flight.

39

Laura tried to act like everything was normal. But sitting across from the woman who'd given her the files wasn't helping. On one of Sixteen's bathroom breaks, Laura scheduled her own. Sixteen told her to leave her alone, her words masked by a flushing toilet sound.

Laura delayed her exit, making sure to leave enough time between her and Sixteen. She returned to the office, a tight space with a new and insufferable silence to it. How could she pretend her life had not been turned upside down by a set of files she hadn't asked to see? She sat down in her chair, barely able to make out the file details on her screen. Taxes and filing failures seemed even more trivial now, given what she'd learned. Whatever issues Earth had, it paled in comparison to those of the Indigenes.

She glanced over at the dark-haired woman who had pushed Laura down a path of lies and experiments, exposing the truth about the real origin of the Indigenes. But looking at her now—head down and eyes on her screen—it was as if their conversation had never happened.

Except it had.

Genesis Code

Then there was Isla Taggart. Laura had peeked inside the already-opened envelopes to find letters written in code. It had been the photo on the micro file of Isla talking to one of the Indigenes that had pushed her to open them. In one picture Isla Taggart was smiling at someone off camera. The picture had been stamped with the words: *Destroy the evidence.*

That wasn't a bad idea.

She would pass the letters on to Bill Taggart, then burn the micro file. But could she destroy the file, knowing what damning evidence it contained? She wasn't even sure why she still kept it. Maybe she'd hoped this was still some twisted joke to break in the new girl.

No, this transcended some silly initiation.

The easiest thing would be to forget she'd seen anything. But that would make her no better than the people she worked for.

☼

After an hour of trying to focus, and processing less files than she knew she could manage, another bathroom break called to her. Laura left her cubicle behind.

Chewing on her thumb, she entered the foyer and turned left for the bathroom. But her distraction missed someone who had her in her sights.

'O'Halloran!'

Laura stiffened when she heard the sharp voice of the CEO. She popped her thumb out of her mouth.

'Oh, hi,' she said.

Gilchrist eyed her. 'You look like you've seen a ghost.'

'What? Oh, it's nothing.'

'Actually I'm glad I ran into you.'

'You are?'

Gilchrist folded her arms. 'Yes. I've noticed the numbers of files you've processed has dropped off this week.'

Good one, Laura. In her efforts to pretend everything was normal, she had forgotten about her work, the one thing that might draw attention to her.

'I'm sorry. I won't let it happen again.'

'Make sure you don't. I didn't promote you so you could slack off.'

'Of course not. I'm grateful for the opportunity.' The words came out weak and pathetic.

'And stop grovelling at my feet.' Laura looked up surprised. She didn't realise she'd been doing that. 'You can let people push you around all your life, or you can take control and stop being a doormat.'

'Excuse me?'

Gilchrist arched a brow. 'If you want any kind of future, you need to show you belong. When the transfer happens, not everyone will get the opportunity. If you want yours, prove you can be a team player.' The CEO assessed her clinically. 'Go home, please. You look like hell.'

Gilchrist walked on. Laura stared after the CEO until she disappeared down a corridor.

Team player? Is that what Gilchrist wanted?

She sucked in a breath on her way back to the office; it bolstered her energy that had been flagging all week. Collecting her coat and bag, she walked to the turbo lift that would take her up and out through the public entrance.

She could be a team player. Who she wanted on that team? She hadn't decided that yet.

40

The ship arrived five minutes early and hovered in the outer perimeter surrounding Earth. Jenny watched and waited alongside fifteen other craft as Cargo Hold 1 in the ship's underside winched open like the jaws of a beast. First in from the HJA-bound vessels, she would be the last to leave with her passengers.

Inside the hold, Jenny tweaked the controls until the landing skids touched the floor. The craft bounced off-course and she quickly corrected the movement with a flick of her hand. When it settled on the floor, she disengaged the thrusters to keep it there. She kept the force field in place while the hold began to pressurise.

Soon after, the ship passengers entered the hold. She observed the ones with a drunken-like stupor who hadn't fully emerged from stasis. Others, like an attractive man in his forties, looked very much awake, but the dark circles under his eyes told her he hadn't slept much. Jenny had never travelled on a passenger ship. She assumed it to be the same as her craft, but without the gut-wrenching turbulence.

From the on-board computer, she downloaded the

manifest from the ship officer's DPad using a unique identification code. Scanning it quickly, she found the name that had turned Stuart's working life upside down. Bob Harris. With everyone on-board, she defied her instructions to not engage with her passengers. She ordered them to strap in, and gave a quick reminder of the turbulence ahead.

'If you feel sick there are bags under your seat.'

Jenny guided her craft out of the hold and headed for Dock 10. Ahead of her, similar vessels heading to HJA descended to Earth. Behind her, others branched off towards their own destinations. She waited fifteen minutes, then contacted the communications operator in HJA and received a clearance for landing. She began her descent, firing all thrusters until the craft had dropped below the outer perimeter shield. There, the final leg of the journey would be dictated by gravitational pull alone.

Her arrival at the docking station minutes later went smoothly, but the docking station had been transformed into a war zone. Crates had been stacked high. Roving cameras hovered around Dock 10. Dozens of military personnel peeked out from behind the crates, while nervous attendants waited to receive passengers off the ship.

She kept the door closed until passengers from the other craft had been processed. Her passengers remained in their seats.

Jenny's onboard communication pinged suddenly. She shoved an earpiece into her ear. 'Yes?' she whispered.

'Captain, is the person of interest on board?' It was the sergeant.

'Bob Harris? Yes he is. I'm looking at the manifest now. How do you want me to proceed?'

'Do nothing, ma'am. This is our operation now.'

She hated it when people called her ma'am. 'Understood,' she said with a shudder.

Outside, the line of passengers outside was moving fast. The order for her to open her doors followed. In her rear-view mirror she spotted two odd-looking passengers wearing navy-blue suits and black Stetsons. Jenny's skin prickled when both men stared at her.

41

They were so close, but a long line and an anxious pilot stood between Stephen and Anton's freedom.

Stephen had caught the pilot's conversation between her and someone in the docking station. The name Bob Harris had been mentioned—his alias.

The people ahead of them began their disembarkation, leaving him little time to come up with a plan.

Anton shot an anxious look at Stephen. *They can't catch both of us,* he said. *Why don't we just make a run for it?*

Because I think they've erected a force field around the building. We won't get far.

Anton shrugged. *So what's left? We can't come this far to give up now.*

I've no intention of giving up. Let me think for a minute.

Stephen ran through the limited options available. The only certainty was they couldn't stay here. He needed a way out of this station and to find the investigator. His gaze flicked to the pilot and the controls he was certain would not respond to his security chip. His idea started with threats and grew to include a control room, which must turn off the security barrier around the station.

I think I have a plan, but it'll be risky.

Anton frowned. *What is it?*

How fast can you run these days?

Almost as fast as you, brother. You need me to go somewhere?

He rushed through his hasty idea. Through the tiny craft windows he saw rows of stacked boxes. Beyond that was a set of double doors that led out.

I don't know where the control room might be, but you should start through that set of doors. To get through security, you'll have to play it cool. A part Stephen was certain he himself would fail at. *And be quick. I don't want be stuck with these humans for longer than necessary.*

The woman behind him inched forward. He flinched.

Don't worry, Stephen. I'll get it done.

Stephen's lips quirked up as the tension in his gut settled. But only a little.

I'm glad you're here. He nudged Anton with his elbow. *Let's stick to the rear of the group. If we're discovered, we use this craft as a plan B.*

The line moved; Stephen gestured for the others to pass him. Both he and Anton stayed to the rear, ready to put their hasty plan into action. It was a risk sending Anton out alone, but if the humans were only looking for one of them, now was the perfect time to separate.

In the dock, military humans materialised from behind shipment crates like ghosts and swarmed around the passengers. He'd picked up on their scents already. Why they'd deemed it necessary to hide he wasn't sure. Bill Taggart had mentioned a Gilchrist and a Deighton.

Were they behind this show of force?

Ahead, the military took up new positions behind the docking-station attendants as they scanned identity chips. Passengers gasped when the extra force made their presence known.

Military ushered cleared passengers out through a set of doors to the rear of the dock. Anton had almost reached the attendant. Stephen's heart pounded thickly in his chest as he watched his friend risk his life for a plan that might not even work.

42

Jenny watched the military hover around Dock 10 from the safety of the cockpit. Just one passenger remained on board: one of the two odd-looking men from before. She walked over to where he stood by the open door.

'Must be serious,' she said placing a hand on his shoulder. 'They don't usually bring out the big guns unless the person they're after is a major target.' The man's tension forced her hand back. 'Stand back from the door, let the place quieten down. The military are always itching to use their damn weapons. I've seen innocents get caught up in their crossfire. It's almost like they have to shoot at something or they'll die of boredom. Wait here a moment.'

She walked back to the cockpit to check with the observation deck. The sound of the craft door sucking closed spun her back around. Her remaining passenger had his finger poised over the door's control panel.

'What the hell are you doing?' She stepped closer. 'Get away from there. Now.'

In the time it took her to blink once, the man was beside her. A flash of metal in his hand caught her eye; bile rose in her throat. Jenny had sensed something was off about him. She should have trusted her instincts.

'Who are you?' her voice barely a whisper now.

The man jammed one end of the metal rod into her back. 'Erect the force field around this craft, or I will hurt you. It's a matter of life and death.'

She tensed up against the pressure of the weapon on her skin. 'For who?'

'For you, for me.' He blinked and shook his head, almost as if he couldn't explain. 'The reasons are beyond your comprehension.'

Jenny drew on her experiences of transporting criminals back in the day. 'Who are you? Tell me why you're here.'

The man shoved her into the cockpit and her seat. 'I said erect the force field around this craft.'

'Why should I?' Her words sounded shaky, weak. She cleared her throat.

'Because I could snap your neck.' *Could,* not *will* snap. 'I need you to find a William Taggart for me.'

The name was not familiar. 'Who's William Taggart? What's this all about?'

He jabbed the rod into her spine again. 'Force field first.'

She knew her odds of survival would be better if she complied. The military personnel had no interest in her or her craft. They were only interested in Bob Harris— whoever he was. She could call the observation deck, but this man's reflexes were off the chart. She'd be dead before anyone made it to her in time.

Jenny pressed a button on her console. 'Done.'

'Find William Taggart.'

The man's cold tone made her shiver. 'Can you at least tell me where I should begin?'

'He was a passenger on the ship I just came from.'

The rod found her rib and she cried out. 'Okay, I'll help you, but please stop hurting me.'

The man reduced the pressure. 'I'm desperate to find him.'

The word "desperate" turned her around to meet the gaze of her assailant.

'What is he to you?' His eyes, a strange brown, were wild but fearful.

'Just find him.'

'I'll help you. Whatever you need.' It's what she'd been taught to say in a hostage situation.

Jenny scanned the ship's computer and found the name her kidnapper wanted. 'He's an ITF investigator. Heading to Sydney. Probably going to the Security Centre, I imagine. Will you let me go now?'

'No. I need you to take me there, but not now. Someone is working on getting us out of here.'

Jenny sat back with a sigh. The sergeant had promised her this would be a straight forward job. On the verge of adding a third strike to her record, she accepted this could be her last flight.

43

Narrowed military gazes flicked from one person in the line to the next. The craft door behind him sucked shut. A nervous Anton waited, hoping to create enough of a diversion to draw attention away from Stephen. But that was the easy part. Getting Stephen through the docking station's force field would be much trickier. He hadn't told his friend he wouldn't be going with him.

Stephen's fear from inside the craft manifested like a shiver down Anton's spine. His friend didn't trust many. Anton couldn't let him down.

A dozen military eyes scanned the faces in the queue. One set of eyes lingered on him for too long. He held his breath; adrenaline set his hands to shake. The military man looked him over, his interested gaze flicking between Anton and the person behind him. Anton rounded his shoulders and tried to look bored, hoping to look like less of a threat.

When the man's interest moved on, Anton straightened up with a sigh. His new artificial skin had passed the human test, but the identity chip would soon reveal who he was to the military. Colin Stipple: a road worker from Exilon 5 and of no interest to them. The pilot had only flagged one fake identity: Stephen's.

Anton drew in new air, in an attempt to slow his pounding pulse. At the top of the line, the attendant motioned him forward. Anton placed his left thumb on the DPad. The name that flashed up sent the military into frenzied overdrive. *Bob Harris.*

He'd mixed up the chips.

Strong arms grabbed him and tried to force him to the ground. Anton stumbled and the military tightened their hold. His speed got him out of their constraints and to the doors to the rear of the dock, before they knew what had happened.

The air crackled with a new energy that nipped at Anton's skin. The static eliminator he carried in his pocket heated up. He rubbed away the sensation on his arm and scooped up a utility knife lying next to a collection of boxes near the exit. Anton crashed through the double doors, chased by ten military humans.

Down a long corridor, up three flights of stairs, and on the other side of the docking station, he found the right room. A sign on the door read: Observation Deck and Control Room. Sensing the confusion of his pursuers like a shiver, he knew he had a good lead on them. He burst into the room, shocking the people inside, and quickly wedged the door shut from the inside. He counted twelve humans; not so many that he couldn't deal with them. None of them carried weapons.

That was a start.

Screens ahead of him showed images of the docking station he'd just left and the craft he needed to get through the security force field.

A young male in uniform stared at him with a mix of curiosity and shock. *A good a place to start as any.* The military would be here soon.

Anton shot over to the young male and looped an arm around his neck. With the tip of the utility knife, he prodded the young man's neck.

'Drop the force field around this station,' he said.

An older man stepped forward. 'Who do you think you are, coming in here and threatening my staff? Let the young lad go before you get into serious trouble.'

'I'm in charge now.' Anton snarled. 'And I *said* drop the force field.' The young man tensed up beneath the knife.

'This is my station,' said the man in charge. 'Now drop the knife and we'll forget this ever happened.'

But Anton couldn't leave.

He needed to show them he was a threat. Nicking the young man's neck, he swapped him out for a female. Anton threatened her with the same knife. Gasps filled the room, and he knew it was his speed that had surprised them.

'What the hell are you?' said the man in charge.

'That craft.' Anton nodded towards the viewing screen showing Dock 10. 'It needs to leave. Drop the force field.'

'Why would I help you? You're threatening my staff.'

'Because I could kill you all before you had time to move.'

The man hesitated. Anton had already shown them he was no ordinary threat.

The leader shouted over to the communications operative. 'Drop the force field.' The operative moved to the nearest control panel and manually shut off the field.

He then nodded at the screen. 'What's on that craft that's so damned important to you, anyway?'

Genesis Code

Anton smiled. 'You have no idea.'

'If anything happens to the pilot, you'll wish things played out differently today. I promise you that.'

A man wearing a uniform dripping in accolades peered out from behind the man in charge. 'You won't get away with this, you know.' He wagged his finger at Anton. 'You are trapped here, you fool. You won't last two minutes when my men get here.'

Anton ignored the threat and spoke to the leader. 'Contact the craft and tell them they can leave.'

With a nod at the communications operative, who then muttered a few words into a microphone, the craft rose and exited Dock 10 with Stephen on board. Anton released a soft sigh. Right on time, the military broke down the door. He shot over to his first victim. The young man covered his neck with his hand. Anton chuckled at the move. In some small way, he understood Stephen's obsession with Ben, but not his aversion to all other humans.

'What are you?' asked the young man.

'If I knew that, human, I wouldn't be here.'

A sudden discharge of electricity set Anton's teeth on edge. He slumped to the ground as the military surrounded him.

44

An exhausted Bill slogged through the public entrance of the Earth Security Centre and headed for the turbo lift at the far end of the foyer. He side-stepped the crowds of eager recruits gathered to hear the history of the building from trained guides. The dazzling glass ceiling panels caused him to squint. Its reflective pigmentation transformed the grey world outside into a blue wonder—another pretty lie that masked the problems on this planet. But the only thing on his mind that day was his debrief.

For things to go his way, he needed to command Gilchrist from the outset. Lose control and respect, and Gilchrist would surely stick him on traffic duty. If he could convince her that the mission could be salvaged, she might keep him on as lead investigator.

A blonde woman walking his way caught his eye. Her guarded expression concerned Bill enough that he raised his defences. A year away was long enough for him to forget this planet, but not his enemies. Had Larry Hunt got wind of his return? Was she a distraction?

Bill stared at her, not seeing the usual distraction techniques—a flirty smile or a lingering look. Maybe it was her hurried step or the trace of fear on her face. Or maybe he'd lost his edge and couldn't tell anymore.

He continued to watch the woman with green eyes and pale skin. Then she looked up. Her eyes widened. That's when he caught a flash of a warning as she passed.

He shook away the moment and arrived at the turbo lift that took him down to Level Seven and the boardroom. With clenched hands, Bill followed Gilchrist's personal assistant inside the boardroom. He had prepared for a full board member turnout that included Deighton. But three people had shown up, not the ten or more he'd expected to see. Gilchrist sat at the top of the long table, while Suzanne Brett and Simon Shaw, his boss from the ITF London office, sat on either side of her.

As if Gilchrist had read his thoughts, she said, 'There won't be anyone else joining us. This is a closed debriefing. The board members will be informed in due course about the outcome of today's meeting.' She gestured to a seat at the other end of the table.

Bill took it, glad for the distance from the others. But he wondered why Deighton had not come.

Gilchrist clasped her hands on the table. 'Let's begin. We've received your files from both meetings and reviewed the evidence. But now I would like to hear your version of events.'

Bill settled his nerves a little before launching into the rehearsed details. He recounted his orders to the military personnel not to approach the target on week one. He kept the anger out of his voice as he explained how their advances after the first meeting had jeopardised the investigation. He mentioned Caldwell and Page by name and their subsequent chase of the alien to the New Victoria Maglev station. What he didn't mention was his own pursuit. Page and Caldwell had already filled Gilchrist in on the detail, but neither knew he had come face-to-face with the Indigene called Stephen. He would keep it that way.

The trio sat in silence. Brett and Shaw nodded. Only Gilchrist asked the occasional question to clarify. Were Brett and Shaw there for show, or as witnesses? After fifteen minutes, he summarised making sure to highlight the progress made.

'Where do you think we should go from here?' said Gilchrist.

Bill had given it a lot of thought on the journey back to Earth. 'It's likely the Indigene won't risk surfacing again for some time. I suggest we wait.'

Gilchrist arched a brow. 'Wait?'

'Yes. A week, a month, and track them when they finally resurface.'

'Is that it?'

'No. My team and I have a list of people on Exilon 5 who've made inadvertent contact with the Indigenes before this. My plan is to talk to them and get a different angle on our investigations. It also appears the Indigenes prefer to hunt at night and have surfaced in locations we are familiar with.' The video with Dr Jameson came to mind. 'It wouldn't take much effort to set up vigils in the wastelands between the cities, to catch them there.'

He knew the solutions he'd offered were weak, but he'd suggest anything to get back to Exilon 5. It was his best shot at finding Isla.

Gilchrist rested a finger on her lips 'You propose some interesting solutions. But I'm not sure we have the time, or personnel, to waste on mere chances we *might* find the aliens.'

To his disappointment, Shaw and Brett nodded. He assumed that at least Simon Shaw, his ITF boss, would back him. Bill scrambled to defend his position.

'Look, whatever you decide, I want to stay on this investigation.'

Gilchrist leaned forward. 'It's not about what you want, Bill. It's about what's best for this mission.'

His thinly veiled calm slipped away. 'With all due respect, Ms Gilchrist, I am what's best for this mission. And you can tell Deighton I said that. Just give me another chance. Let me pick my team this time and—'

'There was nothing wrong with your team. Your poor handling of the situation led to the breakdown of communication. Mr Deighton is aware of your abilities, but he doesn't like failure, not when it relates to a threat of this magnitude. We must get the situation under control.'

Bill said nothing; outbursts got good investigators assigned to traffic duty.

'Thank you, Bill.' Gilchrist stood. 'We'll take your points under consideration. We'll be in touch as soon as we know how to progress.' She smiled, but her words lacked sincerity. 'Head down to the docking station when you're ready. Grab the next craft to your accommodation here on Earth.'

'Where am I going?'

'Washington. Mr Deighton has asked that you stay close to headquarters. He may need to call you in at short notice.'

Bill stood to leave. He glanced at Simon Shaw, who refused to be a man and look him in the eye.

Back in the turbo lift he punched the wall. Gilchrist didn't even let him defend his place on the mission.

At least he wasn't being fired. When the heat died down a little, he would try to talk his way back on to the investigation and convince Deighton of his value.

Bullshit, Taggart. You fucked up. This is the end.

45

An epiphany hit Jenny as her craft lifted high into the skies with her illegal passenger on board. She was done with living in fear. She was done with the authorities telling her what to do, how to live. So what if her actions led to dismissal? Starting from the bottom wasn't the end of the world. Eleanor had done it, she could too.

But the thought of losing a steady wage terrified her as the vessel hurtled back towards Earth, over the docking station in Sydney. Could she start again? Her life recently had been one long drawn-out drama. Deighton had it in for her. So did Gilchrist. Maybe she should restart her independent business and become her own boss again.

The stranger in the seat next to her looked ahead. His posture was stiff. The wide-eyed look told her his life was in tatters, like hers would be soon.

'What happened to you?' she asked him.

The stranger blinked once, moving what looked like a set of brown lenses in his eyes. His skin was a strange shade, varying in colour from face to neck. What had happened for him to disguise himself so heavily?

'Nothing that humans care about,' he snapped.

Humans. An odd choice of words. Her experience of transporting criminals had trained her to be cautious around dangerous types. But this man did not seem dangerous.

'Try me.'

The man looked at her. 'Your government. My planet. It wants us gone.'

She didn't understand. 'What are you, nomads?' That might explain the strange outfit. She'd heard of native communities living off grid on Exilon 5 and that the government was forcing them to be part of the system.

'Something like that.'

'Why do you need to speak with this William Taggart?'

'I just do.' His words came out sharp.

Her training also taught her when not to push.

The on-board computer beeped once signalling their approach to the landing plate. She prepared herself for the last few miles.

'This part gets a little rough.'

The man settled into the seat beside her and closed his eyes. He'd abandoned his weapon, much to her relief.

Their speed increased then the vessel jerked hard as reverse magnetic polarisation brought it to a stop above the plate. Jenny flicked the controls back to her and steered to the disembarkation site. ITF military buzzed around like they had in HJA, but not as intense. In fact, the military appeared to be winding down efforts.

'They don't appear too interested in us. Seems like your friend was their main target.'

The fire in the man's eyes dulled. Softly, he said, 'It would seem so.'

Jenny unhooked herself from her chair. The man did the same and followed her over to the doors. 'Will you be okay from here?'

He nodded. 'I'm sorry for forcing you to take me here. I had no choice.'

'I can see that.' She smiled at him but got a deep frown in return. Something was off about him. She had never been to Exilon 5 before or read much on the pockets of society that didn't follow rules.

'Is my government after you because you refuse to join society?'

The man smiled sadly. 'No. It's after my kind because we tried to.'

His reply confused her. With a shake of her head she opened the door, accepting it might be the only reply she'd get. 'If they ask you why you're here, tell them you have a friend at a termination clinic who's about to end their life. They let the rules slide for compassionate travel.'

The man touched the rim of his Stetson. 'Goodbye, Captain.'

'Wait, what's your name?'

The man turned, gave her a short nod and walked on. Within seconds, an attendant jumped on him and thrust a DPad in his face. She watched, heart in mouth, while her illegal passenger pressed his thumb to the screen. A short conversation ensued that looked friendly enough. Jenny huffed out a breath when the attendant gestured for the man to pass. The attendant switched his narrowed gaze to her stood by her open craft door.

Jenny straightened up and prepared for his arrival. She would confirm her passenger's fake story, because sometimes people needed strangers to stick up for them.

The attendant stopped before her, DPad in hand.

'What is the nature of your visit?'

Jenny pulled in new air and prepared to lie for a man she didn't know. A lie that would be the final strike against her.

46

Daphne dismissed Shaw and Brett the second Bill Taggart stepped through the turbo lift door. Her use of the investigator wasn't personal. She needed a way to distract Deighton from whatever plans he was attempting to put into motion—plans he still hadn't trusted her with. Deighton had an unhealthy fixation with Taggart's wife, Isla. Sending Taggart to Washington would hopefully keep the CEO occupied, while Daphne figured out her next move in all of this.

She relocated from the boardroom to her private office and closed the door behind her. Taking a seat, she flicked the monitor over to the face of a sergeant.

'Well?'

'Yes, we have him in custody. We've transferred him to your secured facility in Washington.'

'Good work, Sergeant. Your superiors will hear about your team's efforts today.'

The sergeant smiled. 'Thank you, Ms Gilchrist.'

'Tell Deighton I'm on my way. Out.' Daphne severed the connection on her end and sat back in her leather chair.

Genesis Code

Taggart hadn't been to blame for the breakdown of the operation on Exilon 5. It had been Deighton's idea to send Caldwell in to stir things up. Bill was getting closer to the truth about the Indigenes and his wife. Military better used to guerrilla tactics than tact had been the logical choice to distract their rogue investigator from the real mission: to drive the Indigenes out of their hiding places. And that's what Taggart and his team had done.

But neither she nor Deighton had prepared for one of them to find his way to Earth.

☼

Within the hour, Daphne arrived in Washington on a specially chartered craft. She crossed the foyer of the World Government headquarters on her way to the restricted-use turbo lift located behind the reception desk.

The lift took seconds to reach the secret levels containing several bunkers. The door opened to reveal three weapon-carrying officers patrolling the bunker security area. While the added firepower wasn't necessary with such top line security, a paranoid Charles Deighton had insisted upon it. His access to the World Government board members made him more powerful than most realised.

And that's what worried her.

The system scanned both of Daphne's chips and sampled and cross-referenced her DNA against the database copy. The dual referencing protected the facility against facial manipulation—a popular procedure in the black market.

Daphne continued to the door at the end of the corridor. She entered the room to find Charles Deighton waiting inside, along with Tom Billings, the overseer for security matters in the World Government. Ahead of her was a flexible membrane containment unit holding a male adult Indigene.

'Ah, Daphne. I see you made it.' Deighton greeted her as if they were old friends, kissing her on both cheeks. 'So good to see you.' The words dripped off the old man's tongue like honey.

Daphne performed for her boss. 'Charles! I hope you haven't started without me. What's with all the extra security measures outside?'

'I thought you might comment on that.' He laughed a throaty cackle and nodded towards the unit where the captured Indigene watched the trio in silence. 'Can't be too careful. You never know who's trying to discover our secrets. Daphne, you remember Tom Billings? He's here to witness proceedings.'

'Ms Gilchrist.' Daphne gave him a quick nod, then turned her attention to the Indigene.

'I've just had a meeting with Bill Taggart.'

'Who?'

'The investigator. He's back on Earth. I've ordered him to this neck of the woods. I thought you'd like to keep an eye on him.'

But Deighton wasn't listening. 'Looks like we've captured a second generation, given his young age. I'm not sure we can lay claim to a product of two Indigenes.' His brows lifted and his mouth down-turned. 'But we've certainly set evolution in motion.'

Daphne moved closer to Deighton, hoping to learn more about his plans. 'What's to be done with this one?'

'This is the perfect time to begin the experiments again. We learned nothing new from the child Indigene before it died. And clearly their race has evolved since we placed them on Exilon 5. This is a rare opportunity to perfect evolution.'

'Evolution?' She kept her tone light. 'What are you suggesting?'

Deighton waved his hand at her—a sign he was done with the topic. 'Billings, you got here before me. Has he said anything?'

'Just grunts,' said the security overseer. 'He's refusing to cooperate.'

'I'm in no hurry,' said Deighton.

'For what?'

Deighton ignored her. Daphne turned her attention to the Indigene. Maybe he could tell her the story her boss was unwilling to share.

47

Laura almost dropped her handbag when she saw Bill Taggart walking towards her in the public section of the ESC. Gilchrist must have called him in. Was the investigation on Exilon 5 over?

Gilchrist had told her to be a team player. Her thoughts shot to the letters and their secret words, hidden in her apartment. She could be one.

Pushing down her nerves, Laura flashed the investigator a warning look. But all Bill Taggart did was respond with a tight nod before walking to the turbo lift. She searched for the roving cameras she knew operated in this part of the ESC. But the place was too packed with people for her to find them. Quickening her pace, she exited the building.

Laura didn't know how long her fists had been clenched by her sides. She unfurled them and shook out her fear at what was to come. Haymarket wasn't far from the ESC, but her shock at seeing the investigator had slowed her walk. It wasn't until she'd reached the outer door to her block that she heard movement behind her.

The grey skies and dark streets added to her fear.

She drew on her limited strength to not turn around. Instead, she fumbled around in her bag for an object that could double up as a weapon.

Groping for anything weapon-like, she calculated the time she'd need to activate the lock on the outer door. It would take her thumbprint to open it, but the delay would give the advantage back to her pursuer. Her skin tingled, as though the person was to near.

Damn, nothing in my bag. Her racing mind scrambled for a plan B; her body braced for an attack from her pursuer.

She turned partially, stopping when a cold hand touched her shoulder.

Her voice shook. 'Don't try anything. I'm armed and dangerous.'

Gathering up her remaining courage, she turned around. A gasp caught in her throat when she saw who stood inches from her face.

'Wh... What do you want from me?' The Indigene, named as Stephen in her files, stood before her. His face was covered by the rim of a Stetson, but it was definitely him.

The Indigene, taller than she'd expected, loomed over her. 'I wouldn't be here if I had another choice. I saw you acknowledge Bill Taggart just now. Please, I need to speak with him urgently. Can you help me?'

48

Bill stepped outside, into the dull Sydney afternoon, and fixed his gel mask in place. His feelings about Earth hit him like a punch to the gut, coating every thought with black despair and regret. He tried to shake off the painful reasons he hadn't wanted to return. One in particular. With every step, his thoughts blackened and made him second-guess his decisions—even the good ones.

The congested streets filled with despondent people added to his pessimism. A better life existed beyond this one, with sunshine and the promise of a fresh start. But none of that would happen while the Indigenes existed. His anger lashed out at his wounded heart, reopening old scars he thought he'd sealed for good. Bill tugged at the edge of his mask.

Just pull it off. End it now.

The dead gazes of the crowd watched him, as though they were willing him to end his miserable life. But their lack of emotion stopped the tugging. He was angry. He had passion—even hope. With fight still in him he would not give up.

Bill quickened his pace on his way to the docking

station at Sydney's harbour front. The sound of footfall behind him—faster than his—put him on high alert. His hands shook from the shot of new adrenaline coursing through him. He kept his eyes forward.

It could only be one of Larry Hunt's henchmen—the powerful businessman Bill had helped to put away. Maybe Hunt's business with Bill wasn't over. He sped up, keen to put distance between him and his pursuer. He didn't want to shake them, just make them follow.

Bill crossed the street, toying between making a run for it or confronting his pursers. But his thoughts, aggravated by fear, had lost their usual clarity. So he kept going, weaving in and out of the crowds on the busy thoroughfare.

His weak plan amounted to luring his pursuers away to somewhere private. After that, he had no idea what to do. He stayed on the street that would lead him to the area known as the Rocks. His mind raced like his pulse as he tried to figure a way out of this mess.

An opportunity presented itself at a road junction. Bill took the road heading west and slowed down for his follower. Confident they'd taken the same route he ducked into a nearby alleyway and hid behind crates stacked outside an unused replication terminal. He watched for the feet of his potential assailants. When only one set passed by, he made his move.

He froze when he saw who it was, but forced his shock to one side. Grabbing the woman from behind, he spun her around and closed one hand around her throat. Her head made a dull thudding sound when he slammed her against the wall.

'Who are you?' The young woman's eyes were squeezed shut. He'd seen her earlier in the foyer of the ESC. She opened her eyes. The terror in them loosened his grip on her throat, but he didn't let go. 'I said who are you? Why are you following me?'

She curled her fingers around his arm. 'Please, you're hurting me!'

'Tell me who you are. I saw you at the Security Centre earlier. I want to know why you're following me. Do you work for Hunt?'

'I don't know anyone called Hunt.' The woman coughed. 'My name is Laura O'Halloran. Please, let me go.'

Seeing only fear, Bill dropped his hand. Laura rubbed her neck and coughed again.

He stepped away from her, embarrassed by his heavy-handedness; her slender frame made her no match for his strength. But he remained on alert. 'Who do you work for?'

Laura coughed a third time. 'I work for the Earth Security Centre. I just needed to talk to you for a moment.'

He tipped his chin at her. 'Prove it.'

'I don't have any way of proving it to you. Unless you have a chip-scanner handy?'

Bill shook his head.

Laura showed him the uniform she wore under her coat. 'They don't give these out to just anyone.' She pointed to the security tags sewn onto the shoulders of her jacket.

Bill tilted one tag to reveal a special code hidden inside the hologram. The code changed hourly, making the security tags near impossible to replicate. It looked real enough. 'You should really think twice about sneaking up on people. I could have killed you.'

'I'll try to remember that for the future.'

'What do you want to talk to me about?'

'Your most recent investigation on Exilon 5.'

Bill's gaze narrowed. 'Why?'

'I've seen information that directly relates to your current case. I also promised someone I would find you and ask for your help.'

'Who? For what exactly?'

Laura looked around. 'I can't say here. Please come with me. I'm taking a risk just by being here. You need to trust me.'

In all his years working for the World Government, not once had anyone asked for his help. He'd been asked *to* help: head up missions, profile criminals, track wanted felons. If this turned out to be a trick, Bill would pay for his trust. But he sensed no malice in the woman's tone, only warmth and compassion. It had been a long time since he'd cared about another's cause.

'I don't know why, but you have my attention, lady. Where are we going?'

'Back to my apartment.'

49

It took less than fifteen minutes to reach a block of apartments in the Haymarket area. Bill kept up his guard as he followed Laura, but he also kept his mind open. He had no reason to trust this woman. So why was he here?

Simple. Curiosity.

He followed her up the stairs to her apartment door. Laura opened it and he stepped inside. She closed the door quickly—to stop him from changing his mind, probably.

The size of her apartment caught his attention that was generous for Earth accommodation. 'How big is this place?'

'Big enough to have a separate bedroom, if that's what you mean,' she said.

He let out a low whistle. 'I've only read about apartments this size on Earth. You can get hold of these easy on Exilon 5, you know. You must be doing well to get this, considering you live alone.'

'I do okay. Job perk, I guess.'

Time for extra security. Bill pulled a sound interrupter out of his pocket, shaped like a rolling dice. He attached it magnetically to the front of her Light Box's hardware unit.

'What's that?' she asked.

'A sound interrupter. So we can talk in private.'

The idea seemed to put her at ease.

'I brought you here to meet someone. Before I bring him out, though, I need you to keep an open mind.'

'An open mind, for what?'

She called out to the empty space. 'It's just me, and I've brought Bill Taggart.'

Bill tensed as the bedroom door creaked open.

A tall figure dressed in a blue suit emerged from the darkened room and took a single step towards them. Bill's body went stiff. His mind flew into overdrive.

'Hello,' said the figure. He was someone Bill would never forget. 'We've met already but I would like to formally introduce myself. My name is Stephen.'

Bill stumbled away from the Indigene standing a foot away from him. His back hit the door with a thud. Laura was close by and he reached for her.

'Laura, I need you to come to me. *Now.* You have no idea how dangerous this Indigene is.'

She took a tentative step towards him, but not in fear. It was as if she were trying to reassure Bill of something.

'He's not dangerous, Bill.'

'Of course he is. He... They killed my...' He couldn't say it. Saying it would make it true.

She took another step forward. 'Your wife?'

Bill's heart hardened. 'What the hell do you know about that?'

'I'm sorry,' Laura said in a calm voice. But her trembling hands said she was anything but. 'I have information and I know you're looking for answers. I need you to understand the Indigenes are not to blame.'

It had to be them. Isla had disappeared while on Exilon 5. 'Who else could it be?' Bill kept his eyes fixed on Stephen, in case he made a move. He swiped at Laura again hoping to catch her arm, but she stayed out of his reach.

'The government, Bill. It's been them all along. Deighton was responsible for Isla's disappearance. The board members ordered her to be killed.'

He dropped his arm and straightened up. Shock widened his eyes. 'What?'

'I'm sorry to tell you this way, but the World Government and the ESC are involved in bad things. Isla got too close to the truth. She got close to the Indigenes and tried to help them.'

'Yes, and the Indigenes turned on her.' He glared at Stephen who had his head lowered, but not his eyes.

'No.' Laura stood between them and placed her hand on Bill's chest. Her touch softened the edges of his rage. 'Listen to me. It wasn't the Indigenes. They had nothing to do with her disappearance. It was Deighton and Gilchrist. She's dead.'

Bill shook his head at her. 'You're lying. If she was dead, they would have told me. Where did you get this information from?'

'Files about the investigation. And letters.'

'Letters?'

Stephen moved suddenly; Bill snapped his attention back to him. He pushed Laura's hand away. But she remained where she was, acting like a buffer between them.

She pleaded with the Indigene. 'Please, I know it's difficult being here with us.'

Stephen lifted his head, eyes on Bill. 'I need to know why you were investigating us. Tell me and I will

Genesis Code

leave.'

'Please, your fight is not in this apartment. It's not with me or the investigator.' Laura grabbed Stephen's arm, like he was an ally—a move that turned Bill's stomach. 'We are all caught up in the government's drama. We are seeking answers, like you. We are fighting for the same thing.'

'Let him go, Laura.' Bill made a tight fist. 'If he wants a fight, I'll give him one.'

'Not until he understands what he is.' She looked at Stephen. 'If you still want to fight us after what I tell you, then go ahead. We don't deserve your forgiveness.'

Bill tensed at her invitation. 'You don't know what you're saying. You have no idea what he's capable of.'

'I know everything about him. His origin, his creation.'

Both he and Stephen stared at Laura.

'His creation?' Bill shook his head. 'What are you talking about? What do you know?'

'If you're going to help each other, you must know everything about him, including where he came from. You have to know what he is. Are you ready for that?'

'Tell me, what is he?' said Bill.

Stephen's stance remained rigid. His wild eyes fixed on Laura, also waiting for her answer.

Her gaze flicked from Stephen to Bill. 'He's human.'

Her words hung in the air.

Bill unclenched his fists. 'He's *what?*'

'Human,' Laura repeated.

'Yes, I know I am,' said Stephen. 'This is not news to me. But why are you also called "human"?'

Bill couldn't believe what he was hearing. He grabbed her arm and shook it. 'Where did you get this information from? How do you know this?'

To her credit Laura kept calm. 'I've recently seen information that I wasn't supposed to know. Trust me I'm not making this up.'

Bill released her and stared ahead of him. None of this made sense. He looked up at the two before him. A more urgent thought entered his mind.

'How many visitors are you permitted to have?' he said.

'What?'

'How many visitors. Think.'

Laura shook her head, confused. 'I don't know. I rarely have any. Why does that matter?'

He shook her arm again. 'How many does this block allow?'

She thought it over. Then her face fell. 'Crap. Only one...'

Bill raced over to the Light Box's hardware control unit and opened a panel at the back. He removed a small disruption device from his pocket and placed it beside the sound interrupter he'd attached upon his arrival. He re-routed the Light Box signal through the disruption device.

'Do you know if they're monitoring your apartment?'

'I... don't know.' Laura stared blankly at the door. 'Will they check?'

'It's likely. This disruption device confuses the Light Box sensors. By re-routing the signal through it, we can predetermine the number of signatures it will detect. It should be picking up just two. But they've probably already detected the three of us. I'd be surprised if they didn't send a team out to check the anomaly.'

Laura looked shocked. 'What do we do?'

'We need to cut our numbers by one. Then I'll

remove both devices before they see them. When I do, there can only be two of us here.' Bill thought of an idea and spoke to Stephen. 'Can you do that fast blurry thing you do?'

Stephen nodded. 'Yes, that should work.' He explained to Laura who looked confused. 'I can move at a speed that renders my form invisible to the human eye. It should fool the sensors long enough for them to not detect my presence.'

'They'll be here shortly.' Bill looked Laura over. Her purple uniform peeked out from under her coat. 'Change out of *that* and into something more casual. Then follow my lead.'

☼

Five minutes later, there was a sharp rap on the door. Stephen took his cue and disappeared into a blurry haze right, before their eyes. Laura gasped then forced her eyes to the door. Bill removed both the signal disruptor and sound interruption device. He hoped the sensors could no longer detect Stephen.

Grabbing hold of a casually dressed Laura, he kissed her on the mouth. She went limp for a second before she tensed up. He held her tightly—probably a little too tight—as he jerked the door open. Two officers stood in the hallway, one male and one female. Both carried Impulse Tasers and Buzz Guns in their hip holsters; Bill noticed their hands were poised over the latter and deadlier of the weapons. Neither officer introduced themselves.

'We have reason to believe you've violated the building safety code,' said the male officer. 'Our sensors register a third person in the apartment. This is a serious offence and punishable by law.'

Bill looped his arm round Laura's shoulders and pulled her even closer. Both her warmth and the apple scent wafting up from her hair did little to ease his tension. 'I'm sorry, officers. That's entirely my fault. You see, it's our anniversary, and I only have two hours with this gorgeous woman before I have to go back to work.' He stroked Laura's hair. She smiled and laid her head on his chest.

The female officer narrowed her gaze at Bill. 'What career line are you in?'

'Shipping. I'm a pilot.'

'Where do you work out of?'

'Sydney, mainly.'

'And what about you?' She turned towards Laura.

Laura hesitated. Sensing her discomfort, Bill gently pushed her away. 'Is this interrogation really necessary? As you can see, it's just us here.'

'Rules are rules,' said the male officer. 'I'm afraid we're going to have to check for ourselves.'

They both stood back from the door and allowed the officers to enter. 'As you wish. You're free to check.'

A nervous Bill scanned the room, but he couldn't see Stephen anywhere. Damn, he was good.

The officers carried out a sweep of the apartment, but couldn't find a third person. The female officer followed up with an independent scan, which still registered just two signatures, besides their own.

'All clear,' she announced warily to her partner. Turning to Bill and Laura she asked, 'This doesn't account for the third person you registered ten minutes ago. Care to explain?'

'I'm so sorry. That was my fault.' Laura laughed and touched a hand to her heart. 'I'd arranged a surprise for my boyfriend. You see, the guy came to install a virtual package upgrade for the Light Box. You know the one where you can holiday in any part of the world without having to leave your armchair?' She shook her head. 'He's addicted to his virtual world. I mean, who isn't, these days?' The male officer mumbled in agreement. 'Well, the guy was supposed to finish up earlier, but got delayed. Then this idiot came home earlier than planned.'

Bill shrugged his shoulders at the officers in a what-can-you-do way.

'Oh, I've heard about that one. Is it any good?' said the male officer.

'I don't know yet. We were planning a quick trip to Bali before you called.' Bill winked at him. 'Sun, sex and margaritas.'

The male officer smiled. His gaze lingered on Laura a little too long. Bill grabbed her hand and gave it a squeeze.

'One last thing,' said the female officer. 'We need to scan your identity chips. For the record, you understand.'

'Is that really necessary? I rarely get time off, these days. I'm on the clock.' Bill sighed hoping to appeal to the male officer's better nature. 'You know how it is, with the crazy work schedules. It's tough enough to get time off at all. Am I right?'

The male officer nodded and laughed. 'I'm just surprised you have the energy. All I want to do is sleep during my free time.' His tone turned serious. 'Everything seems to be in order here. Enjoy your evening.' He pushed his reluctant partner out of the apartment.

As soon as Laura closed the door, Bill removed the disruption device from his pocket and channelled the Light Box signal through it once more. Then he placed the sound interrupter on the front panel again.

His heart thumped too fast. 'That was way too close for comfort. We should be okay for the next two hours. But then they'll expect me to leave.' He spoke to the empty room. 'You can come out now, Stephen.' Turning to Laura he said, 'And you need to start from the beginning.'

50

Two hours ago, Anton had woken up inside a containment unit that heaved with energy. The room smelled like cold and rock, hinting that he was deep beneath the surface. The smooth and rendered walls reminded him of a fancier space than District Three. He hoped his sacrifice had been for something, and that Stephen had not succumbed to the same fate as him.

The Gilchrist woman stood in the middle of the room next to a man called Charles and another man, younger than the pair.

'What a magnificent specimen he is,' she said.

Anton watched all three from his prison. They carried no weapons. If he could escape his containment unit he could probably overpower them. Charles looked to be around Pierre's age, but less agile than the elder. He reached for the invisible barrier surrounding his prison, certain the humans did not know about his high tolerance for pain. The barrier sparked, stinging the tips of his fingers. Grunting, he yanked his hand back.

'The unit is electrically charged,' said Charles. 'Apparently, electricity only slows you down. We're not sure why it doesn't kill you.'

Anton straightened up. Watched. Waited.

'The Indigenes are quick learners,' said Gilchrist to Charles. 'The replica identity chip used to gain access to the passenger ship was virtually identical to an original, right down to the wiring.' Her curious, but also fearful, gaze flicked to Anton. 'I wonder if this second generation is cognitively more advanced than our original creations.'

Anton rushed the barrier. The electricity stung him again and he yowled. His foot slipped, but he righted himself before he fell.

'Look at him! See how he moves like that?' said an excited Charles. 'Their species was much more primitive in the beginning. Closer to our design, really. Time has allowed their abilities to develop naturally, and in such a short space of time, too. How advanced will the next generation be, I wonder?'

A strange, quiet, mood filled the room. The female came closer to his cage. Anton dropped to all fours—his hunting stance.

Gilchrist's eyes grew large and she stopped.

Anton reached out for their thoughts, but the barrier —the electricity—dulled his abilities.

'See what he just did? That hunting stance?' said Charles pointing. 'They didn't do that when we first created them. Primitive animals. Brutes. Couldn't even talk. But they've adapted fast to their new terrain, to their new lives.' He clasped his hands behind his back, pondering something. 'Now, if we can replicate their abilities and apply it to our design, we can remove all uncertainties about our future.'

Gilchrist showed her disagreement through a shiver.

Two armed officers entered the room. Anton dropped to a protective crouch when they neared his prison.

Gilchrist came closer to the containment unit, while both officers shadowed her. She'd shaken off her earlier shock at what he could do. This close, Anton could detect some feelings from her. Her fear, in particular, chilled him, but it was at odds with the confident image she portrayed. Anton sensed it wasn't him she feared.

With a tight smile she said, 'We're not here to hurt you. Think of us as your friends.' She touched a hand to her chest. 'My name is Daphne. I'd like to call you something other than Indigene.'

She waited for his answer. Charles muttered in an excited way. Anton said nothing.

'Not interested in talking?' She dropped the pretence and a new chill entered her friendly tone.

'Perhaps he can't communicate in the same way we can,' said Billings.

'The Indigenes can learn languages.' A puzzled look crossed her face. 'In fact, I'm surprised they haven't created their own by now.'

'What if they have?' said Billings. 'What if they can communicate without words?'

Gilchrist raised an eyebrow.

Even without his full range of skills Anton sensed her desire to be in charge. She also thrived on order. But in her arrogance, she'd missed the point Billings had been astute enough to make.

Her friendly act disappeared. 'You can drop the charade now because I'm not buying it. I can keep calling you Species 31 or Indigene, but I would rather call you by your real name.'

His silence kept him from the truth of why he was here. 'My name is Anton.'

'Anton!' Charles clapped at the back of the room.

'What a human name. Not surprising, I suppose, considering what stock you came from.'

Anton straightened up. 'What do you mean?'

Charles squealed. 'Did you see how fast he just moved there? Marvellous.'

It wasn't the first time the hairs on the back of Anton's neck had stood up. The humans had been looking for Bob Harris. They'd been expecting him, which meant the original Bob Harris must have reported an anomaly with his chip. What bothered him now was the why. Why was Anton here? He worried Stephen was in a similar containment unit, being quizzed in the same way.

But they had yet to mention him by name, real or false. The pilot had only flagged one alias on board—his.

'By the way *Bob Harris*, your use of the chips was very clever. I assume you had an accomplice?' said Gilchrist.

Anton released a quiet breath. They were fishing for information. That meant Stephen must be safe.

He shook his head. 'The human who owned it was careless with his identity chip.'

Gilchrist frowned. 'Why were you in such a hurry to get out of Dock 10 then? Our records show Colin Stipple illegally commandeered the flight out with one of our best pilots on board. Who is he to you?'

'Nobody. A distraction.' How the lies flowed in the face of danger.

'You went to a lot of trouble to create the distraction. What sob story did he give you?'

'A dying relative. A termination clinic.' He shrugged. 'It's the truth.'

An hour ago, Stephen had passed the lie on to him telepathically. He hadn't sensed him close enough to do it. Their heightened fear must have extended their ability to communicate over distance.

Gilchrist laughed once. 'And I don't believe you're that naive.'

His pulse thundered in his ears as he shrugged again. 'I figured you were on to me, so I used the human as a distraction. It almost worked, didn't it?'

'Not really. We were on to you from the moment you set foot on the passenger ship.'

Gilchrist pinned him with a cold hard stare. She was trying to read him: his facial expressions, the way he held his hands, how he stood. Anything that might reveal a hidden clue. While he had no history with these humans, he understood better why Stephen hated them, or why certain Indigenes targeted them for sport.

A smiling Gilchrist applauded his performance. 'You are quite the little actor. Fortunately for you, when we spoke to the pilot she backed up your story. Still can't figure out why she lied.'

'I'm afraid it's no story. Colin Stipple needed my help. I used him to delay my capture.'

Charles stepped forward, hands behind his back. He'd been quiet for a while. Now, he was smiling at the ground. 'You still haven't answered an important question. Why are you here on Earth?'

'You first. What do you want from me?' Gilchrist came closer; his nervous energy spiked.

The old man chuckled, narrowing the gap between them. The uniformed officers shadowed him. Charles was clearly someone important.

'What don't we want from you?' he said. 'The list is too long.'

Gilchrist lifted her chin, to assert dominance in a room where she had none. 'Answer our questions first and we'll answer yours. We caught you trespassing on our planet. You are a risk to our national security. We have one missing identity chip on Exilon 5. But the chips don't work in new hosts. They're set to work with the biology of the original recipient. How long did it take to replicate both chips leave Exilon 5?'

That would remain his secret, for now.

'You attempted to destroy our race once. Now you tail us, trap us. I should be more concerned about you. Do you hold no responsibility for your actions?'

'You can only discard what you already own,' said Charles. 'To destroy is to assume it belongs to someone else.'

Anton shook his head at the old man's riddles. 'Are you going to kill me?' He'd gone into this mission knowing he might not return.

Both Gilchrist and Charles laughed at the same time.

'No, my dear boy,' said Charles. 'What a waste that would be. I have much better plans for you.'

'Care to share them?' said Anton.

'Of course not. Where would be the fun in that?'

51

Laura's shot at transferring to Exilon 5 was over. Gilchrist would make sure of that. But for the first time in her life she was doing something that mattered.

Two people stood in her apartment: one born in a brave new world, the other stuck in one that had to change. Both listened as she explained what she knew to the pair.

'The Indigenes have only been in existence for fifty years. They were created from humans who had lives here, in the beginning.'

'How is that possible?' snapped Stephen. What little control he appeared to have before slipped away. 'Our race has existed for thousands of years, not half a century. You are misinformed.'

Laura touched Stephen's arm; he jerked away from her. 'I wish I was. I couldn't believe it when I saw the data for myself.'

'Where did you get the data from?' said Bill.

'I received it from an anonymous tip. Anonymous, because I don't even know her name.' Laura attempted a laugh. 'There's a woman who works on Level Five, the place I was promoted to, about two weeks ago. Well, she approached me at lunch and handed me a micro file.'

'She didn't say anything?' said Bill. 'What was on it?'

'The data speaks for itself.'

'What did she say?'

'That maybe I'd do the right thing, maybe I wouldn't. But that she couldn't sit on this information any longer.'

Bill frowned. 'At least someone who works there has a conscience. Any idea what her connection might have been?'

'No idea. She wouldn't talk to me after that.'

'Not unexpected behaviour, given the circumstances.'

Laura felt Stephen's eyes on her.

'Wait,' he said, his voice cracked. 'Start from the beginning, please. I came to Earth because your species is still trying to eradicate ours. Why and how did we become another version of you?'

Bill's gaze flicked from Stephen to her. 'Yes, I'd like to know that too.'

Laura sat down. She knew she had to tell them everything, even about the experiments, but knowing and speaking about it were two different things.

Stephen and Bill stood at opposite ends of the sofa, looking uneasy.

She patted the vacant area beside her. 'Please, someone sit with me. You're both making me nervous.'

Bill perched on the edge of the arm-rest while Stephen remained standing.

'In the latter part of the twenty-first century,' she began, 'the World Government appeared to have known about the inherent risks to our planet. The overpopulation had become an issue, the biodiversity was unbalanced and extinction lists were growing at an unmanageable rate. It was what drove the initial investment in space travel.'

Bill nodded. 'Apart from the government's early indications, this is all well known.'

Laura continued. 'Well, as you know, their relentless search for a new exoplanet began shortly afterwards, and then they came across Exilon 5.'

'In 2076.'

'That's right. But what the books don't reveal is that the government in power at the time was digging up other facts isolated from this event. They discovered the planet could support life, but not their own because of incompatible gases. So they looked for other ways to make it happen.'

'Alter its composition?' said Stephen. His eyes were wider than looked comfortable.

'Not at the beginning. While the government worked to come up with a solution, they were secretly putting Plan B into effect. As far back as 2032, the government was carrying out genetic experiments on human test subjects.'

Bill frowned. 'There was an early twenty-first century condition known as hemeralopia that caused day-blindness. Specific cases mentioned it more recently, involving children with eyes that shone bright in the dark.'

'Yes, I read about it too,' said Laura. 'That was one of the early experiments they carried out on children. Tests were done, often without permission. Some were as young as four.'

Stephen's eyes widened further. 'Did these children have superior night vision?'

'Yes,' said Laura. 'They had exceptional vision in darker conditions, but their eyes were more sensitive in daytime light. Why?'

'You have just described the eyesight of every Indigene I know.'

The confirmation made Laura shiver, but this was only the beginning of her story.

'I'm sorry, Stephen,' she said. 'I know this is difficult for you to hear. But you need to know everything.'

52

Bill was buzzing. Yet he hadn't had a coffee all day.

'I'm having trouble understanding exactly where Stephen fits into this.'

Laura sighed. 'As I said, the genetic experiments were carried out long before the planet had even been discovered. From the files, it appears that around 2110, while engineers and ship designers were busy perfecting space travel, the World Government had almost perfected something of their own.' She glanced at Stephen.

Bill looked between the pair. 'Are you seriously telling us...?' He ran his fingers through his hair. They couldn't. They wouldn't. 'No.'

'Yes,' said Laura. 'They created a race that could survive on the planet in its original uninhabitable state. They'd given up hope of humans ever living there and without having discovered more exoplanets, they fell back on their contingency plan for the human race. In their mind, the Earth was beyond saving.'

The last piece slotted into place, and Bill's hate for the Indigenes slipped away. 'So not only did Deighton and the board members create a new breed of human, but they did it without permission?'

'Most likely.' Laura glanced at Stephen. 'He was designed to be a better version of us.'

'Shit.' Bill let out a breath. It all made sense. The last piece of the puzzle clicked into place. The videos he'd watched on board the ship; the young Indigene with the genetic makeup of a twelve-year-old boy. Except for the mutations to his appearance and how he breathed, the boy could have passed for human.

But something else about the story caught his attention. 'And what had they planned to do with the regular humans?'

Laura hesitated. 'The government was placing our future existence in the hands of this superhuman race. What remained of the human race would be wiped out.'

Bill knew the World Government was shady, but this stooped to a new level.

Stephen stepped forward, a move that surprised Bill. He'd almost forgotten about the man in the room who'd been unwittingly caught up in a war not of his making.

'How did we come into existence?' said Stephen. 'Where did my race come from exactly? Please, I need to know.'

Laura nodded. 'In the early days, scientists had advertised for human test subjects to join their gene-splicing and manipulation therapy programmes. It was funded by the World Government.'

'Another non-surprise,' said Bill.

'Some volunteered, but many didn't. Without enough test subjects, they resorted to taking people from the street. The tests succeeded at first, they said. But neither the splicing nor manipulation techniques worked well in those who had inherited genetic diseases from their parents. Their bodies successfully rejected the changes.

Genesis Code

'It was through trial and error that the scientists discovered that anomaly. Later on, when they trialled splicing in people of average intellect with clean DNA structures, the results improved slightly, but showed minimal differences between the before and after test subjects. It wasn't until they tested those with a superior IQ that the genetic splicing and manipulation worked perfectly with their genes. The work done also had a boosting effect on their brain's ability to learn. Take doctors, engineers and professors. Professions with a high IQ. The tests seemed to supercharge their skills somehow.'

Bill had always suspected there was something different, or special, about the indigenous race on Exilon 5. 'So, there really is a race of super-intelligent beings on Exilon 5?'

'You only have to look at Stephen to know that's the case.'

'What's your IQ, Stephen?' asked Bill.

'We don't use human measurements to define our intelligence, but if I was to compare it to your scale, it would be close to two hundred and seventy.'

Bill let out a low whistle. Stephen might still pose a threat, but all he saw before him was a man whose history had been torn to shreds. A man who fitted nowhere.

'So, Stephen is fully human?'

'Yes and no. Stephen is less than fifty years old. Am I right, Stephen?' The Indigene nodded. 'So, essentially he was the product of two superhumans. He's a true indigenous species of the planet. According to the files, those older than fifty would have lived as humans, since there have been no experiments for the last fifty years.'

Stephen gasped suddenly, alarming Bill. 'What is it?'

'Our oldest Central Council members are well over

fifty years old. Are you telling me they were once your kind of human?'

'I'm afraid that's probably the case,' said Laura.

The Indigene shook his head. 'But it's not possible. They have specific memories of being born, of growing up on the planet, and of a life before the one we have now. How can that be?'

'When the government created the early superhumans, it overwrote their memories with new ones. The scientists rewired the neural pathways so they'd forget their old lives. The government scientists created a new existence for the new race, so they'd adapt to the new planet. Because of your age, Stephen, your memories are real. Any recollections of your society earlier than fifty years ago are most likely false.'

One thing still confused Bill. 'Why is the government trying to kill the Indigenes if they are just like us?'

Laura pulled the band out of her hair and ruffled it. When she tucked it behind her ears, Bill could tell she was hoping for a break.

'Their motives appear to have been more innocent at the start,' she said. 'While putting all their hopes for survival into this new race, they accidentally stumbled upon a way to alter the gas composition on Exilon 5. When they realised the planet could house ordinary humans, they knew one race would be sacrificed for another. When the explosions happened, it wasn't just to terraform the planet; it was to destroy their creation. The files mentioned that neither race could discover the other.'

'We did more than survive.' The Indigene snarled. 'We adapted even further.'

'He's right,' said Laura. 'The first superhumans who relocated to the planet resembled us, but were more primitive in behaviour. Their skin was as sturdy as it is now, but their outward appearance was more like how you and I look.' She addressed Stephen. 'I imagine it was the years of living underground that altered your DNA and made your appearance what it is today.'

'Apparently,' said Stephen. 'But the toughened skin, how?'

Laura's rounded shoulders told Bill she had carried this truth for too long. He encouraged her with a touch on her shoulder, and felt her shaking through her clothes. 'I know this is a lot to explain, but please continue. We need to know everything.'

She nodded. 'The genetic manipulation involved experimentation with other species' DNA. Animals, mostly. Think of the toughened exterior of a rhinoceros, for example, or the night vision of a nocturnal animal, or the regenerative properties of a lizard. They tried various permutations to alter the human code so it would mimic the more interesting properties of some animals.'

A pacing Stephen asked, 'What do they plan to do with us?'

'I don't know. They can't carry out any more explosions on the surface, not with a few transferees already living on Exilon 5.'

He stopped pacing. 'What then?'

'I don't know.' She sighed. 'Look, I got no idea of how this would play out. All I can tell you about are the facts on the micro file.'

Bill glanced at a stressed-looking Stephen. 'Sorry for pushing you so hard, Laura. We both appreciate the effort you've made here. Do you still have the file?'

'Yes. I thought about getting rid of it, but for some insane reason I kept it around. It's yours if you want it.'

'This transfer you speak of,' said Stephen with a

frown. 'When did it begin?'

'Around twenty-five years ago,' said Bill. 'Why?'

'And when did it slow down? Far fewer of you have since settled on the planet.'

'I don't know exactly. A few years ago. Why?'

'Well, it seems to correlate with the extra attention paid to our young.' Bill assumed he was referring to the capture of one Indigene, from the videos. 'Could it be their plans have changed?'

'Anything's possible,' said Bill.

'So what do we do about it?' said Laura. 'Can we do anything?'

Bill had no idea. 'All I know is it's not safe for us to stay here. Laura, you need to come with me. Leave your apartment, your life behind.'

Her eyes grew large. 'What? No, I have a job. A career. I can't just leave it.'

'If they find out what you know, you won't live long enough to enjoy it.'

'You don't understand. I need to get on the transfer list to Exilon 5. I can't explain why. If I disappear now, I lose that chance.'

'I expect all future transfers will be placed on hold, anyway. There are more pressing issues at play here. You need to decide which side you're on.'

She stood. 'I'm on this side, of course. Wouldn't I be more useful to you if I was on the inside?'

Bill couldn't see how it would work. She'd be in too much danger.

'I must return to Exilon 5,' Stephen declared, breaking the tension. 'I need to tell the Indigenes what I've learned here. We have much more to fear than I'd first anticipated. We must be ready for when they come.'

Compassion replaced the anger that had consumed

Bill for so long. He'd had it all wrong. He'd been focusing on the wrong enemy. 'Of course. Getting you safely off this planet is our first priority.'

'I have another favour to ask of you, Bill,' said Stephen quietly. 'I didn't come here alone. My friend Anton was captured so I could escape. I need you to find out if he's still alive.'

'If the World Government has him, he may not be.'

'I'm prepared for that. But I would still like you to check.'

'I'll see what I can find out.'

'Thank you.'

Bill ran a hand through his hair. He stopped to touch the bump that remained after his near-suffocation.

'I'm sorry about your head,' said Stephen.

'How do you know about...?' He paused. 'That was you?'

Stephen gave a small smile. 'Actually, it was Anton who convinced me to help. I'm glad I did now.'

A yawn caught Bill by surprise. He'd been so tense about his return to Earth and meeting with Gilchrist that he'd pushed the exhaustion away. This heavy input of new information let it all back in. 'Do you mind if I take a quick nap on your bed?' he said to Laura.

She nodded. 'Take all the time you need. But before you go, there's something else.' She went into her bedroom and returned with three envelopes.

He looked at them, puzzled. 'What are these?'

'Letters from your wife.'

His heart pounded. He stared at the envelopes, then at Laura. 'Where did you get these? What do they say? I mean, did you read them?'

She shook her head. 'I was given them at the same time as the micro file. I can't decipher them. They're coded, I think. Just take them.' She shoved them closer to his hand.

He grabbed the letters from her, swallowing down a lump in his throat. He pulled Stephen aside. Laura read the situation perfectly and gave them space to talk.

'What do you know about the whereabouts of my wife?'

Stephen frowned. 'What was her name?'

'Isla... Isla Taggart. She went missing on Exilon 5. Do your people have her?'

Stephen shook his head. 'There are no humans living in the district. I've never heard our elders mention someone by that name. I'm sorry.'

His eyes said he was telling the truth. Bill let out a long breath. 'I've suspected for a while that I've been looking in the wrong place. I just didn't want to believe it.' To Laura he said, 'Wake me up in an hour. We can't stay here.'

With a heavy heart and clutching the envelopes to his chest, he shut the bedroom door behind him. The truth had drained the anger from him. He still had questions, and he didn't know if he could fully trust the pair in the next room. But he was certain of one thing: the Indigenes were not his enemy. They never had been.

Bill kicked off his boots and lay on the bed. He turned onto his side and hugged the letters close to him. Tears fell. His eyelids drooped with the effort to keep them open.

He needed to rest. He was sick of fighting.

But the fight was just getting started.

53

Anton woke to the sound of buzzing electricity. He sat up, shaking his head to clear the persistent noise from his ears. The lump on the back of his head was fresh.

After he'd refused to tell the humans anything more, the officers shadowing Charles had approached his cage. With the barrier still in place they'd reached a long needle through and jabbed his arm with it, just before he passed out. He must have hit his head on the floor.

He got to his feet. His suit was gone. A pair of loose-legged trousers was all that covered him now.

Anton's hope lifted when he spotted freedom. An opening to the room was all that separated him and the way out. But in his effort to reach it, something slowed him down. A strange energy nipped at his skin. His legs grew heavier, as though he were treading deep waters. He only made it two thirds of the way before an electrical current rooted him to the spot.

Two voices reached him, one belonging to Charles and the other to Gilchrist.

Her voice was low. 'Charles, how long do you plan to keep him here?'

'As long as it takes.'

She laughed once. 'But I'm still not clear on your reasons for holding him. Is he a threat?'

'No, my dear. He is the answer to our problems.'

'Charles, I still don't under—'

'All in good time, Daphne. You worry too much. I promise to tell you everything. Now leave me.'

Anton heard a door close. Charles appeared in the tunnel outside the opening. He whistled a tune.

'Let me... out of... here.' Anton's words were thick and slow, just like his movements. Breathing hurt more than usual. His device! He rolled his tongue over the back of his throat. The flexible membrane shifted in place.

'I'd like to, dear boy, but you're far too valuable to me.'

'Let me... go and I won't... kill... you.'

Charles laughed. 'You won't, because you can't.' He fixed his watery gaze on Anton. 'Daphne is terrified of you. But me, I find you utterly fascinating. She agrees with me in public, but I know she has her reservations about my plans. We cannot live on this planet indefinitely. We cannot live in these broken bodies. We can help each other.'

Anton inched backwards until he had regained mobility. The electrical binds released his hands, allowing him to check for the rest of his filtration device. Finding it calmed him enough for the device to work as it should.

'You've seen what I can do.' Anton huffed out a breath. 'The female is right to fear me. You should too.'

The old human laughed, hard. 'I'm quite sure I'm safe. You won't escape this room unless I turn that thing off.' He swirled one finger in the air. 'That low buzzing noise is an irritation, even to my ordinary ears, but the electricity works wonders to halt you.' He hid his hands behind his back and a small smile settled into place. 'We need each other.'

'How?'

'You need me to survive and I need you to convince the board members of my ambitious plans for the human race.'

Plans?

Anton slowed his breathing down, until the fog in his mind had lifted a little and he could think a little clearer. They had drugged him. His sluggish body and mind were attacking the new substance; it wouldn't be long before his supercharged immune system counteracted its effects. 'My friends, they're coming for me,' he breathed out.

Charles tensed up. He dropped his friendly manner. 'Who is coming for you? Are there more of you on the way?'

Anton considered telling him about Stephen. How he had evaded the authorities and was loose on Earth. He could send them on a wild chase and buy himself more time. But to admit to it would be suicide for both of them. He pursed his lips.

'Yes, that's what I thought.' Charles relaxed his shoulders. One Indigene was apparently enough for this human. 'You've come alone. Or maybe you haven't, it doesn't matter. I only need one of you, anyway.'

Anton slid down to the floor and wrapped his arms around his knees. His bare back pressed against the cool rock. It felt familiar and comfortable, like District Three. He concentrated on his captor's thoughts, but the old human appeared able to block Anton's abilities. Or maybe it was the electricity, or the drugs. He shook his head to clear both.

Would Stephen send for help? Would he live out his

days as a prisoner? Not if he had anything to do with it. But how could he fight against both the drugs and the electricity?

A part of him resigned to his capture. He looked up at the old man. 'What do you need me for, anyway?'

Charles' eyes brightened for a moment, but then he turned and walked away. Anton heard a door open.

'To help keep me alive.' His voice echoed in the open space.

Keep me alive? The three words tumbled about in Anton's mind as the door shut. The faint thread of a thought danced before him; he tugged on it.

Charles needed Anton for something. That meant he had a fighting chance.

54

Their chat had left Laura feeling exhausted. But while Bill slept, she kept an anxious Stephen company.

'Can I get you anything? Water? Food?'

He attempted a smile. 'No thank you. But I do need to leave.'

'There won't be another passenger ship leaving until tomorrow. We have time.'

The Indigene looked away. This weirdness between them bothered her.

She sat down of the sofa. 'I know this isn't what you expected.'

Stephen laughed once. 'No, it is not.'

'But it is what it is.' She patted the seat next to her. 'Can't we at least pretend to be friends?'

'I prefer to stand.'

'Okay.' She stood, despite her exhaustion. 'Then we'll stand.'

Stephen eyed her. It wasn't fear or wariness lodged there, but curiosity. 'You are strange.'

She clasped her hands to the front. 'So are you.'

'Are we... related?'

She didn't think so. 'Distant cousins, maybe. I don't believe our government has a right to claim you, if that's what you're worried about.'

Stephen sighed and his guard appeared to lower. 'We have not asked for any of this.' No they hadn't. 'Why are we being followed now? The experiments you mentioned took place a long time ago. What is the reason for their interest now?'

'I wish I knew, but the investigation—Bill's investigation—obviously triggered a new interest in something. You want the truth?'

'Please.'

Laura focused on the floor. 'We were supposed to transfer to Exilon 5, all humans, all twenty billion of us. While that hasn't happened yet, interest in Exilon 5 remains high. For what purpose, I don't know.' She looked up at him. 'But I don't believe that everyone in charge has the same agenda—whatever that may be.'

Stephen nodded. 'What will become of me if I stay here?'

'You will end up like your friend.'

'I need to find him.'

She touched his arm briefly and smiled. 'And with our help you will.' Gilchrist had told her to be a team player. She hadn't pictured her team to consist of an angry investigator and an Indigene. But she finally trusted her gut. 'We're on the same side. Bill and I won't let anything happen to you.'

Stephen frowned at her. 'How can you make that promise?'

'I can't, but I'm going to damn well try.'

55

Bill hadn't moved from where he'd collapsed on top of Laura's clothes. Sleep had hit him hard but the good feeling hadn't lasted. Bill couldn't remember the last time he'd had a decent night's rest. He checked the time. An hour had passed. Tears and tension had woken him five minutes ago.

The envelopes felt like an extra weight in his hand. He brushed his fingers over the tops of them, brought them up to his nose, and sniffed them. It was faint, but he thought he smelled Isla's perfume.

Panic hit him. Was he ready to read his wife's innermost thoughts? Was he ready to learn she was still in danger, or worse, that the letters might be his last tangible link to her?

She must still be alive. Without the discovery of a body, it was the only proof he had.

The door to Laura's bedroom creaked open. He stuffed the envelopes into his jacket pocket and sat up. More pressing things required his attention, like getting Stephen off this planet. That and leaving the apartment, before the officers returned to ask more questions.

She paused at the door, one hand on it.

'Hey, time for us to go.'

His wife used to stand at the door like that. His raw ache needled at him.

'You shouldn't have let me sleep so long.'

She flinched at his snappy tone. 'You needed the sleep. Excuse me, I'll be outside.' She closed the door behind her.

Bill set his feet on the floor. The envelopes made a crunching sound in his pocket.

'I'm sorry love, but someone needs my help right now.'

She didn't answer him. In fact, she hadn't spoken to him since the passenger ship. After he helped Stephen, his focus would shift to Earth. But he needed to do it fast, before they erased all clues as to Isla's whereabouts.

Bill emerged from the bedroom to see Stephen standing by the front door, his navy-blue suit buttoned and free of wrinkles, his borrowed black Stetson in one hand.

'Are you sure you can get me safe passage off Earth, Bill?' he asked, fitting his hat on his head.

'I'll make damn sure it happens. I just need to make a quick call first. One of my off-grid contacts.' He paused. 'I don't want to see you here again. You understand?'

Stephen smiled. 'If I'm here it means I'm not safe.'

Bill dug his communication device out of his pocket and stuck the earpiece in his ear. He barked instructions to the man.

'Are you sure it will work?... Yeah, ycah. Colin Stipple... It's a hot name right now. People are probably looking for him.'

'Is it for a friend?' the contact asked.

Bill glanced at Stephen. 'Yeah, something like that... Cheers, I owe you one.'

Laura slipped her jacket on and wrapped a scarf around her neck and head, making it into a hood of sorts.

Bill pulled his earpiece out, taking in Laura's appearance. 'And where the hell do you think you're going?'

'I'm coming with you.'

'I won't be responsible for another person going missing,' said Bill.

'He's right, Laura,' said Stephen. 'I don't want you risking your life for me. It was Bill Taggart I needed to find and now I have.'

She turned the collar up on her coat and produced a gel mask from her pocket. 'The last time I checked, neither of you were responsible for me. If I hadn't seen the information on the micro file, you two wouldn't have learned as much as you did. And since you're both in my apartment, I'd say I'm very much involved.'

Laura opened the door and walked out into the communal hall.

When they didn't follow, she turned back.

'Well, are you coming or not?'

Bill shook his head. 'Stubborn,' he muttered, walking past.

'You have no idea just how much, Bill Taggart.'

He had a feeling he was about to find out.

Laura closed the door after Stephen and put on her gel mask. 'Now, let's get Stephen home.'

56

Four days later

Stephen had boarded the passenger ship to Exilon 5 the next day without setting off any alarms, thanks to Bill's contact. The authorities weren't looking for another stowaway. Three days on board and his stolen identity chip hadn't alerted anyone to his presence on the ship.

Sitting in the ship's recreation room and dressed in his blue suit, his skin tightened at his proximity to a group of humans. Chatter echoed around the space. Curious eyes sought him out.

Without Anton, Stephen second guessed every decision he made. Should he stay out of sight? Should he sit on display? He realised his best defence was company not isolation.

The rim of the black Stetson he wore irritated his skin. He sat on his hands to stop himself from adjusting it. Fiddling with his hat would only draw attention to the parts of his arms where the silicone skin had fallen off. The brown contact lenses irritated his dried-out eyes. His filtration device struggled to remove the extra oxygen from the ship's purified air. Ironically, the Earth he'd left behind—the oxygen-starved air and the grey skies—felt more like his old planet had before the changes.

Two men three tables over began a fight with each other over something. Stephen shifted to a table farther away from the roughhousing. Others followed suit. Two officers carrying Buzz Guns entered the room. The air danced with electricity, making Stephen's static eliminator run hot as it drew the static from the air.

The officers got rough with the pair before handcuffing them. Was that how the military had dealt with Anton? His gut twisted thinking about his friend. But his priority was to get home. Despite his logic, the guilt of leaving him there tightened its grip on him. Stephen tugged his jacket around him as a new chill blasted his hot and clammy body.

The officers left the room with the pair, taking the static energy with them. Stephen retreated to his sleeping quarters—the only place left where he felt safe. Inside the dark coffin-like sleeping pod, sleep continued to elude him

☼

Two weeks later

Exilon 5 drifted into view outside the windows of the passenger ship. Stephen joined others at the viewing window to look out at his home that he hadn't seen for four weeks.

Knowing the truth about humans, he now viewed the planet with new eyes. Six minuscule blots on the landscape represented each of the human cities. Roads connecting the cities left tracks in the earth like blood-filled veins. Areas of recently disturbed land meant only one thing: they were preparing to transport more humans to Exilon 5.

The ship slipped into Exilon 5 space in the dead of night. At least he'd have cover and cool temperatures for the final leg of the journey to District Three. The cooling packs inside his jacket helping to regulate his body temperature had stopped working a week ago. The tight and restrictive human clothes he wore irritated his clammy skin.

Alongside the other passengers, he waited in the ship's hold to board a spacecraft destined for New London. As the craft descended to the planet, he planned his escape. Minutes later, it hovered above the magnetised landing plates at the docking station where he and Anton had begun their journey.

The passengers filed off the craft too slowly, which only made Stephen anxious. How he wanted to break out of his human pretence. Ahead of him, an officer was scanning the passengers' identity chips.

His heart slammed against his ribs. Had Bill Taggart's contact made sure his name would not trigger alarms on Exilon 5 too? Putting his safety in the hands of strangers chilled him, but he'd seen no other way.

Stephen scanned the station for the fastest way out. He could make a run for it, but that would draw attention to him.

The line inched forward and brought him one step closer to escape.

Keep it together, Stephen.

The device in his throat struggled to reduce the oxygen levels in the docking station. The humans' heartbeats sounded like a runaway train. Their thoughts were like muffled sounds.

Stay calm, you're almost there.

Keeping to the plan would help Anton too—if he

was still alive.

He shivered as he passed through the identity verification area. The alarm stayed silent.

He released a breath.

'Did you enjoy your visit to Earth, sir?'

Stephen stopped and turned around. The attending officer was speaking to him. 'Is something the matter?'

The officer smiled. 'I'm sorry, sir. I didn't mean to alarm you. Are you returning from a break? Although I wouldn't call Earth a holiday destination. You're better off here, if you ask me.'

Stephen returned the smile, although the attempt felt awkward.

The officer frowned. 'Are you all right, sir?'

'Apologies. I am just tired. I am rested from my break, and happy to be home.'

The officer's frown deepened. Stephen's stomach knotted up—his language was too stiff; humans talked in a more casual way.

'Okay, well, have a good journey.'

He walked on relieved to be home. Something fell out of his coat pocket and he froze.

'Mr Stipple?'

Stephen turned to see the officer holding one of the cooling packs in his hand. 'Mr Stipple, I think this belongs to you.'

He grabbed it from the officer's hand. 'Oh, thank you.'

'What is it? Looks like a cooling pack.'

'It's nothing. It's not important.' He shoved the pack into his pocket and caught up to a group heading for transport that would take them to New London. To his relief, the officer didn't follow.

With the vehicle in sight, Stephen peeled away from

the back of the group and strode towards the flatlands. At a safe distance, he ditched his shoes and pumped his powerful legs. His bare feet glided across the surface and left shallow imprints in the soil. As soon as he'd cleared the immediate area, he dug the chip out of his thumb and crushed it between his fingers. By the time he'd reached his top running speed the gash had healed over.

The communication stone he carried with him should have alerted Pierre and Elise to his arrival back on Exilon 5. He had to reach District Three and warn the elders of the new threats to their society.

The New London streets were eerily quiet, except for a few people out late that night. A wolf howled in the distance. Stephen ran past large parks and grey brick buildings, built by human engineers. The Indigene environs were more accommodating and dynamic, designed to enhance their emotions, and to amplify and control the raw energy from the planet's various rock types. He couldn't imagine his elders once living in a city as basic as New London.

A digital library loomed up ahead, its bright pink neon sign testing the strength of his eye lenses. An advertisement blinked overhead:

GET YOUR DPAD DOWNLOAD OF
NEWLY DISCOVERED
CHAPTERS
IN EXILON 5'S HISTORY

How much did humans know about the secret project their government had created? And that the result lived beneath their feet? The level of building work he'd seen from space hinted that things were set to improve for one race on Exilon 5, and it wasn't the Indigenes.

He reached the New Victoria Maglev station tracks and followed the well-worn path back to the door of District Three. The decontamination procedures began. He clawed at the skin on his neck, sick of the filtration device controlling his breathing. Tired of the artificial skin changing him into something he was not.

The door took too long to open. Stephen jammed his fingers into the door's crevice and winched it open. Safely inside, he dropped to his knees and yanked the filtration device out. His Stetson fell to the ground and he pushed it away. Next, he tore the jacket and shirt from his body and clawed the rest of the silicone skin off his face. Clumps of the pigmented membrane fell to the floor; the remainder clung to his clammy skin in ugly patches.

He was home. Standing over him were Pierre, Leon and Elise.

Where's Anton? Leon frowned at the open door. *Is he following?*

Stephen shook his head as Elise helped him up off the floor. The air grew uncomfortably warm. For once he was grateful for her calming power.

'Don't worry,' she said. 'We'll figure something out. At least you're home and safe.'

Stephen looked each of them in the eye. 'I wish it were that simple. We've got bigger problems.'

☼

Book 2: With the government's lie partly exposed, Bill Taggart and Stephen return in ***Genesis Lie*** to face new challenges in their search for a missing Anton.

CONTINUE THE SERIES WITH GENESIS LIE. BUY IT ON AMAZON.

WORD FROM THE AUTHOR

This is the second edition of a book I first published in 2012 as Becoming Human. It features new scenes for fan favourites and focuses more on the central theme of the story. While I loved the first version, I felt it meandered into subplots a little too much and left key character scenes underdeveloped.

After completing Genesis Cure, Book 7 in the series, I could see the first book needed serious updating to bring it in line with my current writing style. Yes, I'm a completely different writer in 2020 than in 2012! Whether you're a long time fan or new to the series, I hope you enjoyed the new version. I must say I got great pleasure from tearing the story apart and rebuilding it, while keeping the stuff that mattered.

Thank you to Tom, Jessica, and John for road testing the new version for me. When I started writing, I never thought I'd have readers so willing to help me out whenever I asked. I am really and truly grateful for your help.

Reviews! Please leave one if you enjoyed this book. Or if you didn't. It's your opinion. Reviews inform other readers before they buy. Every one of them counts.

PURCHASE OTHER BOOKS IN THE SERIES

Digital only

Genesis (Book 0)

(Get this teaser story for free when you sign up to my mailing list. Check out **www.elizagreenbooks.com** for more information)

Paperback and Digital

Genesis Code (Book 1)
Genesis Lie (Book 2)
Genesis War (Book 3)
Genesis Pact (Book 4)
Genesis Trade (Book 5)
Genesis Variant (Book 6)
Genesis Cure (Book 7)

Standalone series

Duality (a sci-fi mystery)

OTHER PAPERBACKS TO TRY

THE FACILITY: A machine-run facility becomes seventeen-year-old Anya Macklin's last hope of survival. But freedom from the facility comes at a price. To win it back, Anya must compete in all nine of their gruelling trials.

***

DUALITY: Jonathan Farrell is stuck between two realities. Who put him there, and can he escape before he loses his grip on the real world? Read this story with flavours of *The Matrix* and *Inception*.

***

Eliza also writes PARANORMAL ROMANCE under the pen name Kate Gellar.

MAGIC DESTINY: A magical legend chose Abby Brennan to be queen to four demon-fighting men. But this chick doesn't like to follow the rules.

Check out **www.kategellarbooks.com** for more details.

REVIEWS

Word of mouth is crucial for authors. If you enjoyed this book, please consider leaving a review where you purchased it; make it as long or as short as you like. I know review writing can be a hassle, but it's the most effective way to let others know what you thought. Plus, it helps me reach new readers instantly.

GET IN TOUCH

www.elizagreenbooks.com
www.twitter.com/elizagreenbooks
www.facebook.com/elizagreenbooks
www.instagram.com/elizagreenbooks
Goodreads – search for Eliza Green

Printed in Great Britain
by Amazon